Beyond The Horizon

A Novel by
CLIFTON LABREE

FORT LEWIS SERIES

Fort Lewis is a fictional Cree Indian village in the vast Canadian boreal forest on the shores of the beautiful Lake Diamante. It has a Hudson Bay Store, a Catholic Church, a Royal Canadian Mounted Police barracks, and a newly-built infirmary. The Crees are in a transition period trying to adapt to modern civilization. The infirmary was established by Bright Cloud, a beautiful Cree nurse who saw the need for a medical facility to care for her people. For centuries they have survived the brutal winters with plunging temperatures and deep snows. They had traditionally followed the reindeer herds which provided them with sustenance and shelter. Survival has been their greatest achievement. It's a tribute to their woodland skills, undaunted courage, and a triumph of the human spirit.

The four books that make up this series portray a Cree family in cataclysmic events during World Wars I and II, the Korean War, and the Vietnam War. The series pays tribute to the brave men and women who served to defend our right to live as a free people. The beauty and tranquility of Fort Lewis helps to heal their troubled souls. The families return every summer for renewal and spiritual growth.

Dedicated to my wife Pauline, and my family, with thanks for all their support and encouragement

Chapter One

There was a melancholic feeling in the air. The warm waning days of summer had passed, and an uneasy stillness enveloped the wilderness. Warmer clothing felt good. Winter was not far away. Early in the morning you could feel the crisp frost that blanketed the earth. The aurora borealis worked its magic in the cobalt blue voids of the evening heavens, sending its electrically charged mosaic of red, blue and orange strings of fiery color into every corner of the night. At times, the flowing lines looked like water cascading over a rocky ledge, disappearing as quickly as they formed. The erratic movements defied logic.

The cool northwesterly breeze swept the towering branches of spruce, fir and cedar trees, carrying their cleansing fragrance across the land. Fall was a witness to the death of summer. Gone were the carefree days filled with warm sunshine and bright flowers that graced the landscape. For those who made the effort and listened to the heartbeat of the earth, nature was warning them to prepare for the supreme test — winter in the northern forests of Quebec, Canada.

Faith Hamilton sat in an Adirondack-style chair outside her temporary quarters, staring at the boiling sky. She felt the sadness of one more season passing into memory and thought how differently things had turned out for her from what had been expected! The darkness of the night veiled the tears that ran down her face, collecting on the lapels of her jacket. She bared her soul to the night and let the full fury of her despair give way to muffled convulsive sobs, interrupting the silence of the wilderness embracing her.

The chill that cut through the air was an omen of greater things to come in the Canadian wilderness, reminding her that she had expected more than she had a right to hope for. It had all seemed so "right" and "possible!" Now she reeled from the sting of rejection. All of her hopes and dreams had been in vain. She felt alone, insignificant and unwanted. Time was passing her by, and she was still held in bondage to the past.

Faith's blonde hair, sprinkled with streaks of gray, hung loose about her shoulders. She was a slender, energetic woman with a large reservoir of stamina few individuals her age could match. Her healthy tan contrasted with her blonde hair and intense bluish-green eyes. There was a timeless air of wholesomeness about her that made people feel comfortable in her presence. Attractive without being showy, Faith's most endearing quality was her sincere plain-speaking directness. She was a younger-looking woman than her forty-nine years, except for her eyes, which mirrored the sadness and loneliness that had been a large part of her life.

Her beloved husband, Thomas, was killed at the Changjin Reservoir, Korea, November, 1950, nineteen years ago, leaving her, a young widow, with a newborn son which his father had never seen, and precious memories of married bliss. Anger, despair, and apprehension were daily companions through the years that young Tom, Jr. was growing up. She frequently had questioned her ability to raise a son and make a living at the same time. The uncertainty of the future eventually developed into a way of life with no end in sight.

The financial struggle to maintain their home and live a modest life with the barest of essentials had taxed her energy and resourcefulness to the limit. She never regretted the hard work and long hours, for her son was worth any sacrifice on her part. He was a lot like his father — studious, soft spoken and serious; yet, he was a happy child who laughed a lot and enjoyed a large circle of friends. Even at a very young age he was aware of how hard his mother worked to make a life for the two of them. He tried to do his part by mowing neighborhood lawns and working summer vacations at a nearby farm within walking distance from their home in Montpelier, Vermont.

During his high school years, Tom expressed a desire to go to college even though he knew that it would place an even greater financial burden upon his mother. He continued to work at the farm during vacations and summer breaks for as many hours as the farmer would pay him. It all helped to make the dream of an education a reality. Faith had informed him, without equivocation, that if he truly wanted a college education, they would find a way to make it possible.

She had worked her way through the University of Vermont earning a degree in Agronomy. She always had a respect for the land which provides everything man needs for life. Without the shallow layer of soil that covers most of the earth, life as we know it could not exist. After she found a job with the United States Department of Agriculture as a Soil Scientist, she breathed easier. The benefits and security of civil service made it possible for her to continue school on a part-time basis to obtain a master's degree in Hydraulic Engineering where she was especially gifted. Her master's thesis was a valuable contribution to the growing knowledge of the relatively young engineering discipline.

Life seemed good until Bill Savoie, another member of the Soil Conservation Service in Vermont, began to take an intense interest in everything she did. He called her several times a day to chat as if they were old friends. For two years Faith tolerated his unrelenting obsession; then, in desperation, gave up the government job for a position with a privately owned firm in Philadelphia. The move would give her a chance to get rid of the obnoxious admirer. That same year, Tom started school in Burlington to study forestry. Her only regret was that she would have to leave her beloved home in Montpelier behind.

There was an air of professionalism about Hastings Engineering Company that impressed Faith. She enjoyed working as a team member. She was genuinely welcomed into the firm and felt comfortable with the owner, Glenn Hastings, the first time they met. He was a middle-aged man who kept his finger on the pulse of current operations. He had been seriously wounded during the Second World War and had won the Medal of Honor at Normandy. She remembered his eyes the most. They were friendly and direct, but beneath his courteous demeanor, she recognized the sadness and sorrow he held inside. His wife had died giving birth to twin boys, and he had recently been notified of the death of one of his sons in Vietnam at the time she applied for a job. She could relate to his emotional burden for she had been in some of the same places.

Faith's first assignment with the company was at the construction site of a large aluminum processing plant in northern Quebec Province, Canada. She traveled to the site with Glenn, and they ended up falling in love. It was the first time since her husband had been killed that she was attracted to another man, and it filled her heart with anticipation, hope and joy. But the hand of fate had something else in mind. Glenn had suppressed his feelings for Kathleen Cohen, a school teacher in York, Maine, for twenty-five years, and they turned out to be stronger than his newly found feelings for Faith. The news was devastating to Faith. It was one of the most hurtful experiences of her life since her husband was killed. The pain of rejection still lingered, weeks later.

With the onset of cooler weather, Faith's residence at the plant construction site was rapidly coming to an end. Winter weather closed down any possible work on the land. Within a month she would be leaving Quebec Province, returning to the Philadelphia office for her next assignment.

Faith's son, Tom, had completed the forestry summer courses at the University of Vermont and had traveled to Canada to be with his mother until school started the second week in September. Both looked forward to hiking and exploring together in the vast northern wilderness.

Their first outing was planned by Faith long before Tom's arrival. The most memorable moment of her stay in northern Canada was a weekend she had spent with Glenn Hastings, hiking a trail north of the plant, when they were caught in a sudden rainstorm and forced to take refuge in a log cabin belonging to the Cree tribal council at Fort Lewis, an outpost village a few miles to the north. Wet and hungry, they had arrived at the cabin where they found food and dry wood generously provided by the native people of the forest. That night in the wilderness, Faith had watched the dying embers of the fire in the fireplace and freely acknowledged the stirrings within her heart. It had been a long time since she had felt the warmth of caring for a man. It was a wonderful memory, and now she realized that she had taken too much for granted.

Faith and Glenn had promised each other that they would return to the cabin at a later date with provisions to replace those they had used during their stay. It was a long-standing custom of the forest people, and they respected those traditions. She told Glenn as he was about to leave on the helicopter for York, Maine, that she would fulfill their commitment to replenish the supplies, hoping that the excursion would give her some closure to the short-lived relationship.

The day that Tom arrived on the helicopter shuttle, Faith was anxiously waiting for him at the helipad. Tom was all smiles when he saw his mother wave to him. Tall and straight, he moved easily out of the cargo section of the helicopter. He shared his mother's blue eyes and blonde hair. His face was raw-boned and angular, reflecting his Nordic heritage. At first glance a stranger would find him austere and intense, but his ready smile and laughing eyes soon eased first impressions. His reserved demeanor and courteous mannerisms made people feel comfortable around him, but he held a lot back from strangers. His close friends knew that he evaluated people carefully and reserved the privilege of selecting his own circle of friends and acquaintances on his own terms.

"Hi, Mom!" Tom shouted, dropping his suitcase to hug her. "Wow, that helicopter ride was something."

"I thought you'd like it," answered Faith, holding him close. The top of her head just touched his chin, so she stood on her toes to kiss him. "Have you been eating well? You look as if you lost some weight."

"No, Mother. You've been asking me that same question every time we meet for the past year. Actually, I'm heavier than I was a year ago."

"I keep forgetting how tall you've grown," she replied, pointing the way towards her cabin. "You're looking more like your father. I'm so glad to see you."

"Now it's my turn, Mom," said Tom, concerned about her welfare. "Is everything all right with you? You look drained and bothered by something. I was thinking that you would be pleased about the jail sentence Bill Savoie received. He was a creep. I was plotting some kind of mischief against him with a couple of friends at school."

"Tom, you shouldn't think such things," cried Faith indignantly. "You could get yourself into serious legal trouble. Savoie may have been a creep, but he wasn't stupid by any means."

"That was part of the excitement in thinking about it, but his weaknesses settled the problem before we were able to come up with a suitable plan."

"Thank God for that!"

"Is anything wrong, Mom?" Tom asked after a moment of silence.

"No, Tom," Faith replied, not wanting to share her personal experience with her son. "I'm just a little lonely up here on top of the world without my son to keep me company. Here we are at the quarters that I call home. They aren't elaborate, but they're safe and comfortable. I've been able to do my work and live here in a pleasant atmosphere. The workers have been great. I'm the only professional woman on the project, although several females work in the mess facilities. The food is great as you'll find out."

"I never realized how cool it would be up here at this time of year. The air smells fresh and pure. There's a frosty feel to it."

"It has turned out much colder this past week. We're going to take a hike tomorrow if the weather holds good. You'll love the feel and enchantment of the vast boreal forest. The native people of the region have won my respect for their ability to work and survive in such an extreme environment," Faith commented, opening the door to her cabin. She turned to her son and said jokingly; "You'll have to make do with the sofa in the living room where you'll probably overhang a little bit."

"I'll be fine," Tom responded, amused with his mother.

"You can unpack your case using the shelves on the wall beside the couch. If you're hungry, we can get something to eat at the mess hall before you unpack. They're serving the evening meal now."

Faith clung to her son's arm on the way to the mess line where she introduced him to several of her co-workers. Tom was impressed with the courteous and respectful manner they used around his mother. By the time they finished eating, he was seeing his mother in a different light. He always knew that most people liked her for her unpretentious ways and sincerity, which was genuine, yet she had also won the admiration and respect of the male-dominated work force at this remote location. She did it by being an uncomplicated woman and a superb engineer. Tom was proud of her unassuming dignity and professionalism.

The walk back to their cabin was interrupted by one of the supply workers who handed Faith an envelope that had just come in the mail packet. Her heart beat rapidly when she saw that the letter was from Glenn Hastings. Tom watched her rip open the envelope and read the contents:

York, Maine
September 3, 1969

Dear Faith,

A few lines to tell you that more things have happened to me in the past few weeks than I could ever dream possible. Kathleen and I were married yesterday and we want you to share in our happiness. The happiness that I've been searching for has been found with Kathleen.

We owe much of our joy and contentment to you who acted as a catalyst for it to take place. We both thank you for your courage and decency, and for your deep sense of fair play. It pains me to realize that our joy became a reality at your expense.

True happiness cannot be found by making others unhappy. Please forgive me, Faith. I never intended to hurt you, who give so much of yourself to others. God has a plan for all of us, and we pray that you may find the fulfillment and meaning in your life you so richly deserve. I'm sorry that you and I were not meant to be.

Kathleen and I seek your blessings for our marriage, though we understand how difficult it must be for you at this time. May we call you a friend?

Sincerely,
Glenn and
Kathleen Hastings

"Are you all right, Mother?" Tom asked, standing beside her. She lifted her eyes from the letter with a determined look that masked the sad sinking feeling in the pit of her stomach. Tom saw that glint of hopelessness disappear with a tightening of her jaw and a slight tilt of her head. He had seen it many times in the past. It was her way of accepting the inevitable and making the most out of it. His mother was a fighter.

"I'm fine, Tom," Faith answered, folding the letter and placing it in her jacket pocket, thankful that he did not press her for information. She was not in the mood to talk about the details. The letter had nothing to do with her son and everything to do with her personal future. "Without going into specifics, I can truthfully say that this letter closes an episode of my life and opens the door for the future."

Chapter Two

The next morning Faith was up early, debating if she should wake Tom out of a sound sleep or let him wake up on his own. She smiled at his lanky frame stretched across the studio sofa flat on his back with his arms folded across his chest. His feet stuck out from under the blanket hanging over the armrest. She checked her watch - it was 7:00 AM. The mess tent was already serving breakfast, so she aroused her son by playfully running a finger nail the full length of his two bare feet. He awoke with a startled scream, jerking his feet in the air.

"Mom," he cried in protest, "someday I'm going to get even with you."

"You've been saying that ever since you were ten years old," she laughed, delighted to have her son with her. It would give her an opportunity to forget the past for the next few days and concentrate on enjoying Tom's visit. "If you're hungry, you'll have to hurry up and get dressed. The only place to eat up here is the mess tent, unless you want to fill up on candy bars."

"Are you still hoarding those things?" Tom grinned.

"Of course. They've been a lifesaver at times; besides, they're tasty," she giggled, stepping into the bathroom. "You can use the bathroom in a couple of minutes. Dress in comfortable field clothes and sturdy boots. The trail will take us over a lot of rock outcroppings."

"Mother, the full extent of my wardrobe consists of jeans and comfortable foot gear," answered Tom, starting to get dressed.

He was selecting a pair of socks when his mother came out of the bathroom fully dressed for the outing. "You can use it now. While you're getting ready, I'm going to write a letter to my boss so that we can post it on our way to the mess tent." She selected a clipboard with a pad of paper attached and sat on the couch to write a reply to Glenn's letter:

September 7, 1969

Dear Glenn and Kathleen,

I received your letter of the third. Congratulations on your marriage (I mean that sincerely).

When I was notified of the death of my husband in December 1950, I thought that my world had come to an end. It was the beginning of many long days and sleepless nights. I almost lost my sanity! For the last nineteen years I have often wondered if it would ever be possible for me to love another man the way I did Tom, for he was a very special human being. The years passed, and the question remained unanswered until I met you, Glenn.

I was painfully aware that we had known each other for such a short time, and that maybe it was impetuous of me to assume that you had the same feelings for me. At least now, I know that I am capable of falling in love again. I thank you for igniting that awareness. I do not harbor any resentment for the choice that you made. My pride was injured, but no promises or commitments were broken. I have accepted the reality and will get over it.

I've thought a lot about you and Kathleen. What a beautiful love story – twenty-five years of loyalty and remembrance. The two of you deserve the opportunity to share that love without regrets, especially from a virtual stranger such as myself. Seize this moment and don't let anything or anyone stand in your way. It's nice to know that such a love is possible between a man and a woman.

Well, Glenn and Kathleen, I've meandered enough. I just wanted to tell you that I will be proud to be your friend.

Sincerely,
Faith

Faith sealed the envelope, satisfied with her answer to Glenn's letter and stared aimlessly out the window. In the back of her mind, she wondered how this would impact her professional relationship with Glenn, but she dismissed it immediately as a non-issue. They were both professionals, and she was certain that, after a period of time, they would be able to work together on any project without bringing up her feelings of sadness over what might have been.

"Is anything wrong, Mother?" Tom saw his mother looking out the window with a pensive expression on her face.

"No, I was just thinking about where my next assignment might be when winter shuts us down up here."

"It feels like it's not that far off," said Tom, pulling a warm sweatshirt over his head.

"The Canadians tell us we've got about a month before permanent frost and deep snows arrive," answered Faith.

"There's a fascination to this isolated wilderness that's hard to describe. We can't get that same feeling from pictures or movies. A person has to breathe the air and listen to the magnitude of the silence in order to grasp the immensity and depth of the land."

Faith listened to her son. She had felt the same way when she first came to the region. "Do you have any second thoughts about your forestry major?"

"I can't think of anything I'd rather do with my life. The expanding population of the world and the advances in technologies that are becoming more global than ever, places more pressure on the forestry profession to manage the limited forest resources available for more and more uses. And besides, I'll be able to work in the most beautiful and peaceful surroundings a person could ask for."

11

"You've given it a lot of thought, haven't you?" she asked, pleased with his grasp of the big picture.

"I can hardly wait to get back to school. Mom, are you as hungry as I am?"

"Probably not, but a cup of coffee will taste good right now. C'mon, let's get in line."

A heavy dew still remained on the ground that the sun rising above the surrounding trees would soon dry out. Blue skies promised a fair weather day for a walk in the forest. Workers continuously joined the cafeteria line from all points of the compound. The large tent was half full of sturdy workmen satisfying a hunger that the brisk climate actively cultivated. Faith and Tom sat at a table opposite Mike O'Leary, the foreman of the project's heavy equipment operators. He was a tall, thin Irishman with a sharp tongue and a winning smile.

"Mike, I'd like you to meet my son, Tom. Tom, this is Michael O'Leary, our equipment foreman," introduced Faith.

"Hello, Tom. I'm glad to meet you. Your mother speaks a lot about you. Welcome to God's country."

"I'm glad to meet you, Mr. O'Leary. Mother has written about how you've been a good friend."

"Your mother is quite a lady, and she does a pretty good job of taking care of herself. She's a well-qualified engineer and has used me and my boys with professionalism and respect. It's been a pleasure to work with her and reciprocate that respect. We've had some of our most productive work periods under her direction. We've never worked with a hydraulic engineer before. She's shown us a few things we never understood about subsurface water movement. In our book she's first rate. I never told you, Mrs. Hamilton, but the one thing the boys and I have appreciated the most from you is the fact that you never failed to say 'thank you' for a job well done."

"Well," answered Faith, blushing modestly, "thanks for making me look good in front of my son."

"I've got to run," exclaimed Mike O'Leary, collecting empty dishes on his tray. "Duty calls. Nice meeting you, Tom. Take care of your mother on your hike today."

"I will, Mr. O'Leary."

"So long, Mike. Thanks for everything," Faith said.

"There goes a happy Irishman," Tom remarked. "I like him. He knows who he is and stands on his own."

"Mike O'Leary has been a rock of support for my work right from the start, and he's become a good friend. Well, I'm full. Are you ready to get underway?"

"Sure," answered Tom, wrapping a donut in a napkin and placing it in his pocket. "I'll eat it on the trail. It'll be something different than your candy bars." He suppressed a grin.

"Okay, Smarty, I won't offer you any, just for that."

The trail leading north from the processing plant had been used by a number of the workers at the plant since Faith and Glenn had taken their excursion earlier in the summer. The deciduous trees had already started to turn color. Scattered patches of yellow birch leaves mixed with the red and gold of the maples along the brooks and streams where the soils were moist. Pine and spruce trees were dropping their needles, giving the coniferous forest floor a new coat of fresh-smelling cones and a soft mat of golden needles.

Faith had made up two packs of canned food to leave at the cabin. She had also picked up four sandwiches and a thermos of coffee from the mess tent for their lunch.

Tom was quiet on the trail and let his mother set a pace that she was comfortable with. It was the first time he had ever been in the deep wilderness of the spruce-fir type and was awed by the experience, absorbing the vastness and grandeur of the primeval forest with every step they took. Faith pointed out where the glaciers had scoured the area, leaving pockets of small rocks and soil between large areas of bedrock, still showing the scrape marks in a northwestern - southeastern fashion. Evidence of a recent fire could be seen on a distant hilltop. Burned trees still stood like silent sentinels watching over the land. Beneath the black stubs a new forest was regenerating itself with a lush thick growth of white spruce and balsam fir. Nature heals her wounds in a relatively short period of time. Fire was a natural component of the forest community.

Late in the morning, Faith and Tom arrived at the center log cabin and ate their lunch there. A single window on the west wall allowed sunshine to enter the cabin most of the midday and afternoon. They ate lunch on the same wooden table Faith remembered from her visit with Glenn. The large stone fireplace occupied the north wall.

"Wow, look at that," exclaimed Tom, impressed with the construction of the cabin. "A stone fireplace held together with clay and animal hair. Wouldn't it be great to have a private cabin like this to use for hunting and fishing?"

"In these latitudes this cabin serves a vital function for travelers caught in inclement weather," explained Faith. "It could mean the difference between life and death when winter holds the northern forest in its heavy grip. That's why food and ample dry firewood is stockpiled for immediate use."

"I like that tradition of caring for strangers in need," answered Tom. "Where did you say they stored the foodstuff?"

"There's a trapdoor on the floor in front of the fireplace. Light one of the candles and lift the door. You can jump down in the cellar and pack away the food we brought."

"There's quite a bit down here already," Tom discovered. "I'm amazed. They have steel containers marked for coffee, rice and matches. In our so-called civilized world, a stash like this would be vandalized or stolen in a heartbeat."

"You're right, Tom, and it's a sad commentary on the progress of civilization," Faith sighed, picking up the sandwich wrappers and placing them beneath the neatly prepared bundle of shavings and kindling wood in the center of the firebox.

"The bleached out piece of paper on the wall is interesting," Faith directed Tom to the wall near the door. He examined the yellowed document in silence and read:

> Welcome to the center cabin! You are the guests of a tribe of native Cree Indians from the outpost village of Fort Lewis on Lac Diamante. There is food in an earth cellar beneath the floor in front of the fireplace. You are welcome to whatever food or dry wood you may need. We ask that you respect the

generosity of your hosts and leave the cabin as you found it so that the next forest traveler will find a place to take refuge from the elements and partake of food if necessary.

I used this cabin during the winter of 1922 while working on a forest management plan for the Tribal Council at Fort Lewis. They have earned my respect and admiration. I had served in France with a young Army officer from the village, Lieutenant Joseph "Flying Eagle" Mann, who gave his life for freedom. His remains were among the "unknown". I ask in his memory that you use this cabin with respect and responsibility, so that it may always serve as a refuge for body and soul. Thank you.

Captain Mark Leroux, USMC
December 18, 1922

"Wow," cried Tom. "This Captain Leroux must have been a forester and a veteran of World War One. Things were different back then."

"My boss, Glenn Hastings, told me that he knows Mark Leroux. Both of them are Medal Of Honor recipients from the Second World War."

"Have you been any further along the trail toward Fort Lewis?"

"No," Faith replied, thinking about the trip she had made to the cabin with Glenn.

Tom saw the look of remembrance in his mother's eyes and honored her private thoughts by stepping out the door to look around the cabin. She followed him shortly.

"What do you say if we go see what's at Fort Lewis? According to the map it's not very far. We could return to this cabin and stay overnight if we have to," Tom questioned his mother, watching her closely for a reaction.

"I don't know, Tom," replied Faith reluctantly. "I had planned to drop off the supplies here at the cabin. I hadn't thought much beyond that."

"Are you tired, Mother?

"No, I could hike some more without any trouble," she hesitated, looking at Tom's expression of disappointment. "Oh, what the heck! It should be interesting. If we're going to do it, we shouldn't delay. Darkness settles in quickly."

The trail leading to the outpost village of Fort Lewis passed through an area set aside as a cenotaph in honor of a native Cree soldier, Lieutenant Joseph "Flying Eagle" Mann, killed in World War One. The cenotaph was composed of several mature spruce trees that had been pruned to the very tip of the tree creating a long thin spire reaching for the blue sky.

"When Glenn and I visited the cabin, a Royal Canadian Mounted Policeman told us that the memorial spires here before us were a token of the respect and devotion the local tribe had for one of their dead heroes. Constable Jenkins told us that the people in the area believe Flying Eagle's remains are the ones selected for the Tomb of the Unknown Soldier," informed Faith with enthusiasm.

"There's a feeling of peace and harmony here near the cenotaph, almost like that of a church sanctuary."

"Maybe Flying Eagle's spirit is present, and it's his way of letting the world know that he's finally at peace," Faith reflected, continuing along the trail.

The well-worn pathway leading to the village had been eroded in several places by heavy rains of the summer. In one section a steep rocky gully had been created that was hazardous to travelers. Loose boulders the size of softballs filled the ravine. Tom was about to suggest that he and his mother bypass it when she stepped into the eroded area and tripped on a loose boulder, falling to the ground among the rocks with a badly sprained ankle.

"Are you all right, Mom?" Tom hollered in alarm, running to help her.

"Oh, that hurt," she cried out, grasping her ankle.

"Are you injured?"

16

"I'm not sure. My shoulder is bruised a little, but I'm afraid I sprained my ankle," admitted Faith in a discouraging tone. "Tom, give me a hand. Let's see if I can walk on it."

Tom grabbed her around the waist to steady her while she struggled to stand up. Her ankle was already swollen. She knew she could not put pressure on it. "Mom, hold your foot in the air so that we can get you out of this gully. Lean against me and hop on one foot. Easy now, I don't want to drop you. Maybe I could carry you."

"That's not necessary, Tom. I'm way too heavy for you to lift," answered Faith with a wry grin. "Just hold me upright, and I can skip out of here on one foot."

They made it to the wooded section along the trail where Faith sat down against a spruce tree to examine her ankle. Removing the boot and sock was extremely painful. Large black and blue areas were already forming around her lower ankle and foot.

"You better put your boot back on, Mom. If you wait too long you'll never be able to squeeze into it." Tom checked his watch. "If you think you can hop on one foot, I can try to whittle a crutch out of a small tree. I still have the Swiss army knife you gave me. Or, you could rest while I run to the village for some help. What do you think?"

"Probably you should go for some help, Tom. I don't think I could get very far on my own. I'll wait here and enjoy one of my candy bars."

"I saw you put a fistful of them in your pocket before we left. If you don't mind, I'll take one now for quick energy. Don't worry, I'll be back as soon as possible." Tom took the offered Hershey bar and kissed her on the forehead.

"I'll be here waiting. Don't worry about me; it's only a sprained ankle."

Tom took off at a slow trot towards Fort Lewis. He knew that his mother's condition had to be painful or she would never have allowed him to go for help. Fifteen minutes later, Tom could smell the pungent aroma of smoke from wood fires and saw the cabins of Fort Lewis ahead of him. Each of the log cabins looked the same. Not a soul could be seen as he continued running across a small bridge. He was looking for a Mounted Police station and spotted the tall radio antenna mounted on the roof. A young policeman working on a boat tied up to a dock beside the station saw Tom running and hailed him.

"Ahoy there," shouted the policeman. "May I help you?"

"Yes," answered Tom, pausing to catch his breath. "My mother has turned her ankle and is sitting beside the trail leading to the center cabin. I need someone to help me carry her to the village. She can't walk on her own."

"I'm Constable Jenkins," announced the young officer. "We have a four wheel trail machine that's being used by another officer at the moment; however, our school teacher in the village has one at the school behind you."

Tom took a closer look at the village around him. He noted the Catholic Church next to the police station and a Hudson Bay Store built out of large cedar logs beside the police station on the waterfront. Inland several hundred feet stood a large wood frame building with a sign on its front "Eagle Nest." That must be the school, he thought.

"There's Steve Jackson coming out of the Hudson Bay store," said Constable Jenkins, pointing to a middle-aged man with thinning sandy colored hair sprinkled with gray. He walked briskly towards them.

"Hello, Constable. Is anything wrong?"

"This young gentleman has just come into the village looking for help. His mother is back on the trail near the cenotaph."

"She turned her ankle and can't put any pressure on it. I'm Tom Hamilton. We were out for a hike on our way to the village when she fell at an eroded portion of the trail."

"I'm glad to meet you, Tom. I'm Steve Jackson, the local school teacher. The village is relatively empty right now because the men folks are busy harvesting pulpwood on the tribal lands." Steve recognized the urgency of the situation. "If the police trail mule is out, I could run the school machine to fetch Mrs. Hamilton. Is your mother capable of sitting upright?"

"Yes, sir. She would be able to hang onto a trail machine. It's only her ankle."

"If you're going out for her, Steve, I'll notify the infirmary that you'll be coming in with a patient," volunteered Constable Jenkins.

"That's a good idea, Constable," agreed Steve. "Tom Hamilton, you can ride out with me to get your mother, but you'll have to wait there until I come back for you. The machine can only carry two people at a time."

"I'll wait here, Sir. She's sitting on the north side of the trail at the heaviest portion of the washed-out area."

"I'll find her."

"My mother will be terribly embarrassed to be so helpless," confessed Tom truthfully.

"I can drop you off at a place where you'll be comfortable until we return. My in-laws are at a cabin on our way out to the trail. Mr. and Mrs. Leroux will be tickled pink to have a new face with whom to visit."

"The same Mark Leroux who left the note at the center cabin?"

"One and the same," replied Steve in his easy-going manner. They walked toward the three-sided wood storage shed behind the school building where Tom noticed the trail mule. "Climb on behind me and hang onto the bars beside you. I'll point out the infirmary as we go by. It's behind the church on our right. I'll bring your mother there. The Leroux cabin is located off to the right side of the trail after we cross over the bridge at the village water supply."

When Steve turned close to the Leroux cabin they heard a piano being played inside. "That's Mrs. Leroux playing her piano. Just knock on the door and tell them what's going on. We take care of each other up here, young man, so don't worry about your mother. We'll be back as soon as possible."

"Thanks for everything," answered Tom, climbing off the machine. He was a little reluctant to knock on a stranger's door two hundred miles from civilization. Before he had a chance the door was opened by an elderly white-haired man supporting himself with a cane.

"May I help you, young man?" the small-framed man asked in a clear voice. His dark sensitive eyes appraised Tom from top to bottom.

"Hello, I'm Tom Hamilton. Mr. Jackson suggested that I stay here with you while he goes out on the trail to get my mother who injured her ankle. Are you Mr. Mark Leroux?"

"Yes, I'm Mark Leroux, and I'm glad to meet you, Tom Hamilton. Please come in. My wife was playing the piano and didn't hear Steve's machine. She'll be pleased to learn that we have a new visitor."

They entered the great room of the cabin. The first thing Tom noticed was the large fireplace on the north wall. The mantel piece above the fireplace opening was made from a large cedar log sawed in half. Additional rooms were located off each side of the room.

The door of the room to the right was open, and Tom noticed an elderly Indian lady turning on her piano stool to see who was with her husband. Her white hair was done up in two braids that hung down to her waist with a red ribbon tied on each. As she approached them, Tom thought she was one of the most beautiful ladies he had ever seen. Her white hair accented her bronze complexion. Dark sparkling eyes radiating warmth sought out Tom. There was something regal and majestic in the way she walked across the room in a graceful gliding movement.

"Welcome to our cabin," she said in a clear melodious voice.

"Bright Cloud, this is Tom Hamilton," introduced Mark Leroux. "Tom, I'm always proud to show off my wife. We call her by her Cree name Bright Cloud."

"It's a pleasure to meet you, Bright Cloud," Tom answered, struck by her beauty and feeling comfortable with the warmth and sincerity of his reception. "My mother sprained her ankle on the trail. Mr. Jackson has gone out to bring her into the village."

"That's too bad. Please sit and make yourself comfortable. We'll take care of her as soon as they return. You don't sound like a Canadian," said Bright Cloud, directing him to a seat on the couch beside the fireplace.

"I believe I detect a New Englander's clipped dialect," guessed Mark with interest. "We have a home in Maine."

"I'm from Vermont. My mother is an engineer at the aluminum processing plant south of here," answered Tom, looking at the pictures on the half-log mantel piece. Several portraits were of people in uniform.

There were two large framed pictures at the center of the mantel. One was of a young Army Lieutenant, the other was that of a young lady in a Naval Nurse uniform who looked like Bright Cloud. He glanced at Bright Cloud. She recognized his uncertainty and a visible veil of sadness descended on her face and clouded her eyes. Tom thought she was on the verge of tears. A muscle in her neck started to pulsate as if she was suddenly under great tension. Mark reached out for his wife and held her hand with his injured right hand.

"The young lady in the Naval Nurse uniform is our daughter, Bright Star," said Mark in a hesitant voice. "She was killed in Vietnam last year. We're still having a difficult time dealing with the fact that she's never coming home."

Tom felt like an intruder and was touched by the tragedy. "It must be a terrible thing to accept. My father was killed in action in Korea before I was born."

"I apologize for letting our emotions intrude on your visit to our home," said Bright Cloud perceptively, realizing how uncomfortable it made Tom feel. "When Bright Star left for the war zone, we had a feeling that something was going to happen. Seeing you, a tall young man, come into our home the way you did reminded me of our son who was killed in action in the Second World War."

"I had the same thought," Mark replied, still holding Bright Cloud's hand.

Tom noted the show of affection between his two hosts. He never had a chance to observe the interaction between a father and mother, and for the first time in his life he understood how difficult it must have been for his mother to face every crisis in their lives without support from a husband.

"Our lives are not dominated by sorrow. Our granddaughter has been a source of great joy and happiness. She's like a breath of fresh air and gives our lives a new meaning. This is a picture of her at college," Bright Cloud held out a photograph for Tom to see. "We call her Morning Dew."

Tom looked at the picture in disbelief and cried out: "I know her. She works part-time in the school cafeteria with me. Her name is Kimberly Jackson!"

Chapter Three

Steve drove the army surplus trail machine as fast as he dared towards the location of the injured person. When he arrived at the eroded section of the trail, Faith was visible in the distance, standing beside a tree, looking in his direction.

"Hello there," Steve announced himself from the trailside, shutting the machine off so that he could be heard. "Your son said that you had injured your ankle and couldn't walk, Mrs. Hamilton. I'm Steve Jackson. I'm a teacher at Fort Lewis. May I give you a lift to the village?"

"I'm terribly sorry that my inattentiveness to the trail condition caused me to fall. I don't want to be a bother to anyone," explained Faith self-consciously.

"Now, Mrs. Hamilton, you're no bother, as you say. We have a staffed infirmary at Fort Lewis that'll fix you up in no time."

"I appreciate your help, Mr. Jackson. I've been sitting here trying to imagine how I'd get to the village. It would be a long distance and difficult if two people had to carry me on a stretcher or if I was to attempt it on a pair of crutches. Now I see that you have one of those forest trail vehicles. I can ride behind you okay. It'll be much easier than I thought."

"That's the spirit," said Steve, noting her streak of independence. "Let me start up and position the machine so that you can climb on easier. This is the second time I've driven it. It's really quite a lot of fun."

Steve maneuvered the trail vehicle close to the tree where Faith was holding herself upright and jumped off to assist her. She hopped to the mule and backed onto the seat lifting her left leg over the saddle while she braced herself with the two handles beside the seat.

"Your son was concerned about you. I left him at one of the cabins where he could visit with some folks while I came to pick you up," explained Steve, climbing back on the machine in front of her. "Are you going to be all right holding your injured foot against the foot rest?"

"Yes, it doesn't hurt as much now," answered Faith. "We were hoping to make it back to the plant site by darkness or at least to the center cabin. We packed some food supplies to replace what I used on a previous visit earlier in the summer."

"The traditions that prevail in this forested North Country are a part of what makes it such a grand place to be. Don't be afraid, I'll take it easy," promised Steve, starting down the trail towards the village. Neither spoke until the cabins at the village came into view. "Your son is at the cabin on our left. We're headed for the infirmary next to the church a little further down the shore of Lac Diamante."

Steve stopped the machine at a wooden platform beside the infirmary as two Native American nurses pushed a wheelchair through the door for Faith and helped to get her comfortably seated in it. She turned towards Steve as they were pushing her away: "Thank you, Mr. Jackson."

"You're welcome, Mrs. Hamilton. They'll take good care of you. I'll tell your son that you're here."

Steve started the trail mule, drove it to the school and parked it in the woodshed. He entered one of the school classrooms to talk to a young Cree woman working inside.

"How did your mission of mercy turn out, Dad?" asked Morning Dew. She had been working most of the summer painting the interior of the classrooms, and was busy cleaning the paint brushes and her hands with turpentine.

"A lady sprained her ankle walking the trail from the center cabin," Steve explained, watching his daughter with pride. Morning Dew was the only child he and Bright Star, his beloved wife, were blessed with. Dew had inherited her mother's beauty and temperament. Her slender lithe figure moved quickly and deliberately. "Your mother would be proud of you. I'm so glad you came north this summer to work. You've been a good helper. Eagle Nest has never looked better. Now we're ready for the coming season."

"I wanted to help, but I really wanted to be with you this summer more than anything else. When we received word of Mother's death I worried about you, Dad. Grandmother and grandfather did also."

"I'm handling it, Honey. You've helped a lot too. Say, I'm going up to your grandparent's cabin to tell the lady's son that his mother is at the infirmary."

"Are they Cree?"

"No, they're Americans. The woman works at the aluminum plant being built east of us. You look as if you could use a shower. Painting is not a very romantic job, is it?"

"Now that you mention it, no," Dew answered with a smile. She was spontaneous and unpredictable like her mother. "I'll walk with you. I'm finished here for now."

Steve and Dew followed the well-traveled path to Mark and Bright Cloud's cabin. She and her father shared a cabin adjacent to them and closer to the lake. As they approached the cabin, Dew noticed a person carrying firewood inside for her grandparents. He looked familiar to her, but she wasn't certain until they arrived at the door and Tom came out for another armful of firewood. They recognized each other with surprise and wonder.

"Tom, what are you doing up here?" asked Dew.

"I could ask you the same question, Kim," laughed Tom. "I recognized your picture on the mantel. Your grandparents told me that you had been at Fort Lewis for the summer. It's a small world!"

"I'll say. Tom, this is my father, Steven Jackson. Dad, this is Tom Hamilton. We work together part-time at the college cafeteria."

"We've already met. Your mother is at the infirmary, Tom."

"Thanks, Mr. Jackson."

"It's our pleasure, Tom. You know it's getting late in the day. You and your mother are welcome to stay here with us at Fort Lewis for as long as necessary."

"Mr. and Mrs. Leroux have invited us to stay with them. They've made me feel at home. Their woodbox was almost empty, so I'm trying to make myself useful by getting firewood for them," Tom told him.

"I thought you were taking a forestry course for the summer."

"I was until a few days ago. I came up here to be with my mother at the aluminum processing plant."

"Hi, Steve and Dew," greeted Bright Cloud sticking her head out the door. "Why don't you two come over for supper tonight? We have special guests, and it would be nice to make them feel welcome."

"That sounds great," answered Morning Dew. "I've just finished a day of painting, so I'm going to run along and take a shower. I'll see you all later. It's nice to see you again, Tom."

"Me, too," answered Tom, blushing in the presence of her father.

"Young man, if you'd like to check on your mother, she's at the infirmary," said Steve, pointing to the building behind the church. "She's in competent hands, I can assure you."

"Thank you, Sir. I'll carry a few more loads of firewood and see how she's doing. I can promise you that being immobile is going to be a test of her patience."

"Well, I'm going back to the school for a while. Thanks for the invitation, Bright Cloud. It seems that Dew and I eat with you more than we do on our own."

"You know we enjoy your company any time."

Tom completed filling the woodbox and announced to Mark that he was going to the infirmary to check on his mother.

"My Bright Cloud was the founder of the infirmary way back during the First World War. It has improved a great deal with newer and expanded facilities, but the tradition of serving anyone in need of care is a core principle and remains the same today. It has a glowing record of service to the inhabitants of the northern forest of which we're proud. Tell your mother that she has an invitation to share our table and home as if it was her own."

"I will, Mr. Leroux. Thanks again for the hospitality."

Faith was sitting upright in a hospital bed. Her injured ankle was being bandaged by a Cree nurse. She saw Tom when he entered the building. "Hi, Tom. My ambulance was a trail mule," she laughed.

"Your mother will be fine," informed the attending nurse. "The sprain will be painful for a while, but she'll be back on her feet in a couple of days."

"Tom, this is Minnie," introduced Faith. "Minnie, this is my son, Tom."

"I'm glad to meet you, Minnie. It looks as if you have everything under control. It's amazing how everybody at the village has been so helpful to a couple of strangers," answered Tom, pleased to see his mother in such a good frame of mind.

"It's a pleasure to meet you, Tom," Minnie answered, placing the adhesive bandage on Faith's ankle. "No person can stand completely alone. We people of the forest understand that better than most."

Tom thought about what the nurse said for a few seconds and replied thoughtfully, "I believe we have a lot to learn from our northern neighbors. Mother, you and I have been invited to supper with Mr. and Mrs. Leroux. They live in a nearby cabin."

"In that case, Mrs. Hamilton, would you like to try a pair of crutches to get around on? Or would you prefer a wheelchair?"

"Crutches will be easier to use, Minnie. I'm going to be spoiled with all this attention."

The nurse left the room and returned with a pair of crutches capable of being adjusted for different body configurations. She had Faith swing her feet over the bed so that she could touch the floor.

"If you can stand, Mrs. Hamilton, I'll adjust the crutches to fit you. Once you get the hang of them, you'll be able to move around quite easily while your foot is healing."

"How can I thank you for your kindness, Minnie?"

"By getting well soon," the Cree nurse laughed. "I'll keep your boot here at the infirmary until you're ready to leave Fort Lewis, if you don't mind. You'll enjoy your visit with the most respected senior citizens in the village. Mrs. Leroux is called Bright Cloud. They return each summer to visit and help the villagers. They're remarkable people, but I'm sure you'll find that out for yourselves."

"Okay Tom, I'll let you lead the way to the Leroux cabin."

"Thanks again," Tom said, holding the door open for his mother.

Faith was awkward at first, but once she got into a systematic rhythm, she became more confident in her ability to walk with the aid of crutches. She stopped intentionally a few steps from the infirmary and looked around at the village. The church was next door on the shore of Lac Diamante. The water was calm and glistened like a sheet of glass. The large cone-shaped spruce trees that lined the lake's shore stood like majestic sentinels reaching high into the deep blue sky. The sun was sinking fast behind a large rock outcrop west of the village. The mountainous granite formation protected the village from the harsh prevailing northwest winds that swept continuously across the northern landscape. Faith was moved by the serenity and simple beauty of the area.

"It's a beautiful place, isn't it, Tom? It feels so peaceful and in harmony with the world around it."

"I felt the same thing, too, Mother. You're not going to believe what I've got to tell you."

"Good news or bad news?" questioned Faith quickly.

"Surprising news," he declared with a smile. "I just met a student from school up here. She's working in the village at the school house. Her name is Kimberly Jackson. Steve is her father. They call her Morning Dew."

"She's a Native American then."

"Her mother was a full-blooded Cree. She was recently killed in Vietnam."

"That's horrible, Son. The hike that we planned is turning out to be quite an adventure after all!"

Tom led his mother to the Leroux cabin and knocked on the door. Bright Cloud answered swinging the door wide open for Faith's ease of entry. "Welcome to our cabin, Mrs. Hamilton. I'm called Bright Cloud. You've had an unlucky day on the trail."

"Thank you, Bright Cloud. Please call me Faith. They've been wonderful at the infirmary. It's a simple sprained ankle and will be better shortly," Faith responded, entering the cabin's great room.

"Mother, I'd like you to meet Mr. Mark Leroux." Tom was pleased to introduce the elderly gentleman standing near the fireplace where he had just ignited several logs with cedar shavings.

"Hello, Mr. Leroux," acknowledged Faith, anxious to put a face to the person Glenn had spoken about. "My engineering employer, Glenn Hastings, told me that he met you at a Medal Of Honor Society gathering."

"It's nice to meet you, Mrs. Hamilton. Yes, I remember Glenn well. He was horribly wounded."

"Please call me Faith."

"I will if you'll call me Mark," he answered with a smile on his lips and a gleam in his dark sensitive eyes. "Please sit near the fire where you'll be the most comfortable. As soon as the sun goes down at these latitudes a fire feels good regardless of the time of year."

"I love a fireplace," said Faith, putting the crutches on the floor beside the couch in front of the fireplace.

"I hope you and your son like fish. We're having baked salmon for supper," announced Bright Cloud, checking the oven of a kitchen stove on the opposite side of the wall from the fireplace.

"That sounds great. Tom and I both like fish. Is there anything I can do to help? I feel quite helpless."

"No, I'm all set, Faith. You just rest awhile. Steve and our granddaughter will also be joining us for supper."

Faith perceived the hospitality to be sincere, but she was still concerned about where they were going to stay for the night. Mark predicted her uncertainty and tried to put her at ease.

"Bright Cloud and I would be honored to have you and Tom stay with us as guests for as long as your ankle takes to heal."

"You read my mind, Mark. We appreciate the hospitality offered. We were fortunate to have been so close to Fort Lewis when the mishap took place."

Steve and Morning Dew announced themselves from the door. Dew ran to give her grandfather a hug and kiss on the cheek, then did the same thing to Bright Cloud. "Something smells good, Grandmother."

"Kimberly, this is Tom's mother, Faith Hamilton. Faith, meet our granddaughter, Kimberly," said Bright Cloud.

"Up here we call her Morning Dew," Steve introduced. "Morning Dew is like the soft sparkle of ice crystals at the beginning of a new day. A promise of a fresh start. Sometimes she's a big pest, too."

"Dad, that's not funny," said Dew with feigned indignation. "I'm happy to meet you, Mrs. Hamilton. Tom and I worked together at the school cafeteria. It was quite a surprise to see him walk out of the wilderness like he did."

"I'm glad to meet you. You have a beautiful name. What are you studying at school, Morning Dew?"

"I'm working towards a degree in education. I'd like to be a teacher like my father," she answered seriously.

Faith studied the young lady with interest. She looked a lot like Bright Cloud. Tom had told his mother about the time one of the students in the cafeteria had made a remark about her being a half-breed. Kimberly defended her heritage with passion and conviction by stating that she had the blood of chiefs in her veins on her mother's side, and on her father's side she had the blood of a brave warrior and a gentle teacher, and if the ignorant name-caller didn't like it, then he could simply avoid being around her. Not long after the outbreak, Tom and Kimberly became good friends.

"Does your husband work at the Trails End plant, Mrs. Hamilton?" asked Steve.

"No," responded Faith quickly. "Tom's father was killed at the Chosin Reservoir in Korea, 1950. He never knew his son. He was an Army captain, a company commander."

"I'm sorry, I didn't know," Steve apologized regretfully. "It must have been difficult for you to raise a son without a father."

"My mother has always been reluctant to talk about herself. Her passion for privacy is deeply felt," Tom added, giving his Mother a wink. "I can tell all of you that it has been very difficult for her, and I know that for a fact. Yet, she never complains or stops fighting. I'm proud of her accomplishments. She's going to be angry at me for talking, so I ask for your forgiveness, Mom. She maintained a home for us by working long hours and never made me feel that I was a burden to her. She was always at school events cheering me on the sidelines when I played baseball and basketball. And through it all she earned a Master's Degree in Hydraulic Engineering at the University of Vermont in her spare time. What son wouldn't be proud of a mother like that?"

Faith was blushing before Tom finished. The look she gave her son showed those in the cabin just how much she loved him.

"Bravo, Tom," shouted Mark, impressed by the sincere tone. "A moving tribute to a lovely lady. You grace our home with your presence, Faith."

"Thank you, Tom and Mark, for the kind words. When Thomas was killed, it would have been easy to have given up, but a little baby boy filled my heart with love and turned my life around. Over the years he has always made his mom proud and I'm sure that, in that land beyond the horizon, his father is proud of the young man his son has become."

Bright Cloud listened with interest to the exchanges in the great room. She understood the feelings that were being discussed, and it was all she could do to suppress her tears. Memories filled her heart. Twenty-five years ago, their son

Daniel-Joseph (DJ became his preferred nickname) was killed in the Second World War at the Battle of the Bulge. The wound made by the loss never completely healed. She and Mark had learned to live with it, but sometimes in the stillness of the night a longing to hear his footstep on the porch or hear him talk and laugh became so intense and immediate that she had trouble catching her breath. Tears had frequently stained her pillowcase through the years.

It was natural for Bright Cloud to picture DJ riding his bicycle or working with his father, tall and straight with a serious demeanor that made him appear older than he actually was. His memory was just as real to Bright Cloud and Mark as it was the day they were informed about his death in combat. Faith's light blue eyes sought out Bright Cloud. In that fraction of a second when their eyes met, a common bond was formed between the two strangers. They knew and appreciated what each other felt. They were a part of that silent brigade of mourners that carried the burden of sorrow for a nation's monumental sacrifice of young men who remain forever young. Human virtues of loyalty, courage, and selflessness sustained them. Probably very few of the mourners could describe what it was like to carry such a heavy burden, but when they saw it in others, they were quick to recognize it and shared their sorrow.

The evening meal was eaten in an informal atmosphere. Faith was amazed at how comfortable she felt in the company of her new acquaintances. The great room was filled with warmth, harmony, and love. The attraction and affection that still existed between Mark and Bright Cloud was evident to everyone. Whenever Bright Cloud left the room, Mark searched for her. His eyes lit up when she returned, acknowledging each other with a subtle smile.

Faith observed their mutual commitment, and it sparked a feeling of melancholy within her, rekindling the loneliness that had been her daily lot for years.

After the meal, Faith insisted on helping Bright Cloud and Morning Dew clear away the table. She sat on a stool and wiped the dishes for Bright Cloud, feeling as if they had known each other for a long time. The men were directed to take their seats closer to the fireplace in the great room out of their way. They no more than sat down when a loud sucking sound enveloped the cabin. It was a helicopter at almost the same level as the treetops surrounding the cabins in the village. The noise was frightening. Steve knew what was happening, and a curse passed his lips as he bolted for the door.

"Damn, it's Joe, again!" he shouted. "I'll be right back."

"What's going on?" asked Tom, startled over the sudden appearance of a helicopter over the village after darkness. A minute later, the helicopter dropped heavily to a landing on the Mounted Police wharf.

"It's an old friend of my father, Joe Lance," explained Dew, flushed with concern at how potentially dangerous the pilot's judgment had been. "Dad will be furious with him."

Steve ran as fast as he could to the wharf, seething with anger at the pilot. He was not disappointed at what he found opening the door of the helicopter to shut the engine off. When Steve stepped back from the fuselage, the pilot toppled out headfirst and landed on the dock. The cabin of the machine wreaked of cheap alcohol. The pilot was in a drunken stupor!

Chapter Four

Steve tried to catch Joe, but was unable to act fast enough to prevent the inebriated pilot from banging his head on the deck hard enough to break the skin above his eye.

"You fool, Joe! You showed some stupid judgment on this flight," Steve screamed, straightening him out on the wooden platform. "What an irresponsible stunt! You may not be able to comprehend what I'm telling you right now, but you've just gotten yourself grounded for a long time, buddy boy!"

"Is he all right, Steve?" asked Constable Jenkins, running onto the dock with a flashlight.

"He's as drunk as a skunk, Constable. It's a miracle he didn't kill himself and others with such a maneuver. Would you help me carry him to the infirmary? He's going to have to sleep this one off for a while. God, he stinks of that cheap rotgut stuff he's been getting out in the bush."

"I'd like to know his source. We've been looking hard for it, but haven't found anything lately," Jenkins shook his head. "Sure, I'll give you a hand with him. When they're in the condition Joe's in, they seem to weigh twice as much as normal."

"You've got it," Steve was so angry at his friend that he had trouble talking coherently. "You should probably cite him for this violation, Constable. He knows more than anyone that there are serious consequences to idiotic behavior behind the controls of an aircraft."

The two men struggled to carry the drunken pilot into the infirmary where they placed him on a bed next to a window overlooking the lake. Minnie was still on duty and helped them remove his flight suit and outer clothing. "Just let him sleep it off, Minnie," suggested Steve. "I'll be back first thing in the morning to have a talk with him."

"That's probably the best way to handle it," agreed Minnie. "He's not going anywhere."

Before Steve left the infirmary, he glanced one last time at his friend and shook his head in disgust and amazement that Joe had deteriorated to such a level. It hurt to see what Colonel Joe Lance, a superb marine pilot, had become an alcoholic who would kill himself one day if he did not change his ways. The cool outside air felt good against Steve's face. He paused beside the lake, watching the way the moonlight cast fluttering shadows across the water, remembering that Joe Lance had not always been this way.

Steve's most vivid memory of Joe was from Korea, November, 1950, in the Changjin Mountains when they were both young Captains. Steve was on a strafing and bombing mission near the Yalu River, leading his squadron of P-51 Mustangs to an assigned target when they came across a flight of marine Corsairs flying cover for a downed pilot, Captain Joe Lance. Steve's flight carried out their mission and rushed back to the crash site of the Corsair determined to fly cover until a rescue helicopter could be dispatched to pick him up. The Corsairs had already left because of low fuel tanks. The Mustangs did not have enough fuel to stay on station for the estimated arrival of the helicopter, so Steve had landed his plane on a cart track near the crashed Corsair and picked up Joe who sat in his lap and handled the stick on the flight back to base.

The Mustang received small arms fire from the ground as they were lifting off the causeway, destroying their compass and instrument panel. They had to be guided by the other planes in the squadron. En route to the base in Wonsan, Korea, an urgent call for ground support was requested from a marine battalion in danger of being overrun. Steve dispatched the rest of the squadron planes to answer the call for help, leaving him and Joe dependent on visual recognition of ground features. They intended to fly to the coast and turn south along the coast until they came to Wonsan. It would not have been a difficult thing to do because each of the pilots were familiar with the territory. However, they ran into a dense fog bank and quickly became completely disoriented.

It was impossible to determine if the plane was over land or water. The two experienced pilots became extremely anxious when, suddenly, a powerful beam of light illuminated the cockpit and pointed in a different direction from what they were traveling. Steve had a feeling that they were being guided by Divine intervention and didn't hesitate to follow the light beam. They ran out of gasoline just as they arrived over the airfield at Wonsan. The euphoria they felt upon landing safely forged a bond between the two aviators. From that day to the present, Steve and Joe Lance had been close friends, spending a lot of spare time together.

When the Korean War ended, Steve's New York Air National Guard squadron was rotated to an inactive status, and he returned to his civilian job as a teacher at the Fort Lewis School. Joe had continued to fly in the Marine Corps until 1962 when his twenty-five years of service was completed, and he retired from military life with the rank of colonel. Joe and his wife, Kay, visited Steve and Bright Star often after his discharge. Steve and Bright Star always took time off in the summer to visit Steve's mother at her home on Lake George, New York, where they met with Joe and Kay frequently.

After retirement, Joe took a job with a flying service company working out of northern New York. It was primarily a charter service hauling freight to remote areas in the booming Canadian north. Joe became a certified pilot on helicopters specializing in commercial transport of large bulky items such as electric transmission towers and small buildings. Kay had been looking forward to a more stabilized life style once Joe retired. Their only child, Marshall, was a young graduate from West Point currently serving in the Army in Vietnam as a platoon leader.

Joe spent more and more time flying on special jobs. Kay left him abruptly for another man without any warning or foreknowledge on his part that his marriage of twenty-three years was in trouble. The breakup came in 1968, two years after Marshall graduated from the Military Academy. The swiftness and finality of her desertion almost destroyed Joe. He began to drown his sorrows in alcohol.

"Are you all right, Daddy?" asked Morning Dew, approaching her father in the darkness.

"You surprised me, Sweetheart," replied Steve. "I was just thinking about Joe's problem. He could have killed himself tonight. I wish I knew what it would take to ease his pain of loss and rejection. He's a good person and deserves more out of life than he's getting now."

"Nothing is going to help until he finds the courage to stop drinking, Dad."

"I know," Steve confirmed with a long sigh. "I remember him as one of the best combat pilots our country ever had. He was born to fly and showed courage and heroism every time he flew one of his ground support missions in Korea. I never thought Kay would do such a thing. If Marshall knew what his father was doing to himself he'd be sick about it."

"Thank God he sat the chopper down without getting hurt."

"It had to have been his instincts that did that for him tonight, because his brain certainly was not piloting that helicopter. We'll wait until he comes around in the morning. C'mon Dew, let's get back to our new visitors. Tom seems like a decent young man."

"He's sort of quiet and reserved," described Dew. "Most everyone at school likes him. He works hard and gets good grades. His mother is a lot more outspoken than he is, but she's a pleasant lady."

"It's quite a coincidence meeting one of your school mates way up here. I expect your grandparents will be worried about Joe." Steve placed his arm around Dew's shoulders and they walked back to the cabin.

Steve explained to Mark and Bright Cloud what happened to Joe as they sat around the fireplace getting better acquainted with their guests. Later in the evening, Faith and Tom were given two guest rooms on the east side of the great room. Faith was exhausted. It would feel good to stretch out on the bed and rest.

The small room was neat and clean with a slight scent of cedar. Two windows looked out on the lake and the infirmary. Bright Cloud had insisted that Faith accept her offer of a bathrobe and a change of clean clothes. The room contained a twin bed built out of small cedar poles. It had been Bright Star's room. Faith noticed several pictures of Bright Star on a small dresser beside the bed. One showed her in a Naval Nurse uniform standing beside a younger Steve in his Air Force blues. She curiously picked up the picture and examined it carefully. They were a handsome couple. She saw love and contentment on their faces. The tragedy of her death must have been horrific for Steve. Faith was an expert on those kind of feelings.

Faith shut off the light and sat beside the window counting the stars that punctured the dark blue sky. She thought of her job at the plant and wondered how long it would take for the ankle sprain to feel good enough for her to walk on it again. The lights were on at the infirmary. Faith noticed a movement through one of the windows. It was a man sitting at the side of a bed with a bathrobe wrapped around him holding his head in the palms of his hands. It looked to her as if he was crying. He was a study in dejection and disgust. She assumed that the patient was the pilot, Joe Lance, and remarked to herself that, "A pilot with a drinking problem was a combination that spelled disaster sooner or later". A nurse helped the patient lay down on the bed and placed a blanket over him. He covered his eyes with his right arm just as the light was turned off.

Early the next morning Faith woke to hear Tom and Mr. Leroux talking low as they passed beneath her window. She climbed out of bed to find out what was going on. She saw Tom carrying two fishing poles walking behind Mark Leroux. They were going fishing!

Her foot still throbbed when she moved about getting dressed. The aroma of brewing coffee filtered into the room from the kitchen. She opened the door and walked out to the great room on her crutches.

"Good morning, Faith," greeted Bright Cloud dressed in a long bathrobe sitting at the table. "Tom and Mark have gone fishing on the lake. Mark promised to reveal some of his favorite fishing holes to your son. He keeps a small punt down on the shore. It's more stable for him to use than a canoe. Come sit down and share a coffee with me."

"Thanks, Bright Cloud. I saw the two of them out the window. Tom loves to fish."

"May I fix you something to eat? There are some bran muffins still warm on the stove."

"They would taste good," answered Faith, taking a seat next to Bright Cloud, placing her crutches on the floor.

"Your Tom has been good for Mark. He hasn't gone fishing first thing in the morning for ages. I saw enthusiasm in his eyes this morning that's been missing lately."

"I'm glad. Tom has been denied a lot of male companionship. He never knew his father, and my father passed away when he was very small. No matter how hard I tried, I could never be a father and a mother at the same time," lamented Faith.

"You've done a wonderful job with him, Faith. It's refreshing to see a young man with manners. So many of today's generation fall short in that department. Tom reminds Mark and me of our son Daniel-Joseph."

"You and your husband have been through a lot," reflected Faith buttering her muffin. "Sometimes I forget, when I start feeling sorry for myself, that others have suffered also."

"It's hard to accept that they're never coming home. Many years have passed since we lost DJ; yet, I can still hear his voice as vividly as if he was calling me from the next room. I think Mark has accepted their deaths better than I have."

"It's impossible to completely shut them out of your mind," Faith admitted truthfully.

"Your love for your husband must have been strong," said Bright Cloud, hesitant to pry into Faith's private life. "It's none of my business, but an attractive lady such as yourself must be surrounded by potential suitors."

"You flatter me, Bright Cloud," Faith was determined to not openly discuss her personal feelings. "Maybe my expectations are too high and maybe I'm too independent, but there hasn't been a whole lot of time in my life for serious relationships. Very few men measure up to my husband."

A knock sounded at the door of the cabin. Bright Cloud remained seated at the table and invited the person at the door to come in.

"Mrs. Leroux, it's me, Joe Lance. Steve suggested that I come over here to use your bathroom to shower and shave, if you don't mind. I need both badly. Morning Dew is busy in his and you know how lengthy she can be."

"Come in, Joe," exclaimed Bright Cloud, standing up to greet him. "Of course you're welcome to use the bathroom. We have a guest with us this morning. Faith, this is Joe Lance, the pilot who flew the helicopter last night. Joe, this is Mrs. Faith Hamilton, an engineer from the aluminum plant. She sprained her ankle and is recuperating with us until it's healed."

"I'm glad to meet you, Mr. Lance," said Faith, offering her hand.

"It's my pleasure, Mrs. Hamilton. I apologize for my unkempt appearance. I guess Steve told you."

"Yes, he did, Joe," answered Bright Cloud. "I won't stand in judgment of you, but it seems to be a terrible waste. You disappoint all of us and we value your friendship too much not to be concerned about a destructive behavior that's tearing you apart. Please feel free to use the bathroom. As soon as you're finished, I'll put on a fresh pot of coffee for all of us."

"I appreciate that, Mrs. Leroux. I'm embarrassed to meet you under these conditions, Mrs. Hamilton," Joe said, avoiding her inquiring stare. He was a small dark-skinned wiry man with deep searching eyes. Joe used his hands a lot to emphasize what he was talking about and walked quickly to the bathroom just as Steve entered the cabin.

"Did Joe just stop by?" Steve asked. "Good morning, Mrs. Hamilton, I hope you slept well. I'll mooch one of your muffins if you can spare one, Bright Cloud."

"You know I can," she smiled, setting a plate for him on the table. "If you don't mind waiting a few minutes, I'm making a new pot of coffee. Joe's in the bathroom."

"I dropped by to give him a clean change of clothes he had left at our cabin. How's your foot, Mrs. Hamilton?"

"It's improving, but still hurts. I hope it doesn't hold me up for too long. I have work that needs to be done at the plant. I'm going to be spoiled after all of this pampering," Faith smiled, making room for him to sit beside her.

"Within a few days I'll have to fly Morning Dew back to Vermont so that she can get ready for school. I could drop you off at Lac St. Jean on the way," offered Steve. "Then you can catch their daily shuttle to the plant site. There aren't any water bodies close to the plant where I can land my float plane."

"So you're a pilot as well as a trail mule driver," Faith acknowledged with a grin.

"I'm a jack of all trades," replied Steve, taking the seat beside her.

"Our Steven is also a very serious school teacher and school administrator. He flew fighter planes in the Second World War and Korea."

"You might have flown ground support for my husband's unit in Korea. He was assigned to the 31st Regimental Combat Team as an infantry company commander. They were badly cut up by the Chinese Communists in their first attack."

"Did your husband ever mention a battalion commander by the name of Scott Taylor?" Steve asked.

"Why yes, do you know him?" asked Faith, surprised to recognize the name of an officer Thomas had considered his best friend in the Army.

"We know him well," cut in Bright Cloud. "He was my son's commanding officer in the Battle of the Bulge where DJ was killed in action."

"What a small world. Thomas and Scott were very close friends. They attended an Army Staff School at Carlisle Barracks together. As a matter of fact, his last letter to me mentioned that Scott was married a few days before the Korean War started."

"His wife, Marie, taught school here at Fort Lewis. She was blind when she started to teach. One day she fell on the rocks beside the dock and banged her head. The blow restored her sight. It was a miracle," Steve explained. "She was a gifted teacher."

"A few days after my husband's death, Scott telephoned me from a hospital in Japan to tell me how Thomas was killed. I treasure the silver star that Scott recommended for him, but I was not surprised. Thomas was the kind of person who took his responsibilities seriously. He had a strong sense of duty and honor. His son is a lot like him," Faith recalled, feeling a chill talking about her dead husband.

Joe Lance had cleaned himself up and changed into the clothes Steve had placed in a chair beside the bathroom door. The shower erased the stench of whiskey that had permeated Joe's old clothing, and a close shave made him feel more presentable again. He quietly unlatched the bathroom door and walked out into the great room, approaching the kitchen table with some uncertainty, unsure of the reception that awaited him.

"Well," Steve noticed Joe out of the corner of his eye. "Have a seat, Joe, and share a cup of coffee with us."

"Yes, Joe, come and sit down," Bright Cloud pointed to a chair beside her. "There are some warm bran muffins on the stove. Would you like some?"

"I would appreciate that, Mrs. Leroux," Joe answered nervously. "I haven't eaten anything for a couple of days. I just drank."

"My friend," Steve began forcefully. "Now that you brought the subject up, I want you to understand that what you did last night was inexcusable. You endangered every person in the village. You didn't land that helicopter on the dock. Your

42

blind instincts did it for you, and you were lucky. If you were in my command I'd court-martial you on the spot, friend or no friend. What in hell were you trying to prove, Joe?"

"I don't have any excuses, Steve," Joe avoided his eyes and stared at the cup of coffee Bright Cloud placed on the table in front of him. His hands shook nervously. "Thank you, Mrs. Leroux. Lately, the pain has been getting harder and harder to handle. Everywhere I go I see Kay's face staring down at me. I keep searching for some logical explanation. I can't be much if she so easily tossed what we had aside for someone else."

"You're making excuses and feeling sorry for yourself, Joe. That has nothing to do with responsibility in the cockpit, and I don't have to tell you that. How would you feel if Marshall had seen you last night? Smarten up, Joe."

Faith watched Joe's eyes as he quietly listened to what Steve was saying. He did not like being criticized in front of people, especially strangers. Joe stood up to confront Steve, defiantly straightening his shoulders and replied in a menacing tone. "How do you know how I feel? Have you experienced the same thing? If the answer is no, I suggest you stop playing God. Sure, I had too much to drink. I admit it. I've been a pilot as long as you have, and if it makes you feel any better, last night I even scared myself. I'm not stupid, and I'm not a child, so back off and save your breath. I don't need you or anybody else to pass judgment on my conduct. I'm capable of doing that all by myself."

"Please, Joe and Steve!" exclaimed Bright Cloud, uncomfortable with the volatility of the conversation.

"I don't know you, Mr. Lance, but I recognize when a person is filled with pain and doesn't know which way to turn for relief. All of us have been there at one time or another, and it's very difficult. I'm sure Steve is concerned for your welfare as any good friend should be. Sometimes close friends act the way they do because they're frightened and feel powerless to help," Faith watched Joe's eyes fill with tears.

"I'm sorry, Joe," admitted Steve, confronting his friend. "Faith is correct. Last night I was scared for you."

"I know that," Joe sobbed embracing Steve. "You're the best friend I've ever had. There isn't a day that goes by that I don't think about Korea. I thought I was a dead man when my Corsair crashed in that rice paddy. Then you swept the area around me with machine gun fire, and I had hope that maybe I was going to make it out. The most heart-warming sight these bloodshot eyes ever saw was watching that beautiful Mustang dropping its wheels to land on a cart trail nearby. I had trouble believing my eyes. Forgive me, Steve. Please don't tell Marshall."

An anxious knock sounded at the door interrupting Joe. "Excuse me, Mrs. Leroux," said Constable Jenkins excitedly. "We have an emergency. A Royal Canadian Air Force transport plane has crashed with six people on board. They're looking for any available aircraft in the area to help locate it."

Chapter Five

"I'm available, Constable," Joe volunteered without hesitation. "I'll have to refuel at the aluminum plant. If you need a lift back to the plant, Mrs. Hamilton, you can go with me."

"My son is on the lake fishing with Mr. Leroux."

"You head out, Joe," Steve suggested. "We'll worry about getting them back later. My Norseman is ready for a few hours of flying before I need fuel. I'll be right behind you."

Joe and Steve ran as hard as they could to the wharf where the helicopter was sitting and Steve's float-equipped aircraft was secured.

"As soon as you become airborne, Joe, contact the rescue command post and tell them I'll be available to fly some of their search grid. It'll take me a few minutes to do a preflight check."

The helicopter had a broken limb from a spruce tree lodged in its undercarriage. They both noticed it as they approached the wharf. Joe quickly seized the branch and threw it on the deck, giving Steve an apologetic glance.

"Don't worry about me, Steve. I'll be all right."

Without another word, Joe yanked the cockpit door of his helicopter open and jumped into the seat. He started the engine and pulled on his helmet, plugging the radio set into the jack on the instrument panel. Turning to the frequency given by Constable Jenkins, Joe reported his availability.

"Air Force Rescue Command, this is Red Dog One helicopter responding from the village of Fort Lewis. Do you read me?"

"This is Rescue Command Post. We are reading you loud and clear, Red Dog. We need all the help we can get. Plane is down somewhere east of James Bay and west of Mistassinni Lake. According to the plane's flight plan, it was following a course of 76 degrees longitude. We lost them on the radar screen close to the fifty second parallel. Out."

"Roger, I'm heading for the new aluminum processing plant site to refuel. As soon as I top off, I'll follow 76 degrees northward toward last known location of transport. I'll stay on this frequency and report when I am located on point of search. Bluebird One, a Norseman float plane out of Fort Lewis is getting ready to assist in the search as we speak. He'll be on this same frequency. Red Dog out."

The helicopter pad at the plant site had been monitoring the transmissions and was ready for Joe to land and be refueled. A downed pilot in the North Woods was a serious situation. Everyone in the area made themselves available. A close-knit brotherhood of airmen were responsible for opening up the Canadian northern wilderness, and a rapid response to an accident demanded and received first priority. No one never knew which of them might be on the casualty list next time.

While his helicopter was being fueled, a jeep rolled up to the pad. A young man in a white shirt and apron jumped out of the jeep and ran to the cockpit door.

"We got a call from Mrs. Hamilton at Fort Lewis," the man hollered as Joe opened his door. "She said that you had not eaten for a couple of days, and that we should have a thermos of coffee and several sandwiches ready when you landed. Here you are, mister. Good luck on your search."

"Thank you, son," responded a surprised Joe.

Within a few minutes the refueling foreman gave him a thumbs up, and Joe lifted the craft straight up before heading north at full throttle. At about one hundred feet elevation he leveled off to pour himself a cup of coffee. As soon as he intersected the assumed flight path of the downed plane, Joe throttled down to a slower speed so that he would have time to visually sweep both sides of the helicopter looking for any unnatural disturbance of the forest below or visible remnants of the aircraft itself.

Joe ate two ham sandwiches and wolfed down a cup of coffee just as soon as he slowed for the search pattern. The food settled his nervous stomach and rejuvenated him. The thoughtfulness of a stranger he had just met also warmed him. Leaning his head against the back rest of his seat he carefully scanned the landscape on both sides of his flight path. He rolled his window down. The wind was bitterly cold and had the potential of chilling a body rapidly, but it improved his visibility of the ground. He was determined to withstand the cold for as long as possible.

"Rescue Command, this is Red Dog. I'm now on the anticipated flight path of transport heading north, doing a visual sweep of one to two miles laterally. Out."

"Red Dog, this is Bluebird. Rescue One has vectored me to your west. I'm running a northern sweep approximately three miles parallel to the 76th latitude line. Out."

"Bluebird, this is Red Dog. Would you thank the lady at the Leroux cabin who ordered sandwiches and coffee for me at the plant site? They're greatly appreciated."

"This is Bluebird. I'll be glad to. Good luck, Red Dog. Out."

Visibility started to become impaired minutes after Joe and Steve began to fly the rescue grid. Scattered cumulous clouds had dominated the area earlier, now they were being displaced by a weather front with a heavy overcast. Joe had trouble seeing the ground in front of him. Narrowing the distance between his helicopter and the ground helped him to see better even though it cut down on the limits of acceptable risk to a dangerous level.

"Red Dog to Rescue One."

"This is Rescue One, come in, Red Dog."

"This is Red Dog. Weather ceiling is drastically limiting visibility on my trajectory northward. I am dropping to a lower level and will continue the search. If Bluebird is monitoring this transaction, how is the weather to my west? Red Dog out."

"This is Bluebird. Weather front is extensive. I am now experiencing light rain. If visibility gets any worse I won't be able to see the ground and will have to abort the sweep to the north."

"This is Red Dog. Attention! Attention! I've just spotted a portion of the downed plane. It's on the correct flight path. I am turning on my homing beacon and will remain on station. The weather is closing in. Am looking for a place to set down near the crash site. I'm at tree level now. I see no evidence of movement at the site. Remnants of the wings are scattered over a large impact area. The fuselage appears to be relatively intact."

"This is Rescue One. We are dispatching two helicopters to your location. Use caution in dropping to the ground. Out."

"Red Dog to Rescue One. A portion of the nose of the plane is hanging out over a ledge. It may need to be secured before it can be entered. Therefore, send ropes and slings with the first helicopter. I repeat, send ropes and slings with first helicopter. I believe I've found an opening near the crash site where the trees were pushed over or sliced off. I'm going in. Red Dog out."

The struggle against the increased winds made it difficult to control the aircraft. Joe was sweating profusely. Once he made the judgment call to land the helicopter at the site, he never hesitated. The sturdy helicopter landed lightly in the midst of a devastated field of crash debris. He double-checked to see that his homing beacon was functioning properly and jumped out of the cockpit to examine the battered plane's fuselage. It had landed on a relatively level wooded plain with no visible obstacles except the small diameter trees. The cabin and nose of the aircraft had come to a stop at the edge of a ravine which dropped off precipitously to a large stream. He thought that the main fuselage probably still had some structural integrity even if it had been badly damaged.

Upon closer examination, Joe saw that the plane was teetering on the brink of the cliff and was in danger of sliding off into the stream below. He tried in vain to open the twisted door of the transport's body, screaming as loud as he could to alert anyone inside, but heard no response. Joe ran back to the tool compartment of his helicopter to get a first aid kit and an ax. He was able to pry open the airplane's door with the ax.

"Hello, can anyone hear me? Speak to me if you can hear me or pound on something so that I'll know that someone has survived the crash."

"I hear you," answered a weak voice beneath the tangle of boxes and rubble that shattered the plane's interior. "The pilot is dead. I'm badly hurt. My legs are broken and it hurts when I breathe..."

"Try to relax, airman. Help is on its way." Joe hollered. Then he felt the front portion of the fuselage start to tilt downward. He tossed the first aid kit towards the sound of the man's voice and darted out the door to counteract the slide over the cliff by climbing on the outer extremity of the tail of the plane. As soon as he was in a position that successfully tilted the rear of the plane back down on the ground, he tried to reassure the surviving airmen in the fuselage.

"You guys in the transport, hold tight for a while. Search and Rescue is on its way to bring you home. If you are capable of moving, try to make your way towards the rear of the body. We've got to stabilize this thing somehow."

Nervously clinging to the tail of the plane, Joe waited for the arrival of the Royal Canadian Air Force retrieval team, which he knew was as good as any in the world. In the meantime, he thought of how the nose could be supported enough for the dead and injured to be extracted from the unstable fuselage. Dragging the plane backwards was impossible because several broken tree stubs prevented movement to the rear.

Minutes after locating the crash site a plane circled overhead. Joe would recognize that engine anywhere. It was Steve in his powerful Norseman. Joe waved to him and pointed to the front of the crashed plane in hopes that he would understand the predicament they were up against. Steve wiggled his wings several times to acknowledge that he understood, then he pulled up to an elevation higher than the rescue helicopters would use and flew in a circular pattern around the crash site in case he was needed.

Two RCAF medical helicopters approached the crash site as soon as Steve lifted out of the area. Two medics lowered themselves by ropes to the ground while other lines and slings were thrown from the side door.

"There are survivors inside the fuselage, but if we don't stabilize the nose quickly, we're going to lose it," Joe exclaimed.

"What do you suggest?" asked a burly sergeant looking over the situation on the ground.

"Take the ropes and slings you brought with you and place them under and over the nose of the plane. We can hook a line to one of the helicopters to take up the slack and hold the craft in place while you get the men out."

"Our helicopters don't have the lift to do that, Sir," answered the Sergeant authoritatively.

"Then as soon as you guys fasten that sling around the nose, the heavier of you come back here to hold onto the tail section while I bring my machine into position for you to fasten a loop around the lifting ring. I'm sure mine can do the job."

"Yes, Sir."

"As soon as you've finished with the sling, tell your pilots to clear the area above us so that I can lift off to a holding position. One of them can land in the spot I'm occupying. Tell them to be ready to rush the fuselage as soon as I take up the slack on the slings. I'll hold it on station as long as I can until you're clear. Do you understand?"

"I've got you, Sir." The Sergeant relayed to the helicopters what Joe had suggested by way of a radio fastened to his shoulder strap.

The two air medics gently threw a sling around the front portion of the plane's nose, being careful not to interfere with the precarious balance of the fuselage. One of the airmen held the loose end of the strap while the heavier of the two relieved Joe of his position on the tail section.

"When I drop low enough, you can attach the strap to the lifting ring beneath the helicopter." Joe ordered in a deliberate precise tone as he approached his helicopter. "As soon as you have attached it, stand off where I can see you and give me a signal to take up the slack."

"Yes, Sir, I understand. Good luck."

Joe climbed into the cockpit, fastened his helmet, adjusted his radio mouthpiece, and started the engine. The last thing Joe wanted to do was create any more dust and swirling debris at the crash scene than was necessary so he started to lift with the slowest engine revolutions possible. The doughty airman crouched beneath the hovering craft until he could reach the lifting ring. After securing the strap, he rolled to one side of the helicopter and gave Joe a thumbs-up hand signal to start his lift.

The commercial helicopter was heavier and more powerful than the smaller RCAF models. Joe was confident that he could at least take up enough tension on the nose of the damaged plane to hold it from tumbling down into the ravine. He lifted gently until he felt resistance. It was a delicate task to hold the machine on station while applying slight tension to the sling. The wind was increasing by the minute as the weather situation quickly deteriorated.

"Red Dog to rescue helicopters. Get into that fuselage as fast as you can and remove the bodies of the airmen. I'm not sure how long I can hold steady in this new weather front breaking upon us. If I'm blown off station, your lives and the lives of the men inside will be in jeopardy. Crack to it now!"

"Red Dog, we're on our way. One helicopter has already landed in your previous location, and crews are now entering plane. Hold steady, Red Dog, I'll keep you informed. Medics claim there are three alive in the fuselage. The pilot, copilot and navigator are dead. I've instructed ground personnel to evacuate the body of the plane as soon as possible. We'll load and treat the survivors after they've been removed from the fuselage. How's your fuel, Red Dog?"

"This is Red Dog. Fuel is fifty percent. I'm having trouble staying aloft. Have your second helicopter stay well clear of the site so as to keep air turbulence at a minimum. Red Dog out."

A dense fog bank from the northwest was blowing into the crash site. Joe grimaced at how much more difficult it would be to extricate the injured men in the heavy fog. The weather continued to get worse. The fog was accompanied by heavy rain squalls. Joe was worried about the violent wind gusts within the front.

"Bluebird to Red Dog and rescue helicopters. I'm returning to base. Fuel is low. Good luck. I know how focused and busy you are right now, Red Dog. Only a superb aviator could do what you're doing. I'm proud of you, my friend. Out." Steve reluctantly turned his Norseman towards Fort Lewis guided by the homing signal of the Mounted Police radio tower.

A few miles west of the crash site, Steve encountered more turbulent winds and heavier rain squalls with low ceilings and almost zero visibility. "Red Dog and Rescue helicopters, this is Bluebird. The front that is now encompassing the crash site has high winds and heavy rains. Be on the lookout for erratic wind sheer forces. The front is extended at least fifty miles to your west and traveling approximately one hundred degrees azimuth. Out."

Joe's forehead was covered with sweat beads even though his cockpit was damp and cold. His grip on the controls necessary to maintain a hover position taxed every bit of skill and experience he had learned in twenty-eight years of flying. He could feel the fuselage of the transport plane slowly creeping towards the edge of the cliff, and he worried that the helicopter may not have the lifting power to hold it in midair if it moved from the edge it was now teetering on.

"Rescue One this is Red Dog. I am having trouble holding. I may have to abort."

"Red Dog, this is Rescue One. The last patient has a broken back. We're attaching him to a basket litter and should be clear of the fuselage within two minutes."

Visibility instantly got worse. Joe had positioned one of his mirrors so that he could observe the body of the plane and the Canadian airman who remained in view on the ground in case he had to give Joe hand signals. Two minutes seemed an eternity to Joe. He watched the rolling fog bank engulf the rescue scene and prayed that he could hold a little longer.

Suddenly the gusting winds rocked his helicopter sideways before he could counter the erratic move. The fuselage of the crashed plane moved further down the slope. All Joe could do was increase power and lifting ability to stay above the surrounding tree tops.

"Red Dog, patient is clear. Repeat. Patient is clear. It looks as if. . ."

Joe did not hear the last transmission. The rains made the ground more slippery than usual, and the battered transport's fuselage rapidly moved over the edge of the cliff. The medics leaped to the ground, rolling the litter basket ahead of them just as remnants of the fuselage dropped over the edge of the cliff, pulling Joe's helicopter below the canopy of the tree line. He was being pulled into the ravine with his rotors churning the air at full power. The immediate area was filled with broken pieces of branches and leaves being smashed and severed by the whirling blades.

Chapter Six

Visibility was obscured by broken pieces of debris being blown about by the slashing rotor blades. Joe thought that his time to die had arrived, and cried out: "Oh Lord, remember me." He was struggling to pull the release lever of the lifting ring located behind his seat as the helicopter dropped over the edge of the cliff. If he couldn't get to it in time, the heavy transport body was going to pull him all the way to the bottom or drag him into the face of the cliff. Suddenly, his downward plunge was reversed and the helicopter miraculously started to rise. The transport's damaged fuselage smashed its way to the bottom of the ravine landing in the middle of the river.

"Thank you, Lord," he screamed at the top of his lungs.

The Canadian Airmen on the ground were busy attending to the injured when the helicopter dropped from sight. They rushed to the brink of the cliff just as Joe was able to lift free of the transport's fuselage. They stood in awe as Joe lifted clear of the crash site. "That pilot has got some guts," stated the husky sergeant. "I'd fly with him anywhere, anytime."

"Rescue to Red Dog. Are you all right? Out."

"Red Dog to Rescue. I hope so. I just had a scare I don't ever want to repeat. I'm feeling a little more vibrations than normal. The rotors took a vicious beating. I'm sure we're out of balance. I plan to return to Fort Lewis where I can set down and evaluate my situation. Would you monitor my return to base? Red Dog out."

"Rescue to Red Dog. It will be a privilege to monitor and escort you back to your base. If you make the decision to set down between here and base, rest assured we'll pick you up. You have demonstrated some exceptional flying skill, and the

Royal Canadian Air Force salutes you, Colonel Lance. Rescue out."

"This is Red Dog. Thanks, I appreciate the kind words. I believe that I can make it to base if I keep my rotor revs low enough to stay airborne. Red Dog out."

The weather continued to deteriorate. Winds blew in gusts as high as sixty miles per hour, plastering the windshield of his helicopter with rain blowing sideways. Keeping on a charted course was difficult. Joe turned his radio to the strongest homing signal he could pick up. It turned out to be the police radio tower at Fort Lewis.

Joe's commercial helicopter was capable of flying long hours with a minimum of maintenance. The rotors which lifted and propelled the aircraft were as strong as the manufacturer could make them, but the rotors and the adjoining transmission were the most fragile link in the propulsion system. They were much like a fine watch where balance and synchronization were delicately computed. Anything that upset that relationship could cause premature failure or self-destruction.

Praying for the machinery to hold together until he reached Fort Lewis was the only alternative available to setting down in a storm with zero visibility. Straining to maintain the craft at about five hundred feet above the ground was rapidly draining him of energy. Joe was in deep trouble if his instruments were malfunctioning.

"Red Dog, this is Fort Lewis Mounted Police. We've been monitoring your transmissions. Bluebird is assembling every available source of light at the village to light up the wharf in order to give you some visibility to land safely. Good luck. Out."

"Red Dog to Fort Lewis. Thank you, Constable. The helicopter is vibrating badly and getting worse by the minute. I have enough fuel to make it. I anticipate being at Fort Lewis within a half hour. Red Dog out."

"Message received, out."

While Joe was fighting his way through the storm with a crippled aircraft, Steve had assembled all of the motorized trail machines available at the village in a half circle so that they could train their lights on the Mounted Police wharf. The Police station and the nearby Hudson Bay store each had a powerful spot light also capable of reaching the landing dock. Steve was hoping that everything combined would illuminate the area enough that Joe could see it from a distance and follow the light to relative safety.

Tom and Morning Dew were waiting in the doorway of the station prepared to turn on the trail mule lights as soon as Steve told them to do so. Constable Jenkins continued to monitor the frequency Joe was on. Out of the pouring rain a lone figure appeared at the door, carrying a thermos bottle of hot coffee. It was Mark.

"Mr. Leroux, what are you doing out in this weather?" asked Tom who recognized him first.

"Yes, Grandfather, you could catch pneumonia on a night like this," Dew claimed, wrapping her arm around him, and pulling him inside the station.

"I'm old enough to enjoy your concern," admitted Mark, watching Steve and Constable Jenkins listening intently at the radio. "Bright Cloud and Faith are preparing some hot food for all of you. I brought some hot coffee for Joe when he lands. I've been worried about him ever since young Tom and I came in from our fishing expedition this morning to learn that he and Steve had responded to a search request. It's bad flying weather, isn't it, Steve?"

"It is, Colonel," answered Steve. Throughout the years, Steve called his father-in-law Mister or Colonel Leroux out of respect and admiration. "If anyone can make it, Joe can. This has been one of those kind of days that divide mortal man into different categories. I'd say that, today, our friend, Joe Lance, has earned our gratitude and our respect. He's lucky to be alive."

"Listen," said Morning Dew softly. "I think I hear something." They all scrambled out the door and faced northward where they picked up the rhythmic pulsation of helicopter blades slicing through the rain-saturated air overhead.

Dew and Tom ran to the trail machines and started flipping on their lights. The dock was completely illuminated even though the fog was still thick. Steve was reassured that the additional lights gave Joe a clearer picture of his landing area. They held their breaths as the ungainly aircraft shot straight towards the lighted area. Joe maintained a level hover while he brought the nose of the helicopter around pointing towards the village and gently touched down in the center of the wharf.

Steve was the first to reach the cockpit door and opened it to help Joe exit the craft. An interior light shone on Joe with his head leaned back on the headrest and his eyes closed.

"Are you all right, Joe?" asked Steve, reaching to unfasten his seat belt. "You had us worried. Thank God you're here safe."

"I'm exhausted," Joe answered, removing his helmet and unplugging the radio earphones. "I don't mind telling you I've been a little worried too, Steve. It's been a long day."

"Come on, friend. Let's get you up to the cabin."

"Give me a few minutes to unwind, Steve," requested Joe.

"I've got a hot cup of coffee for you, Joe," offered Mark from the passenger side door of the helicopter. He slowly climbed into the seat beside Joe and removed the cap on the thermos bottle. "I'm proud of you, Joe. Semper Fi."

"Semper Fi, Sir. I can't think of anything I'd rather have right now than a cup of Bright Cloud's coffee. Thank you." Joe accepted the cup with shaking hands and drank some of the warm liquid. It instantly refreshed him. "Ah, that tastes good. Today was the second time in my life when I was sure I was going to die. God I was scared, Sir."

"Every man is capable of fear, Joe. Those who claim to never feel it are liars. I was always frightened in combat during the two world wars," Mark freely admitted.

"Today is a day I'll always remember," recounted Joe, grasping Steve's shoulder. "My irresponsible drinking has been way out of line. I promise, on my honor as an officer, that it'll never happen again. Something happened out there today. I prayed harder than I've ever prayed in my life, and my prayers were answered."

"God works in different ways, Joe," added Mark. "I'm not surprised that he watched over you today. You've always been in our prayers."

"I know that, Sir, and I disappointed a lot of people with my drinking over the past months. I'm positive that any helicopter which dropped into the hole that transport fuselage dragged me into would have self-destructed in seconds, but mine held together! God has given me another chance and I'm going to take it."

"I hear my old friend, Joe Lance, again," said Steve, relieved that the man he had come to love like a brother was determined to do better.

"I could have set the helicopter down in a number of places, but I wanted to return to Fort Lewis. This place has been a refuge for me, but most of all I wanted to be with my friends. You won't have to worry about me anymore. You have my word on it. That coffee really hit the right spot, Colonel Leroux. I've been running on nerves all day." Joe held out the empty cup for Mark to refill for him. The fresh coffee aroma filled the damp cockpit. Joe drank the second cup slowly with pleasure.

Morning Dew and Tom witnessed what had taken place. Dew stepped up to the door held open by her father and said: "Uncle Joe, I want you to know that we're so proud of you. We were worried about you in this terrible weather." She hugged him as he climbed out of the aircraft. "I'm sure that Marshall will be proud of his Dad, also."

"It really wasn't that difficult, besides there was no other way to get those injured airmen out of the plane. Thanks for your thoughts, Dew. Marshall would have been disgusted with me if he had seen me last night. It's getting raw out here. A warm shower and hot meal will be appreciated."

Joe buttoned up the front of his jacket and looked around the wharf to see if Mark had climbed out of the helicopter without slipping in the rain. They both retired from the Marine

Corps with the rank of Colonel, but their friendship went deeper than that. It was almost like a father-son relationship. The months since Kay left him for another man, the Leroux's had sat and listened for hours at a time while Joe bared his soul to them trying to work his way through the traumatic period he was experiencing. He appreciated their kindness and unselfishness in making themselves available when he needed someone to talk to. Joe saw Mark almost fall getting out of the helicopter.

"Colonel Leroux," exclaimed Joe as he and Steve rushed to Mark's side. "You're going to get soaked."

"Well, I've been wet a lot of times in my life, once more won't make much difference," answered Mark with a determined tone in his voice. "It'll just make us appreciate a warm fire all the more when we get inside."

Tom knew that Mark could not walk as fast as the rest of the group at the wharf, so he rushed to the Hudson Bay Store where the factor loaned him an umbrella to help keep Mark from getting a chill in the pounding rain.

"I've got an umbrella for you, Mr. Leroux," announced Tom, positioning himself at Mark's right side so that he could shelter the elderly gentleman from the rain. Dew linked her arm around his left arm to guide and steady him while Mark used the cane in his right.

"I'm surprised that Grandmother let you out in this weather, Grandfather." Dew was seriously concerned for him.

"You know, young lady," replied Mark in his independent whimsical way. "There are some things a man just has to do whether others like it or not. I wanted to be present when my friend, Joe Lance, safely landed, and I wanted him to know that we're proud to be his friends."

Dew smiled and shook her head at the frail man slowly making his way towards the cabin. "I love you, Grandfather."

"This weather is not fit for man or beast," said Steve, following behind Mark. "I'm sure that Bright Cloud is going to insist that her husband change his wet clothes and take a warm shower when he gets home. Why don't you come to our cabin for the same treatment, Joe. Then we can all get together for supper with Bright Cloud and Colonel Leroux."

"That sounds great to me, Steve. How pleasant it is to be back in the company of people who care."

Bright Cloud planned a dinner centered around the beautiful string of whitefish Mark and Tom had caught that morning. Since it was a damp raw day outside, she decided to bake the fish in her cast iron wood stove which would heat the cabin and cook their supper at the same time. She wanted to make sure that the cabin was warm for Mark's return from greeting Joe at the landing.

Faith insisted on helping Bright Cloud prepare the meal, volunteering to mix up a batch of drop biscuits, placing them in a large bake sheet. Together they peeled potatoes and carrots at the small kitchen table in the corner beside the wood stove. Faith could not help thinking how remarkably easy it was for her to feel comfortable and at ease with her new-found friend. She had never felt as welcome in any home as readily as the gracious white-haired Bright Cloud and the courtly Mark Leroux made her feel. Faith understood how difficult it was to lose a husband, but her two hosts had lost a son and a daughter! She shuddered at the impact of such a tragedy.

"I'm so glad that you came to Fort Lewis, Faith," remarked Bright Cloud in a soft melodious voice. "It's been nice to have new faces around. I feel bad that you had to sprain your ankle though. Mark seemed to grow younger today when he came back from the lake with Tom."

"I think both benefited from the opportunity to spend time together," said Faith. "I don't know how you and Mark have been able to handle the loss of two children. My heart goes out to both of you. Your family has served our country with much sacrifice."

"Accepting the loss of your own children is hard. Sometimes, I think of something I want to share with Bright Star, and the emptiness continues to linger. . . I went through the same thing with Daniel-Joseph. For years I swore that I could hear his footsteps on the porch of our house at Wells.

Once it was so real I even got out of bed to turn on the lights for him. Coming face to face with reality like that alone in the middle of the night almost destroyed me. I miss them just as much today. Mark handled it differently. He's a much more private person than I am. He held his grief in silence and spent a great deal of time in the forest at home in Wells and here at Fort Lewis. The forest has been an important sanctuary and salvation for my husband. I'm thankful that he has been able to draw strength from the serenity and solitude that has been such an important part of his life. He and DJ went hunting and fishing together a lot. I think Tom brings back some of those happier memories to Mark."

When Tom and Mark came through the door, Bright Cloud escorted Mark to the bathroom where she had laid out dry clothes for him. Faith was amused to notice how Bright Cloud's eyes lit up when her husband came through the door. Mark looked tired when he first entered the room, but there was also a victorious look in his eyes. He had accomplished what he wanted to do even if the effort exhausted him. Without a word, Tom checked the wood boxes by the fireplace and the kitchen stove. They were half empty, so he filled them from the firewood supply under the lean-to shelter behind the cabin. The small cedar log cabin had been built for Mark and Bright Cloud by the tribal council soon after they were married, and the Council still maintained an adequate amount of seasoned firewood for their annual use.

Steve, Dew, and Joe showed up at the Leroux cabin just as Mark had completed his shower and change of clothes. Joe embraced Bright Cloud and gave her a kiss on the cheek.

"It's nice to be back in your home," Joe said in a serious tone. He deliberately turned to Faith and said: "Mrs. Hamilton, I want to thank you for ordering coffee and sandwiches for me this morning at the plant site. I appreciate the thoughtfulness. They made it possible for me to do what had to be done."

"You're welcome, Mr. Lance," answered Faith, seeing a calmer, more positive Joe Lance than she had seen that morning. He did not have to apologize for anything tonight. He was relaxed and was glad to be in the company of friends.

Bright Cloud pointed to the table. "Why don't you men folks sit at the table and us girls will serve dinner."

That evening after the dishes were completed, they were sitting in front of the fireplace enjoying an evening of fellowship. Bright Cloud had been playing the piano while the rest of the gang joined in song. She played a few of the popular songs of the period such as *Moon River, Love Letters in the Sand, Strangers in the Night and Green Berets.*

Mark requested his all-time favorite, *Danny Boy.* "Would you sing it for me, Dew? It's such a beautiful song and it deserves a voice like yours."

"If you really want, Grandfather," Morning Dew shyly agreed.

Bright Cloud patted her on the arm. "I love to hear you sing, Dew. Your Grandfather has good taste. Here we go now."

The ancient Irish folk song told a sad story of a soldier going off to war. Dew sang it with feeling in a clear soprano voice, effortlessly reaching the highest notes which she held for a long time without faltering. She made eye contact with Tom when she sung the second stanza:

"But come ye back when summer's in the meadow,
Or when the valley's hushed and white with snow.
'Tis I'll be there in sunshine or in shadow.
Oh Danny boy, Oh Danny boy, I love you so."

The last line caused Tom to blush. He thought Dew was the most beautiful person in the world. She touched his heart with the music. Everyone clapped their hands. Tom enthusiastically joined in. He looked across the room at his mother who had been watching him.

Talk in the cabin came around to the fact that Steve was going to take Dew back to college soon. They planned to make a visit to Steve's mother and her husband at Lake George, when a knock came at the door.

"Come in," invited Mark in a raised voice.

"Hello, folks," announced Constable Jenkins. "I always seem to be barging in on your gatherings. Maybe this could have waited until morning, but I thought that you would want to know about the message that just came in over the wire." Jenkins placed a piece of paper in Steve's hand. He read it in silence and handed it to Mark and Bright Cloud who held it so that Dew could also read the message:

> Commanding Officer
> New England Naval District
> Boston, Mass.

Subject: Internment of Captain Dawn 'Bright Star' Jackson, USN.

Dear Mr. Jackson;

I have received notification that the last remains of your wife are scheduled to arrive in the United States next week. According to our records you have requested that she be buried at Wells, Maine. Please contact us so that we can schedule a color guard for the funeral ceremony.

This department is available to assist you in any way. Our sympathies are with you and your family.

> Sincerely
> Commander AL Jones, USN

Chapter Seven

"We always knew that this day would come," Mark said so low that few heard him. "It's time that she was brought home."

An air of sadness filled the room as each person searched for answers in the flames leaping from the burning birch logs. Mark and Bright Cloud saw Bright Star's face looking back at them through the flickering flames and long wisps of smoke. Her dark eyes were like glowing coals. There was a smile on her face and she seemed to be at peace. Her long black hair was done up in two braids that hung down across the front of her shoulders the way Bright Cloud had frequently fixed it for her when she was a little girl. Two red silk ribbons were tied in a bow at the end of each braid. Her image was so real that Bright Cloud cleared her throat and was about to speak when the vision disappeared as quickly as it had appeared. Mark placed his arm around Bright Cloud, holding back the tears.

Steve sat beside Morning Dew on the long couch and reflected in a wavering voice: "I remember the day your mother left. She made me promise that if something was to happen to her, we would remember the good times we all had together." Morning Dew placed her head on his shoulder and cried softly. Stroking her long black hair, Steve continued: "Going to the combat zone was something she wanted to do. At the time, I thought I understood it. . . Now, I'm not so sure."

"Bright Star's internment will be a difficult day, but it should help give everybody some closure," Joe added, deliberately walking to the front of the fireplace, knocking the ashes from his pipe on one of the fireplace andirons. He noted Mark and Bright Cloud's agony and felt powerless to comfort Steve, his best friend. "What beautiful memories we all have of her. It's hard to imagine that the energetic and vibrant Bright Star is no longer with us. The first time I met her was in Korea on a hospital ship off the coast of Wonsan. You and I went aboard together, Steve. She was the most dedicated nurse I've ever known and had the soul of a saint. It's sad to think that her time with us was cut short in the prime of her life. I've never experienced such a loss, so I don't know how you really feel deep inside. Your pain and grief is shared by those of us who are newcomers to your family circle. To have known Bright Star was to love her. Now that she's gone I pray that the void in your hearts will be filled with thanksgiving for having shared part of her life for as long as you did. Mourning her passing is natural, but like she told you, Steve, remember the good times, for we are blessed with a bountiful measure of them. She embraced the future with a passion and determination that defined her life. She would expect nothing less of the loved ones she left behind." Joe walked around behind Steve's chair and placed his hands on his shoulder.

Sitting quietly listening to what was being said, Faith glanced around the room. Mark and Bright Cloud grimly held each other feeling alone and forsaken. They stared expectantly at the extended flames on the burning logs as if Bright Star was still looking back at them. Images of days past flashed through their minds. Morning Dew continued to vent her grief as her father held her tightly in his arms. Faith noticed Tom watching Dew. He was distraught that she was weeping so openly. His eyes met his mother's. She quickly looked away, not wanting him to know that she saw what was in his heart. He cared for Morning Dew!

"I sympathize with your sorrow and pray that you will discover a resolve worthy of Bright Star's sacrifice. If my own experience is any guide, the only thing that eases the pain is time and a commitment to the future as Mr. Lance so eloquently stated," Faith reflected.

"Faith and Joe are correct," admitted Bright Cloud. "The hourglass of time for my gentle Mark and myself has fewer and fewer grains of sand remaining, so it's not as easy for us to close a chapter of our lives, but we too must make the effort. Steven and our beloved Dew have the opportunity, maybe even the responsibility, of making of their lives anything they desire. By doing that, they will know in their hearts that Bright Star will be watching over them with approval of their decisions."

The somber mood of the evening was broken when Joe mentioned that he would have to contact his company and make arrangements to repair the rotor on his helicopter. Faith was surprised to learn that the daily helicopter shuttle from Lac St. Jean to the plant site was conducted by the same company he worked for. Joe mentioned that he had flown the shuttle flight on several occasions during the first part of the summer.

"Do you think it would be possible for the shuttle to come to Fort Lewis to pick up Tom and me?" asked Faith, still wondering how she was going to get back to her work project. "I can do what remains to be done with these crutches if I have to. Things would go a lot better for me if I didn't lose any more time, because I was planning on going to Vermont with Tom when he started college. I also wanted to check on our vacant home there."

"I'm sure the shuttle crew would be glad to bring you back to your work, Mrs. Hamilton," assured Joe. "As a matter of fact, I should call dispatch before the evening is over to give them an update on my situation, and I'll relay your request. You can assume they'll be picking you up in the morning unless I tell you different. Well, Mr. and Mrs. Leroux, thanks again for a delicious meal and wonderful evening. I appreciate your support. I'll see you back at your cabin, Steve and Dew. Goodnight, Mrs. Hamilton and you too, Tom. Good luck in your school year."

"I've got a rain slicker you can use, Joe," said Mark, walking to a cedar-lined closet beside the kitchen. "It's still raining hard out, and you've been wet enough tonight."

"Thank you, Sir."

"Goodnight, Mr. Lance. I appreciate your notifying the shuttle for us," answered Faith.

"It's my pleasure. I owe you one for the coffee and sandwiches. Again, thanks for your thoughtfulness," Joe smiled, accepting the rain gear from Mark and letting himself out the door.

"I think we should be turning in, also," commented Steve, stepping up to the fireplace, turning his back to the warming glow of the embers. "The fire does feel good. Thanks to you two ladies for a great supper. I hope that your foot gets well soon, Mrs. Hamilton. When Dew and I are ready to depart for Burlington, maybe it would work out for you to join us. I'll keep you posted at the plant and you can decide later."

"That would be nice. I feel as if I've known all of you for a long time instead of just a weekend. I'm anxious to return home for a while. Our house is in Montpelier and I want to be sure everything is in order. I appreciate your offer."

Tom heard his mother conditionally accept Steve's offer and turned to smile at Dew who was putting on her parka.

"That would be great," exclaimed Dew, returning Tom's smile. "Maybe you'll have a chance to meet Aunt Michelle and Uncle Arlo who live at Lake George. He's a marine like Uncle Joe and Grandfather. Poor Dad, he always gets outvoted when they gang up on him." Dew laughed the way she often did, throwing her head backwards to let it roll easily out of her mouth.

"That would be swell. I hope it works out. It's been a nice surprise running into you way up here. Maybe we'll see you in the morning," added Tom, his eyes remaining fixed on Dew.

"Yes, I'll see you before you leave. Goodnight, Mrs. Hamilton. Tom has talked a lot about you. I'm glad to have met you. It would be nice flying to Vermont together."

"Thank you, Morning Dew. My misfortune has given me the opportunity to add all of you to my list of friends, and I'm the richer for it. Goodnight, young lady," Faith answered.

After Steve and Dew left, Mark selected a log from the woodbox and placed it on the dying embers of the fireplace. Everyone watched the smoke rise from the log for several seconds before it burst into flames. Faith could not shake the warm feeling she felt in Mark and Bright Cloud's living room. The atmosphere was enhanced by the glow of the flames of the fire, but the real source of the warmth that permeated the room came from the hearts of those present. It had touched Faith that first evening and still lingered. It made her feel comfortable and at ease; yet, a melancholic feeling embraced her, reinforcing the fact that she was alone. Sharing her thoughts with someone who cared was a luxury she often missed. The fellowship of the evening readily turned her thoughts to her deceased husband. She missed him the most at those times when she was the most content and unable to share her happiness and pleasure with him. His death still left an empty void in her life.

"Well, Tom, it won't be long before you start hitting the books again. Do you enjoy your forestry studies?" Mark asked, lighting his corn cob pipe.

"Yes, Sir. This semester I'll start to get into the real forestry subjects like silviculture and mensuration. At the end of the second year they have a four-week summer field course where we survey and inventory a tract of land and develop a forest management plan. Usually it's a parcel of land donated to the University by wealthy benefactors. I'm really looking forward to it. It should be a lot of fun."

"It's a rewarding profession, young man," Mark told him. It was a subject he felt passionately about. "I've always been proud to call myself a marine officer, but I must admit that I've been more proud to call myself a professional forester. It's a unique profession filled with quiet visionaries. Most foresters I've met have been independent-minded people who work at their best beneath the hushed solitude of a forest canopy. The land belongs to all of mankind, and it's the forester's job to protect it from fire, insects and disease, and even man himself. If the forests of the world are managed wisely by those who, at heart, are a part of the forest, then they will be perpetuated for those generations yet unborn."

"You make it sound like a noble profession, Mr. Leroux." Faith was impressed with the reflections of the gentle war hero sitting across from her. "I'm so glad that Tom has selected

68

forestry, too. I've known a number of foresters within the group of environmental specialists that I normally work with. As a group, they have displayed a vision and an inherent outlook further into the future than individuals in most other fields of endeavor."

"I've felt the same way," added Bright Cloud, quietly listening to her husband share his thoughts with their new-found friends.

"With all of your experience in the profession, Mr. Leroux, what has impressed you the most?" Tom asked.

Mark smiled at the studious young man sitting beside his mother on the couch and thought for a second before answering. "That's not an easy question to answer, Tom. I believe that I've been the most impressed over the years with the infinite capacity of the forest to produce valuable forest products for mankind and to reproduce and sustain itself with very little assistance from man. It didn't matter if it was the white pine region of central New England or the boreal spruce-fir forest type in northern Canada; the infinite capacity of the forest to heal itself has always fascinated me.

"I was naturally attracted to the forest. It was right at the back door of the home in Maine where I grew up. My father was a hard-working man who built and operated a sawmill most of his life. I worked with him as often as I could until I went to France in the First War. I always felt privileged to be in the forest and was inspired by its serenity. I firmly believe that it was responsible for giving me back my emotional well-being, saving me from a potential life of mental illness."

Mark paused in his response, watching the flames on the log. Bright Cloud reached out to hold his hand. A tinge of sadness filled Mark's eyes for a second, but when he met those of his wife, a smile appeared across his face. It was a poignant moment, and Faith felt privileged to share it with them.

"The harmony one feels within the forest is really a contradiction, for within the forest community there's a dynamic struggle competing for soil, water, and sunlight in a life-and-death contest for dominance and survival. My respect and awe for the continuity of Nature reinforces my belief in a benevolent and all-knowing God whose handy work surrounds us no matter where we go in this world."

"You're an inspiration for my son, Mr. Leroux," said Faith, understanding why her soft-spoken host was admired by so many.

"I don't know about anyone else," yawned Bright Cloud, getting up from the couch. "I'm tired and am going to turn in for the night. These rainy evenings put me to sleep easy."

"I believe I'll follow you, Bright Cloud," Faith added, picking up her crutches. "Thanks again for being so kind and letting Tom and me share your home."

"Rarely do we have guests. The chance to get to know you better has been special for us, too," answered Bright Cloud, taking Faith into her arms. "Rest well, Faith, and sleep as late as you want. Are you going to stay up a little longer, Mark?"

"I'll watch the logs burn down. If Tom wants, he's welcome to keep me company. Do you play cribbage?"

"Yes, I like to play the game. Mom beat me badly the last time we played."

"Well, I bet you two men will use up another log," anticipated Bright Cloud with a soft chuckle, placing a small log on the fire.

"Goodnight, Mrs. Leroux. I'll see you in the morning, Mom. I hope your ankle is better by then," Tom told her, positioning a chair beside Mark and the small table at the end of the couch. A beautifully polished red cedar cribbage board was already on the table.

Bright Cloud rummaged through a drawer in the kitchen for a new deck of cards and placed them on the cribbage board. "People don't play cards as much as we used to years ago. There are more ways to entertain oneself today. Goodnight, everyone."

Tom and Mark played until the embers of the last log that Bright Cloud had placed on the fire turned to gray ash. Tom was the first to peg the sixty-first hole on the board to win a game. Mark took the second game when they agreed that one more game would determine the evening's winner. Tom had not played cribbage long enough to be confident of all the rules, but Mark was very well versed in the rules of the game. Luck was with Tom. He won the third round pegging the sixty-first hole before Mark got to twenty-one. Mark laughed heartily as he placed the carved ivory pegs in a small compartment at the end of the cribbage board.

"If you tell Bright Cloud that you won two out of three games, she won't let me forget it for the rest of the day," Mark told him with a twinkle in his eye.

"Then we'll keep it between the two of us," grinned Tom. "Goodnight, Sir. I'll see you in the morning. Do you want me to bank the wood stove in the kitchen?"

"If you don't mind, Tom. A fire feels good at this time of year. It has been a pleasant evening. It's nice having young people around. I hope you sleep well. Goodnight."

A hot bed of coals remained in the kitchen stove. Tom filled the firebox with split wood from the small storage box next to the sink, and turned the flue damper so that it was partially closed. He shut the draft at the front of the stove so that the logs would burn longer throughout the night.

That evening when all had retired, the rain and wind subsided so that the constant fretful yipping of foxes in the distance could be heard. Suddenly the lonely call of a wolf penetrated the still night from the high rock outcrop west of the village. Across Lac Diamante an answer from the rest of the pack echoed throughout the landscape as the nocturnal creatures took over the night. The symphony of sound was punctuated by the sad, mournful cry of loons preparing for their flight to the south to escape the perils of a winter in the northern forest. The heavy overcast that had plunged the evening into darkness was beginning to lift. In between the breaks of the clouds, stars shone brightly against the blue void of the night. A chill settled over the landscape filling the air with a promise of more to come. Nature was preparing for the long dormant winter months when life seemed to stand still. It was a time when the earth gathered its living in sheltered places for the supreme test of winter. Those that survived and came forth in new glory with the promise of spring were strengthened and tempered by their simple test of survival.

Chapter Eight

The next morning Lac Diamante was covered with thick banks of rolling fog and mist. The somber beauty of the evening was slowly ebbing. Joe was up while it was still pitch dark outside. He had always enjoyed that brief period between the heavy darkness of the night and the shadowy beginning of a new day at dawn. The solitude that surrounded him gave birth to a better understanding of, and acquaintance with, himself. It was a special time of day for him. Decisions that had to be made came easier in the cool fresh air and the peace of morning's first light.

A light breeze out of the west was slowly dissipating the fog on the lake as he climbed up onto the rotor transmission of his helicopter. He removed an inspection panel, checking for evidence of damage. Portions of one rotor were missing, and each of the others were bent and cracked. It was a miracle that he made it back to Fort Lewis in one piece. His initial guess that all of the rotors would need to be replaced was confirmed. Other than the badly damaged blades Joe did not see any exterior evidence to indicate that the helicopter transmission was damaged.

Now that he could see how close he came to disaster, Joe reflected on his long career as a pilot. It seemed like yesterday when he climbed into the cockpit of a plane for the first time. It was in 1938, and he was twenty years old with two years of college behind him. The plane was an old Army surplus Boeing twin engine aircraft. He was broke and looking for a job, any kind of a job, where he could earn enough to survive. Both of his parents had died in the Asian flu epidemic that ravaged the country in 1919 when he was a child.

A friend from Syracuse University had offered Joe a summer job doing ground maintenance and helping around the airplanes at a field in northern New York. His friend's father had recently been awarded a government contract to fly the mail from Plattsburg to Boston, New York City, Albany, and back to Plattsburg. The nine hundred mile loop to the three cities took two days to cover. It gave him a chance to occasionally ride the route as a passenger on those days when he was not working. The first day that he flew, the pilot let him control the plane for a short distance. He had discovered that there was nothing else in the world he'd rather do than fly. It ignited a passion in him that still existed.

Joe learned to fly that summer. Instead of returning to college in the fall he remained working at the airfield and took formal flight instruction. In 1940 he became a licensed pilot and joined the only military service that would take him at that time, the Marine Corps. They sent him to the Naval Air School at Pensacola where he graduated as a second lieutenant ten months later, wearing the prestigious gold wings of a naval aviator. From that moment to the present, aviation had been an important part of his life. He could not imagine a life without the exhilaration he felt every time he lifted an aircraft from Mother Earth into the rarefied atmosphere. His hero was John Magee, an RAF pilot killed during the Battle of Britain when courageous British fighter pilots took to the skies in defense of England against the German Luftwaffe onslaught. Joe had long memorized the immortal lines Magee wrote before he was killed:

> Up, up long delirious burning blue
> I've topped the wind-swept heights with easy grace
> Where never lark or even eagle flew,
> And while with silent, lifting mind I've trod
> The high untrespassed sanctity of space,
> Put out my hand, and touched the face of God.

The first rays of the new day sun reflected from the scattered cumulous clouds onto the waters of Lac Diamante, painting a pageantry of color that interrupted Joe's inspection of the helicopter. He became completely absorbed in the placid scene. The eastern sky was alive with yellow and red hues radiating from the rising sun. Joe never tired of the beauty and brilliance of a sunrise above the sixtieth parallel.

Suddenly out of the corner of his eye he saw a movement near the infirmary to his left. He looked closer to see if it was one of the Mounted Policemen, but it was Faith standing on the shore balancing on her crutches, completely transfixed by the array of color against the eastern shore of the lake. She stood motionless for minutes unaware that he was walking along the shore towards her.

"Good morning, Mrs. Hamilton," Joe greeted her. She was startled and turned away from him. She was crying and avoided his inquiring eyes. "I'm sorry. I didn't mean to intrude."

"I'm all right, Mr. Lance. The sunrise hypnotized me with its beauty. I was wishing that I could share it with my husband. Excuse the tears. I don't know what has happened to me these past few days."

"Did you ever think that your husband might be sharing the moment with you?" Joe asked in a reassuring voice.

"Yes, I've felt that it could be possible. This weekend has been such a pleasant outing even with the ankle. For some reason I've felt his loss more than usual."

"You don't have to apologize to me. I was enjoying the sunrise, too. The further north you go, the crisper and more colorful it becomes. I've always been an early riser so that I could start the day with its birth at sunrise. Frequently it's the only time I can sort things out with a rational mind."

"I've often felt the same way. . ." answered Faith, blowing her nose with a white handkerchief.

"Just before I noticed you standing here I was reminiscing about the lines of a dead RAF pilot. He wrote the simple and eloquent words most pilots feel in the freedom of space."

"Oh, I think I know the verse you're talking about. 'The long delirious burning blue; I've topped the wind-swept heights with easy grace; where never lark, or even eagle flew...' Those lines have comforted me ever since I was a young soldier's wife during World War Two."

"He's one of my favorite heroes. Incidentally, Mrs. Hamilton, I spoke to the dispatch center last night. The shuttle will come to Fort Lewis to pick you up as soon as it unloads its cargo at the plant. They were glad to do it for their star engineer," Joe said with a grin.

"Thank you for arranging it for Tom and me," she responded, returning his smile. "I'm the only female at the site and try to do my job with a minimum of fuss. The project people have been great to work with."

"Could you and I make a deal?" asked Joe.

"I think so... It all depends," answered Faith, caught slightly off guard by his question.

"If you'll call me Joe, I'll call you Faith, if you don't mind."

"No, I don't mind, Joe. Please do call me Faith. I apologize for my emotional outbreak."

"Then Faith it is. Don't apologize to me or anyone else for those things you hold close to your heart. As you know, my wife left me two years ago, and I haven't been the same man since the breakup. I can't seem to let go, and I don't know why," said Joe, surprised at his confession. It was the first time he had put into words the agony that possessed him. "I found comfort and shelter in alcohol and for a while was able to convince myself that I had found the magic solution for coping with problems. I'm not going to promise that it will never happen again because I've already done that to Steve and Mr. and Mrs. Leroux several times and broke my vow each time; however, I can say with honest conviction that I will try harder than ever to get the demons off my back and overcome the weakness. I think I've got God on my side this time," Joe exclaimed with conviction.

"I'm sure God will be with you, Joe," assured Faith. "He works in different ways. It's only natural for humans to seek relief from pain. Sometimes we look for relief in the wrong places."

"Your husband must have been a fine person to have earned such faithfulness and loyalty."

"Yes, he was a good man," she admitted, unwilling to elaborate further. It was her private world, and she did not wish to share it with a recent acquaintance. "He would have liked this place. Fort Lewis has been filled with surprises for Tom and me. I can understand why Bright Cloud and Mark return year after year."

"It was her birthplace and ancestral home. You would have loved their daughter, Bright Star. She was a youthful version of Bright Cloud in many ways. She and Steve had a wonderful life together. He's still traumatized by the tragedy," Joe replied.

Faith used her crutches to move closer to the water's edge where she sat down on a large rock, holding her feet above the water line. It was then that she noticed the helicopter sitting on the dock. "Does your helicopter need many repairs?"

"More than I expected. At a minimum, we'll have to replace the complete rotor wheel. The shuttle helicopter can bring that over to us on its next trip. A mechanic will accompany them. I'll assist him in replacing the assembly. We won't know about the ultimate disposition of the transmission until I start it up with the new rotors. Even if it appears to be in complete balance, I'll take it back to our base facility in northern New York State for a complete overhaul. In aviation you don't take any more chances than are necessary. Well, I'll get back to my work. The fact that you're up so early is a good sign that your ankle is healing."

"It does feel better. I think I'll be able to discard the crutches tomorrow."

"I wish you luck, Faith." Joe started to walk away.

"Joe," cried Faith hastily. "May I ask you some questions about Korea?"

Joe turned to confront her and saw an anguished look on her face as if she was afraid of something. "If I can help, I'll be glad to answer any question you may have."

"I was wondering if you could describe the conditions you observed on the eastern side of the Chosin Reservoir when our forces were completely destroyed. I know that Steve and you were giving ground support to the Army unit that my husband was a part of."

"Are you sure you want to know, Faith?" Joe questioned her request. He was reluctant to describe the tragic circumstances surrounding her husband's death.

"Yes. I want to know everything you can tell me about the destruction of the Army Regimental Combat Team. My husband commanded an infantry company, and as far as I know was killed on the last day of their defense when they were overrun. A few survivors were able to escape to the marine perimeter across the ice. All I know is what our friend Colonel Scott Taylor told me a year after it happened. Anything you can add will help me put the bad dreams to rest," begged Faith.

"I flew with the last sortie to give ground support on that final day of organized resistance. The remaining men were in small defensive postures near a bridge. Their wounded were loaded on the few serviceable trucks ready for a breakout to the marine base across the reservoir ice. We mustered every available aircraft at Wonsan including a few South African Mustangs so that we could maintain a steady level of support for that last rush to the relative safety of the marine perimeter. Then everything seemed to go wrong!" Joe replied, looking across Lac Diamante, reliving the nightmare of that day nineteen years ago.

"You mean the short drop of napalm on our troops from the lead Corsairs?" asked Faith firmly.

"Yes, there was a short drop on some of the trucks. We could see that it created pandemonium on the ground. The Chinese troops were on both sides of the road and bridge. We never knew for certain which plane dropped the bombs that landed short of their intended mark. We were trying to hit targets of opportunity within fifty feet of the road. The enemy was everywhere. We were too late to give much assistance to the brave Americans on the ground." Joe turned to look directly at Faith. His taught facial features registered the agony that filled his soul. She was afraid that she had asked too much of him.

"It may have been me that dropped that load of bombs, I don't know, but it could have been. . . We were helpless to keep the enemy from destroying what was left of the stalled convoy," Joe continued. "There were just too many of them. We fired our machine guns right up until we started to hit the vehicles, but it didn't help. Our time on target was very limited because we did not carry auxiliary fuel tanks. We carried ordnance instead of extra gas. When I was ordered by our group leader to break contact and return to base, I saw that the few remaining Army survivors were desperately trying to reach the marine perimeter across the frozen reservoir." Joe took a deep breath, leaning against the rock for support, struggling to contain the desolate feeling of inadequacy which generally accompanied memories of that final sortie. "We were too late to save them. Anything we might have done would not have been enough at that time."

Faith listened intently, watching Joe relive an agonizing time in his life, and regretted having asked him for information. "I'm sorry, Joe. I didn't mean to dredge up hurtful memories. I just thought that the more I knew of the way Thomas died would help me accept it easier."

"There isn't a night that goes by that I don't think about our last mission to help the beleaguered troops. The nightmare recurs often and I'm still not sure if I'm the one who pulled the bomb release lever too soon! I may be the one who killed your husband!" cried Joe. Beads of sweat formed just below the hair line on his forehead. A muscle on the left side of his neck throbbed profusely. "I don't believe I can tell you anymore than that." Joe stood up from the rock and started to walk away.

"Please don't go, Joe," pleaded Faith. "It was selfish of me to even think that I was the only one to be burdened with what happened on that tragic day. Now I know that others are equally troubled, and I'm sorry that I asked. Please forgive me, I wasn't thinking."

"All of the men in that formation were heroes. My God, they held their ground for four days and five nights without giving up, even when they ran out of ammunition and medical supplies," Joe continued, looking into Faith's eyes. "You have every right to be proud of what your husband achieved. Their valor purchased valuable time for the marine division on the other side of the Chosin Reservoir to concentrate and collect their forces. They eventually made a successful retreat down the single road to the coast where the navy was waiting to evacuate them. It is probably safe to say that without the sacrifice of the men in your husband's outfit, the marine division might have met the same fate. Before I finish, you should know that everything humanly possible was done to save the situation. We tried, but we were just too late!"

"I accept and appreciate that. I never doubted for a second that the air groups did all that mortal man could do. I already knew about the short drop of napalm. It was not my intention to assign blame to anyone for the death of Tom's father," Faith quickly replied, hoping to alleviate his discomfort. "All we can do is blame the war. I'm sorry I brought up the subject."

"Would you forgive me if I was the one who dropped the bomb that killed your husband?"

"I know that you and Steve served our country with courage and distinction. Nobody can deny that. The question you pose is a cruel attempt to place blame and I refuse to do any such thing. How could I hold you responsible for his death? No one knows for certain when he died, and I accepted that fact a long time ago. No, Joe Lance, I don't blame you. Please stop punishing yourself with such cruel thoughts," begged Faith, anxious to change the subject. "Come, Joe, why don't we go back to the cabin? I'll bet Bright Cloud has got a pot of coffee brewing."

"I think I'd like that," replied a relieved Joe. "Since we're on the subject, there's something I'd like to share with you. I've never mentioned it to Steve or anyone else. I was a witness to the hopeless situation the men in your husband's outfit found themselves through no fault of their own. They made all

Americans feel proud. I'm a proud marine officer and would have been honored if my son had wanted to share that privilege with me. Instead he chose to enter the Military Academy at West Point. At first I was disappointed, until I thought about the caliber of men, like your husband, who faced certain death because there was no relief available, yet they fought valiantly to the very end. I thought that if the Army can produce such men, then my son made a wise choice. The day he received his commission on the sacred plains beside the Hudson River was the proudest day of my life."

"Of course you're proud of him. I wouldn't be surprised that your son, Marshall, may be equally proud of his dad. Thank you for sharing that with me, Joe."

"A cup of coffee does sound good." Joe helped Faith get down from the rock.

The smell of wood smoke filled the air beneath the tall spruce trees as the villagers started their stoves for the first meal of the day. Tom had already eaten the breakfast Bright Cloud had served him. She was beaming as she watched the young man consume a large number of pancakes. Mark had tried to match him but quickly reached his limit while Tom was only half full.

"I like to see people sit up to the table and eat heartily," explained Bright Cloud.

"The pancakes and maple syrup were delicious, Mrs. Leroux. Thank you," said Tom. "If I may be excused, I'm going to work off some of the food by filling the woodboxes."

"You're going to spoil me, Tom," declared Mark, lighting his corn cob pipe. "But I won't complain if you really want the exercise."

The large wood storage area on the south side of the cabin was filled with two different lengths of wood. The longer two foot lengths were for the fireplace. The wood cook stove in the kitchen area required wood half as long and split into smaller pieces so as to regulate the temperature easier depending on what was being cooked on the stove. Tom started to load up his left arm with fireplace logs when he saw Morning Dew walk towards her grandparents' cabin.

"Good morning, Kimberly," he shouted to get her attention.

"Hi Tom," answered Dew, surprised to see him at work so early. "I'll help you bring in a load. Which name do you prefer to call me, Kimberly or Morning Dew?"

"I don't believe it matters what I think," Tom replied. "It's what you prefer. Morning Dew has a nice sound to it with connotations of something fresh and pure. There's something serene and peaceful about the image it creates in the mind. I think Kimberly is a nice name, too. It doesn't matter which I like better; it's what you feel comfortable with that's important."

"Have you ever heard anyone call me a half-breed?" asked Dew deliberately.

"Why are you asking me these things, Dew?" Tom was bewildered and upset by her directness. "If I ever heard anyone call you a half-breed, I'd make them take it back and apologize. You have two wonderful parents and should be proud of the heritage and legacies they've passed on to you. As for me, I'm proud to call you my friend. I think you're the most beautiful girl in the world!"

Chapter Nine

Morning Dew heard what Tom had said and turned to look at him. Tom, wondering if he had gone too far in declaring himself, continued piling wood in his arm, afraid to meet her inquiring glance.

"Thank you, Tom," she said, flattered by his response. For some time she had the feeling that Tom liked her, but his comment indicated that it might go deeper than that. He was a quiet, serious young man not given to rash statements. "I'm glad you and I are friends. I'm also pleased that you've had a chance to see first-hand where some of my roots are. It has been nice meeting your mother. She's a lovely lady. Have you had breakfast?"

"Yes, your grandmother loaded me up with pancakes. Maybe I ate all of them," laughed Tom, heading towards the cabin with an arm full of wood, relieved to change the subject.

"You better not have because I'm starved," replied Dew, following behind him with a small handful of wood for the kitchen stove.

Bright Cloud placed the heavy cast iron pancake griddle to the front of the stove as soon as she heard Dew's voice coming through the door. Mark turned to watch the two young people stack their wood in the appropriate wood boxes. Their energy and enthusiasm was contagious. Dew reminded him and Bright Cloud of their beloved Bright Star. It was almost as if she had never gone away.

"Pancakes are on, Dew," announced Bright Cloud. "Is your dad up yet?"

"No, Grandmother. He was up most of the evening sitting in the dark. I doubt if he slept very much last night. He told me he wanted to be alone for a while. I checked on him this morning, and he's sleeping soundly."

"Sometimes a person has to have time and space to work through things," Mark quietly said to himself. "Come, dear girl. Sit down and let your grandmother fill you up. I'm ready to burst, and our new friend Tom has done justice to her cooking."

Before Tom could answer, his mother and Joe entered the cabin. They were both in a sober mood. Tom could tell from her swollen eyes that his mother had been crying. She smiled at him as if to let him know that everything was all right. Bright Cloud volunteered to do pancakes for everybody, and invited them to sit down at the table.

"You're just in time, Faith and Joe. I've another coffee pot ready on the back of the stove. Make yourselves comfortable."

"I'm not in the habit of being waited on like this, Bright Cloud," confirmed Faith. "So I insist on cleaning up and doing the dishes afterward."

"I'll help you, Mrs. Hamilton," volunteered Dew.

"And I'll let you two do it," Bright Cloud added, pouring coffee for Faith and Joe.

"What's the situation with your helicopter, Joe?" asked Mark.

"The rotors are junk, but I don't see anything else in need of replacement. We'll have to rev up the motor after the new rotors are installed before we'll be certain about the transmission," Joe replied.

When everyone was finished eating, Faith and Dew affectionately escorted Bright Cloud out of the kitchen into her favorite chair in the living room while they took over the job of cleaning the kitchen and the dishes. The three men took the hint and joined her. Faith was able to move about in the compact kitchen area on her swollen ankle without the crutches.

"I don't know when I've enjoyed a weekend as much as this one," she said, wiping the sink dry after Dew took the last dish and placed it in the cupboard. "It has been nice meeting you, Dew. Tom has mentioned you in some of his letters to me. Are you anxious to go back to school?"

"I always enjoy my summers here in Fort Lewis, but I'm ready to return to school in the fall. Daddy comes to Vermont to visit me once in a while. I was homesick at first, but I've adjusted to the college routine. It's exciting meeting new friends. Tom spoke often about you, Mrs. Hamilton. He's one of my best friends on campus."

"I'm glad for that. Sometimes his shyness keeps him from joining in as wholeheartedly as most young men. He's a lot like his father."

The pulsating throb of the shuttle helicopter interrupted Faith. It made a turn around the village and landed on the Hudson Bay trading post's loading dock. Faith and Tom hurriedly said their good-byes to everyone and rushed to the waiting aircraft. Dew and Joe accompanied them. Joe requested that the pilot make a loop up and around the lookout rock west of the village before heading to the aluminum plant site. Tom helped his mother climb aboard the helicopter and took a seat beside her. His eyes met those of Dew. She hollered something to him but he could not make it out. She shrugged her shoulders and waved to them. Joe gave an all clear thumbs-up to the pilot and waved to Tom and Faith. The helicopter lifted rapidly, gaining adequate height to climb above the rock formation that sheltered the village of Fort Lewis from the harsh prevailing westerly winds during the winter months. The "look-out" was the village's most prominent landmark.

Faith and Tom returned to the Trails End anxious to complete the initial phase of Faith's responsibility for the first season of construction. The most pressing project in need of completion was the establishment of permanent bench markers throughout the site. The day after they arrived, Faith was able to get around without her crutches. She enlisted Tom as her assistant to hold the stadia rod while she operated the transit. Precision was a necessity for the documentation of the markers. Every measurement in the future would be referred to them, and new data would be computed based upon their accuracy.

For two days they worked diligently completing the task. All that remained to be done was to create a new map showing the locations of each bench marker and its elevation. When it was finished they would be free to leave the plant site at their discretion for Vermont.

Steve left a message at the office for Faith that their plans called for a tentative departure date early Friday morning if weather permitted. He informed her that his Norseman was capable of carrying four passengers and their luggage with ease. Faith confirmed her receipt of the message and told Steve that the shuttle would make a special run to lift her and Tom to Fort Lewis at any hour they wanted to go. It rained all day on Thursday, so she didn't have much faith that the next day would be any better for flying. She rose at two o'clock in the morning on Friday and opened her apartment door to check the sky. It was all aglow with glistening stars and the ubiquitous northern lights arching from horizon to horizon. The weather looked perfect for flying to her. Faith was excited about the prospect of going home. It had been a long summer's work. She had learned much about herself since she came to northern Canada. She had the comforting feeling that she was leaving the wilderness a better person than she was on first arrival.

The memory of Glenn Hastings was still there, but the sting of rebuttal did not hurt as much. For years her grief had been at the center of everything that she did. It had controlled her relationship with others. She was aware that she had developed a selfish attitude as if she was the only person to have suffered. The weekend stay at Fort Lewis had shown her how other people handled the tragedies in their lives. She honored the memory of her beloved Thomas and hoped that she did not create a temple of exclusivity where he was elevated to the role of a God, which he was not. She liked to believe that the best testament to his memory was to live her life in such a way that she maintained her integrity and honor.

She thought of Bright Cloud and Mark who had lost two adult children on the field of battle. The two elder citizens of Fort Lewis were a model of grace and courage in the face of devastating heartbreak. Faith could relate to the sorrow Steve was carrying over the death of his wife, Bright Star. They had shared twenty-five years of marriage. To suddenly lose such a partner and continue with his life was a testament to the love they shared and to Steve's courage to live as Star would have wanted him to. Even Joe's rejection by his wife of almost thirty years could be construed as more difficult to accept than if she had been killed in the line of duty.

The morning shuttle arrived at Trails End at three-thirty in the morning while it was still dark. The pilot called Faith's quarters requesting that she get ready as soon as possible because the helicopter was scheduled for duty further north in the Province. Fifteen minutes later, Faith and Tom rushed to the helicopter pad with suitcases in hand. The chopper lifted off the helipad. A few minutes later it set down on the Hudson Bay wharf at Fort Lewis where they were met by an excited Morning Dew.

"Good morning, Mrs. Hamilton and Tom. It's awful early to be underway. There's been a last minute change of plans. Last night my father came down with a temperature of one hundred four degrees. He's in the infirmary now. Uncle Joe was flown in last night by the Mounted Police. He's taking us to Vermont in my father's plane."

"How serious is your father's illness?" asked Tom.

"We don't know. He hasn't been taking very good care of himself lately. His eating and resting habits have changed. I think he's just plain worn out with a low resistance to every strange bug that comes along."

"That sounds logical, Dew," said Faith, looking around at the village. It was pitch dark except for the spotlight over the entrance of the police station.

"Let me help you with your bags, Mrs. Hamilton," requested Dew, holding a flashlight to illuminate the way to the waiting Norseman airplane sitting in the water beside the police wharf.

Joe's helicopter was still sitting on the wharf evidently in need of more repairs than Joe anticipated. Dew guided them around an assortment of tool boxes to the Norseman which had a light on in the cabin. Joe was standing on the outside float conducting a preflight inspection.

"Hello," greeted Joe. "I hope that our spur of the moment change of time and pilot hasn't upset your plans."

"No," replied Faith. "Tom and I were ready to leave on a short notice anyway. We were rushed before coffee, but I've always got a few candy bars to satisfy a growling stomach if needed."

"Well, I had a feeling you would not have time for coffee, so I requested that the police supply us with a couple of thermos bottles and some of Bright Cloud's muffins, made last night just for us," explained Joe, climbing into the cabin. "We're ready for takeoff. If you'll give me your cases, I'll store them in the compartment behind the seats. Dew's stuff is already on board. Dew has offered the front seat beside the pilot to you, Faith. It's considered the seat of honor. She and Tom can use the back seats."

Joe used his flashlight to secure the bags in the storage compartment. Once everyone was in their assigned seats, Joe released the mooring lines and pushed the plane as far away from the dock as possible. Returning to the pilot's seat, he asked everyone to buckle up their seat belts. He reached above his head for a radio headband and turned on extra lights inside the cabin to explain its use:

"The plane is equipped with an internal communication system that will allow us to talk to each other through a microphone. You'll notice it on the ceiling above your seat. Place them over your ears adjusting the thin microphone slightly below your chin. It'll pick up anything you say and won't be in your way. Any questions?"

"Thanks for the coffee," responded Faith, adjusting the head set.

"I owe you a cup of coffee, remember?" Joe grinned and started the plane's engine. "I'll taxi out to the center of the lake before we start our take-off run. Shifts in wind direction can be tricky for a float-equipped plane. I can detect wind patterns better the further we are from shore. At this point I want to admit that this whole business of starting so early in the morning was my idea. I apologize for the rush, but as soon as we take off and climb a few thousand feet in elevation, I'll show you a sight I hope you find worth the effort."

The sturdy single-engine Norseman aircraft bounced from wave to wave as it picked up speed enough to break the static tension of the floats free of the water. The instant lift-off took place, the engine changed pitch and settled into a steady hum. The cabin became relatively quiet, but the individual microphones eliminated the need for anyone to have to shout to be heard. Joe turned on the aircraft running lights so that the passengers could see the lake drop away from the plane.

The plane was heading east with a tail assist from the prevailing westerly winds. Joe gently pulled the craft up to three thousand feet and checked his compass to make sure he was on a true easterly track; then he turned off all the lights on the airplane, continuing to climb at a fast rate. He kept quiet, letting the scene before them unfold without interruption.

Faith was the first to see it and gasped, holding her breath at its sudden appearance. The black void that had been all around them suddenly disappeared and was replaced with an ethereal, dreamlike panorama of brilliant red and orange colors that filled the eastern sky before them. It was almost as if the passengers were detached from the plane and had become an integral part of the luminous rays reaching out from the sun moments before it first lifted a small portion of its head above the black horizon. The passengers saw it at the highest elevation. A few feet below there was no hint of the change taking place. The sudden richness of the color was its most striking element.

Below the horizon a straight line delineated the colorful display from Mother Earth which was still an indistinguishable black mass. As the craft sped toward the East, the heavens filled more and more with bright rays of sunshine reflecting off the scattered low hanging cumulous clouds looking like islands of white against a tableau of red-orange hues. It looked as if the sky was on fire and that the relatively fragile aircraft was going to run into the cauldron of color.

"Oh my Lord, it's a beautiful sight!" cried Faith, unable to contain her enthusiasm. "The birth of a new day."

Joe and Morning Dew had witnessed the phenomenon before. It never failed to quicken their pulse and give pleasure to the heart. Tom was spellbound like his mother. The darkness of the craft and the surrounding burst of light added to the illusion that they were about to be immersed in the vista. Tom held his breath at first, not knowing what to expect, but his misgivings soon melted away when he viewed the magnitude of the rich color from the other side of the world.

Joe maintained the easterly track for twenty minutes before turning the Norseman to the South with all running lights on again. Within that time, daylight had spread from the east to the west in a steady progression of light dissipating the dark of night.

"Was it worth being rousted out of bed so early in the morning?" asked Joe, glancing at Faith.

"Oh, yes! It was a wonderful surprise, Joe," Faith replied, adjusting her microphone. "What a wonderful experience. Thank you for sharing it with us. I've never seen such an expanse of color in my life. From now on I'll look at a normal sunrise with a renewed respect."

"I remember a class I had in English," acknowledged Tom excitedly. "In one of the windows of the classroom we could read a sign on the marquee which read 'RESTROOM'. The view of the marquee from a different window read, 'CRESTROOM'. It was a simple lesson in perspectives and points of view. Our vantage point in the plane turned a beautiful sunrise into a spiritual experience."

"What did you think the first time you saw the sunrise, Joe?" Faith asked, sensing that there was more depth and perception to the man than her first impression indicated.

"Up here in the northern latitudes, the transition from night to day, and the reverse, are more pronounced and take place much quicker than down in the states. My first thought was a remembrance of the poem we talked about by John Magee, especially the last line: 'Put out my hand, and touched the face of God'. Each time I experience the sunrise, it's as if I'm seeing it for the first time."

"You love to fly, don't you?" she asked. It showed on his face. He was a man completely at peace behind the controls of the airplane.

"Is it that obvious?"

"Yes, it is. I envy anyone that's able to experience a level of satisfaction with their occupation where everything seems right with the world. It's an important achievement to recognize and find that gift."

"Don't forget," reminded Joe honestly. "There have been times in my life where I've sunk to the lowest level of humanity. I've always known that I had an affinity for alcohol. Over the years I've been able to exercise restraint so that it never became a problem. I was a walking alcoholic, but never a drunk, until things started to fall apart with my life. I'm not proud of what I've done since Kay decided she wanted out from the marriage."

"Don't be too harsh on yourself, Uncle Joe," interrupted Morning Dew. "Next to my father I think you're the kindest, most considerate person I've ever known. I'm proud of you. Daddy thinks so, too, or he would have thought twice about you flying us to school, but he didn't."

"I appreciate the confidence and trust all of you have placed in me. Now, our first stop is going to be at the Mounted Police Station at Lac St. Jean. We'll be able to grab a bite to eat while we get refueled. Our second refueling will be at Greenville, Maine on Moosehead Lake." Joe looked at the passengers in the plane with a smug set to his jaw. "When Steve called me to make the trip to Vermont, I took the liberty of arranging for the sunrise and another stop that I won't mention until we get there."

Joe landed the plane at the Mounted Police Barracks where they used the restroom facilities and ate a light lunch while the plane was being refueled. It had taken them two hours to fly from Fort Lewis. It would take another two hours to travel to Moosehead Lake. Joe requested police dispatch to notify Fort Lewis of their arrival and gave the aircraft a thorough visual check before lifting off again. He checked his flight plan and steered to a southerly setting. Two hours later they were refueling at Folsom's Air Service in Greenville, Maine. Joe ran into the office where he made a phone call while the passengers used the opportunity to stretch their legs with a short walk along the shore of Moosehead Lake.

The day remained sunny with excellent visibility. They recognized that the temperature was several degrees warmer than when they left Fort Lewis. The noon day sun felt good. When the refueling was completed, Joe left the office with a large grin on his face. He instantly made another preflight check of the aircraft before climbing into his seat.

"I'm sure that everybody must be hungry. Be patient a little longer and we can have a leisurely meal at some old friends," announced Joe.

"Old friends?" questioned Faith.

"Yes, and that's all I'm going to tell you. Morning Dew is bursting to tell you our destination. I hope it will be a surprise you'll enjoy." Joe lifted the plane from the water. Faith could not imagine what Joe was up to or who he was talking about. He was pleased to spring a surprise on her, and he was like a little boy having trouble keeping a secret.

The small town of Monson was located ten miles south of Moosehead Lake on the eastern shore of Lake Hebron. The surrounding countryside was dotted with several large deep holes where slate had been quarried for the last one hundred years. Immense piles of slate dumps stood in silent testimony to the vast amount of material that had been removed from the cavernous tunnels that ran laterally from the large centrally driven pit. The pits were now filled with water several hundred feet deep.

They flew above the village laid out along the single highway leading to Greenville as Joe pointed the airplane along the east-west axis of the lake to check the surface for the presence of swimmers or boaters that could be endangered by the landing of the float plane. Satisfied that the water was okay for landing, he turned around toward the village and landed as quickly as possible, keeping the craft in a straight line. Once on the water he slowly steered the plane to the southern shore where they noticed a man and a woman waiting on a wooden dock, waving to them.

Faith strained her eyes to look at the couple. She was convinced that she had never seen the woman before. The man was instantly recognizable. Tall, muscular with a military bearing that made him stand out in a crowd, she cried out loud: "That man looks like Colonel Scott Taylor."

Chapter Ten

Scott Taylor secured the airplane to the dock and opened the door to help Faith out of the plane. He was tall and athletic in appearance, looking like the soldier that he was. He had prominent facial features and eyes that could be intimidating, but Faith always remembered them as being kind and studious. He and her beloved Thomas had been the best of friends for years. They were of similar temperaments.

"Welcome to our home, Faith. I must say that the years have been kind to you," said Scott, holding out his arms to her. She eagerly sought his embrace and fought hard to hold back the tears. The last time she had seen him was in 1951 when he stopped by her home in Vermont to bring her up to date on what happened to the Task Force and her husband, Captain Thomas Hamilton.

"I couldn't imagine where Joe was bringing us," cried Faith openly. "He said it would be a surprise. It's more like a shock. How nice it is to see you again, Scott. You're holding up under the ravages of age rather well."

"Faith, this is my wife, Marie. We married right after Thomas and I graduated from Staff and Command School at Carlisle. Marie, meet an old friend, Faith Hamilton. Her husband was killed at the Chosin, one of the bravest men I've ever known."

"Scott has talked a lot about your husband and the times they studied together at your apartment when they were in school. I'm so glad to finally meet you. Welcome to our home," Marie answered, hugging her with warmth and sincerity. She was a short energetic woman, barely reaching to his chin. She had brown hair combed loose about her shoulders and dark glowing eyes that reflected the contentment she and Scott shared with each other. Her energy was contagious and she complimented Scott's serious nature with her spontaneous love of life.

"I'm overwhelmed," explained Faith, wiping her eyes with a handkerchief. "I'd like you to meet my son, Tom. I was pregnant when Thomas left for Korea with you."

"Hello, Tom," welcomed Scott. "You look a lot like your father. He was one of my best friends."

"Mother has spoken often about my father and you, Mr. Taylor," responded Tom, feeling the power in Scott's handshake. "I'm glad to meet you and Mrs. Taylor."

Dew and Joe were old friends. Marie told them that she had taught school at Fort Lewis when Dew was born at the infirmary. Bright Cloud delivered her when Star's time came. "Marie and I usually get up to Fort Lewis at least once a year. I just completed a tour in Vietnam, so we didn't have a chance this summer. How are Bright Cloud and Mark doing?" Scott asked, leading the way up the hill toward their home.

"They're doing well, Uncle Scott," answered Dew, linking her arm around his for the walk to the house.

"Every time I see you, Kimberly, you look more and more like your mother," remarked Marie soberly. "How is your father doing? There isn't a day that goes by that I don't recall how wonderful they were to me when I was there."

"Mother's remains are coming," volunteered Kimberly in a low voice. "The Navy sent a telegram. It will be soon."

"I was there at the cabin when Mark and Bright Cloud read the telegram," commented Faith, walking behind Scott and Kimberly. "How much longer are you going to stay in the Army, Scott?"

"I'll have thirty years service in another year. I think it's enough. I plan to retire at that time. I feel my age lately."

"Faith, he didn't tell you that he was just promoted to Major General," informed Joe, walking beside her.

"My Uncle Arlo and Uncle Scott are both general officers," exclaimed Kimberly proudly.

"We have a lunch prepared at the house," interrupted Marie. "Whenever Scott's at home he likes to take over the cooking duties on the barbecue grill when the weather is good. We have some steaks and fresh shrimp from the coast ready for his masterful touch. I hope you're all hungry."

"I'm starved," laughed Kimberly. "Uncle Joe has pushed us pretty hard this morning. I think he wanted to hold our appetite until we arrived here."

Joe was quieter than usual, enjoying the fact that he had pleasantly surprised Faith with this visit. There was a strong bond of friendship between the two warriors. Joe had flown several support missions for the heroic Army unit Scott commanded at the Chosin Reservoir. Joe and Kay had been frequent guests at the Taylor home. Scott and Marie had not seen Joe since his wife had left him.

"Joe, I haven't had a chance to talk with you since we heard about Kay. We're surprised like everybody else. How are you holding up?" Scott placed an arm around Joe's shoulder.

"I've had better days, Scott, but I really think that I'm handling it better now than I did a while ago. The suddenness of her betrayal was a shocker to me," Joe answered. It was not something he talked easily about.

Marie placed her arms around his neck and kissed him on the cheek. "Our good friend, I feel bad that she used you so shabbily, but she's the loser. I believe that my dear Scott owes his life to flyers like you and Steve. For that I always include you in our prayers. How's Marshall doing? Is he in Vietnam?"

"Yes, I received a letter from him the other day. He seems to be doing fine. He recently received his First Lieutenant commission. If I didn't have him to be concerned about, I'm not sure how well I'd be doing, but I'm working on it. Thanks for asking."

"Now, the grill has been on for a while and I'm taking orders for T-bone steaks and shrimp on a kabob. If anyone wants hot dogs or hamburgers, we have those, too," Scott announced, climbing the stairs to their open porch with a commanding view of the lake.

Joe and Faith preferred steaks. Tom and Morning Dew asked for hot dogs. Marie had laid out a buffet including several types of salads, cheeses and fruits on a large table against the wall of the house. Cold drinks were available in a large tub of ice along with an iced tea dispenser. Scott tied on his chef's apron and placed four large steaks on the hot grill.

"Help yourselves to the drinks and salads on the table behind me. Marie likes to see friends and guests eat heartily. She doesn't like leftovers either. Faith and Joe, there's a couple of beers there if you want one," instructed Scott, pointing to the table with the drinks.

"Thanks, but I'm going to stick to iced tea," Joe said self-consciously. "I scared myself this past week. The booze was getting to me, Scott. I had the closest call I've ever had in my flying career, and I've made a pact with the Chief upstairs to leave it alone. I'm trying."

"You can do it, Joe," Faith supported his efforts. "Here, I'll pour some iced tea for you. I love the stuff. This is a wonderful surprise. It's so nice to meet an old friend again. Thank you for your thoughtfulness."

"They're my friends, too," replied Joe, accepting the tall glass of tea from Faith.

A few minutes later, Scott served the steaks he had been tending to the adults and turned to Dew and Tom, shaking his head with a grin. "I can't believe you two gave up juicy steaks for hot dogs, but here they are, hot and ready. There's more where they came from if you want."

Tom held out his plate for two hot dogs shrugging his shoulders. "Thank you, Sir. I guess I just like them better than steaks."

"Eat and enjoy, Tom. It's nice to have you as a guest and to see your mother again. What are you taking at school?" asked Scott.

"I'm studying for a degree in Forestry and hope to take four years of Army ROTC. If you were my age, which branch would you select, infantry, artillery or engineering?"

"I've always loved the infantry, but you have to decide that for yourself as you get more involved in your studies. Your forestry training would make you more suitable for the engineers. Sometimes they see more combat than the infantry. Our son, Scott, Jr., is studying engineering at the University of Maine. I was hoping that he would be interested in West Point, but he preferred the University. He's also taking ROTC. Some of the most courageous and brilliant officers I know have come to the service of our country through ROTC. Colonel Mark Leroux is a good example, and your father started a fine tradition at Vermont in ROTC. Best of luck in your career."

"Thank you, Sir," Tom said, blushing slightly. "Maybe later I'll graduate to steaks." They both laughed.

Two hours later, Joe herded his passengers aboard the Norseman for the final leg of their journey. They left behind some warm memories of gracious hospitality and friendship with Scott and Marie Taylor.

Faith had talked at length with Marie about her experience teaching at Fort Lewis. Marie described the period as one of the most rewarding times of her life. The response from the children and the inhabitants of the northern wilderness made her feel special and needed. Marie had taught at several Army posts after she married Scott, but the people at Fort Lewis responded to her efforts much more than any other location. She went back to teach on a temporary basis for one year when Scott was involved with United Nations and NATO affairs overseas.

The visit with Scott brought back a lot of memories to Faith. She was much quieter on the remainder of the flight. Seeing Scott naturally reminded her of how it had been for her. The silent vigil of an empty home with fleeting memories of brief reunions and heart-wrenching good-byes. At times she could still feel the terror that had filled her days and nights.

Now that Tom was committed to his future and needed her less on a day-to-day basis, Faith reflected more and more on her own future and what she wanted to do with her life. She lacked a clear strategy for the days ahead. It never bothered her while she worked and cared for Tom, but the years were beginning to mount, and youth had long passed her by. These things had been bothering Faith for the past year, but the visit to Fort Lewis highlighted her status.

"We're coming up to the outskirts of Montpelier," announced Joe, handing her a map of Vermont. "Do you want to see what your place looks like from the air?"

"Oh, yes, that would be fun," she answered, unfolding the map. "Our home is located north of Montpelier on a road that branches from the main thoroughfare towards the Worcester Mountains. We're right here." Faith pointed a pencil at a spot on the map.

"I've got it," responded Joe, picking up the road leading north.

"There are about twenty acres of land with it. The open fields around the house are still mowed annually by a neighbor. That way we can maintain the field without any out-of-pocket-expense. That's the place down there, Joe. The small brown bungalow-style house with an attached barn," she exclaimed.

"Can you see it, Dew?" pointed Tom through his window.

"Yes. The view of the mountains from the house must be beautiful," Dew answered. "The fall colors are starting to change. What a nice setting for a home."

"We always thought of it as a comfortable country home where we could take refuge from the rest of the world," Faith added wistfully. "I can see that our farmer neighbor has picked up all of his bales of hay from the fields."

"A country home sounds nice," reflected Joe. "It takes love and sharing to turn a house into a home. I thought Kay and I had that, but I was wrong. I envy your attention to the values found in rural America."

"The same values are found all over the country, wherever we want to look for them, Joe. People are people, no matter where they live."

"You're right, Faith," he admitted in a low voice. "Burlington will be coming up in a few minutes. I'm going to land in the middle of the lake and taxi to the Coast Guard base on the Burlington, Vermont waterfront. We can leave the plane there while Tom gets your car. How far away is it, Tom?"

"I can catch a taxi and be back to the waterfront in twenty minutes," responded Tom positively.

"Do you have the necessary paper-work for your dormitory room, Dew?" asked Faith, turning to look at her.

"Yes, Mrs. Hamilton. All of the arrangements have been made. I have the receipt in my purse."

"What plans did you have for the evening, Joe?"

"I'm just the chauffeur," he laughed. "If we had more light, I would have dropped down to Lake George to visit with Steve's mother and her husband, General Korsman, but it's too late for that. We could locate a good place to eat after Tom and Dew get settled in their dormitories. In the morning I've got to contact my company about parts for the helicopter."

"I know that you're anxious to check out the house, Mother," suggested Tom. "Maybe we could all go there for the night and return in the morning to register at the dorms."

"That sounds like fun, I'd like that," exclaimed Dew.

"Well, Joe, what do you think?" asked Faith with a questioning look on her face. "We could pick up a few things at a grocery store for sandwiches tonight and breakfast in the morning. The house will only need a light airing after being closed up for the summer months. There's plenty of room for everybody."

"I'd like that," said Joe. "The plane will be safe at the dock overnight."

"Now I can see where Tom lived," Dew mentioned with enthusiasm.

A half hour after they secured the plane at the Coast Guard Base, they were on their way toward Montpelier, stopping briefly at a grocery store to get food and drink for the evening and the next morning. Faith was thrilled to be returning home and insisted on driving the Ford Falcon. Much had happened to her since she left in the spring to take the job at Hastings Engineering. The trip to her bungalow in the shadow of the Worcester Mountains filled Faith with an eager anticipation. It was always a comfort to return, no matter how long or far the journey. It opened a floodgate of memories for her.

"A home gives a person roots," she remarked. "I had forgotten how much it meant to me until we left Burlington. It's not much, but it's been a sanctuary for body and soul for a lot of years. At times it has been a financial struggle to keep it, but Tom and I were able to prevail, thanks to a lot of friends and great neighbors."

"I envy you for having a place that means that much to you, Faith. My career in the Marine Corps kept us moving around quite a bit. I retired a year and half ago after twenty-eight years of service. It was always my intention to find a place in upper-state New York after retirement. I had visions of becoming a country gentleman and living off my own land. A place where I could permanently hang my hat. So much for dreams!"

"You don't have to apologize to me, Joe," added Faith. "I understand how easy it is to selfishly think that we're the only ones burdened by such problems. I've been there too, yet, it's never too late if one really wants to follow their dreams. We're still in control of our lives."

Joe listened to Faith, knowing that she was correct, but found it amazing to hear it come from a woman who had lost a husband nineteen years ago, raised a son to manhood and maintained a home all on her own initiative and hard work. Who was he to complain? His wife had proved to be unfaithful, leaving him and his son a year and half ago for another man. In comparison, he was looking like a cry-baby, Joe mused to himself.

Faith turned onto Mountain Road which led past her house, leading to the summit of Worcester Mountain. Four miles after leaving the main highway, she pulled into a long driveway to a brown bungalow nestled between several large sugar maple trees in the early stages of fall foliage colors of yellow and orange. The house had a porch on the west side where the sun was starting to sink behind the mountain's massive granite formations. The compact two-story house contained three bedrooms upstairs with a master bedroom located over the porch with large full-length sliding windows looking out on the view. A small barn was attached to the house by a two-car garage.

"Here we are," declared Faith, jumping out of the car. "Home at last. I'm anxious to see if it's musty inside. It'll only take a few minutes to air out. Tom has checked it out through the summer, but we haven't lived in it since early June. Tom, would you please take the flashlight and go down to the cellar to turn on the water pump and throw the switch for the hot water heater?"

"Sure, Mom. I don't need a flashlight," answered Tom, opening a side door next to the garage, flipping on an outside flood light.

"It's a lovely location for a house, Mrs. Hamilton," said Dew, looking at the sunset in the distance. "I can see why you're anxious to come back to it."

"I agree, Dew." Joe grabbed the two grocery bags from the trunk of the Falcon. "I'll get the luggage on the next trip."

"You can put the bags on the table, Joe," Faith suggested, turning the lights on in the kitchen, living room, and the bathroom located between them. "I'll have to turn on the water supply from the bathroom. The house doesn't smell too bad. What do you think, Dew?"

"Not at all, Mrs. Hamilton. As a matter of a fact, I'm going to ask for the use of your bathroom, if you don't mind," Dew requested shyly.

"Of course, Honey," exclaimed Faith. "Here, I'll just turn on the water, and you can let the faucets run for a minute or two before shutting them. It's all yours."

"Thanks."

"Make yourself comfortable, Joe. Would you like some coffee?" asked Faith, noticing that he had returned with the luggage.

"That would taste great," he answered, placing the luggage in the living room. "Is there anything I can do to help? What a cozy and inviting kitchen, Faith. You seem to have control of the house." Joe looked the room over closely.

The walls were paneled in knotty white pine boards which gave it a rustic setting. There was a brick fireplace on the east wall of the kitchen with a high-backed love seat and rocker chair on either side. The mantel was half of a log with pictures of Tom as a young boy and one of his parents. A young Faith was wearing a print dress with her hair piled high on her head. She had her arm around an Army captain. Thomas was a tall husky framed man with an easy smile on his face. Joe assumed that it was after World War Two, because he saw evidence of that haunting stare in Thomas's eyes that categorized combat veterans of that era.

The white ceiling was divided by two large white oak beams crossing at right angles to each other in the center of the room. The sink, cupboard and counter section were opposite the fireplace. Joe backed himself up to the front of the fireplace and surveyed the rest of the room. Several pictures of farm scenes at different seasons of the year hung on the walls.

"Why would anybody leave a place like this?" Joe asked as much to himself as to Faith, who heard him clearly.

"One has to make a living."

"I understand how difficult it must have been for you, Faith. This is a home in every meaning of the word. I'm impressed by the amount of hard work it represents."

"You do what has to be done without thinking about any long range plans. I always knew that I'd come back here. That fact makes it possible to leave when it becomes necessary. Would you like to start the fireplace?"

"Sure."

"You'll find wood and kindling in the barn. Go through the garage, there's a light switch to the left of the door leading to the barn. The wood pile is on the right."

"I'm not much good in the kitchen, but this I can do," responded Joe, glad to be able to help out.

The barn was neat and orderly like the house. A couple of well-seasoned cords of wood were stacked against the wall. Joe noticed a World War Two vintage Jeep sitting in the barn with an attached snow plow on the front. He hadn't seen one of those in years.

By the time darkness filled the valley between the house and the mountains, Joe had a fire crackling in the fireplace. Faith was setting the table for them to eat ham and cheese sandwiches. Coffee was ready, and the aroma filled the kitchen. Tom was a heavy coffee drinker like his mother. Morning Dew had a preference for hot cocoa. Faith boiled some water and prepared her a steaming mug, announcing; "It's hardly gourmet dining, but it will hold us until morning." Faith grinned, taking a seat at the table.

"I noticed the Jeep in the barn. I remember using ones like that in the service."

"It still runs great," informed Tom enthusiastically. "It's fun plowing snow with it. Mother watches me closely to see that I don't abuse it."

"The Jeep is like a member of the family. We get heavy snows in this area and need some means of moving snow from the long driveway. Feel free to use the phone, Joe, and you also, Dew. Your dad will be worrying about you and will be relieved to know that you've arrived in Vermont."

"We can call the Police Station and they'll get the message to Dad. Do you want to call, Uncle Joe?" Dew asked.

"You call, Dew. Just tell him that the plane performed well and is at the Coast Guard Station in Burlington."

Dew excused herself from the table and placed a call to Fort Lewis. Constable Jenkins answered the phone and promised to pass the message on to Steve. He mentioned that they had word from the Navy Department about her mother's burial and asked her where she was calling from in case her father wanted to contact them. Dew returned to the table and whispered in a sober voice: "Someone will call back about mother's funeral." She started to cry and turned away from the table.

Faith rushed to gather Dew in her arms. "My dearest girl. I can never know all the pain you're feeling right now. No matter what other people say, it doesn't make the hurt any less, but I do know that there is comfort in knowing that others share your sorrow and care about your welfare. Your grandmother told me that you're a lot like your mother. That tells me that she must have been a wonderful person. It's only natural to mourn someone so special, so if it feels right to let it out, go ahead, dear child."

Chapter Eleven

That night, Faith lay in her familiar bed and reviewed the events of the past few days. Her heart went out to Morning Dew. There was something fragile and vulnerable about the young lady that touched Faith's maternal instincts. Mark Leroux had called them a few minutes after Dew spoke to Constable Jenkins to inform them that the Navy was bringing Bright Star home from Vietnam in a few days. Steve, Mark and Bright Cloud were leaving Fort Lewis for Wells, Maine the next day. Steve had not fully recovered from his illness but insisted on accompanying them anyway.

Bright Star was scheduled to be buried beside DJ's grave at Wells. The local church and American Legion Post were helping to make preparations for the event. Bright Star, the brave Naval Nurse, was coming home to rest in eternal communion next to her brother, two young Crees who had placed their lives on the line in defense of freedom and liberty.

Joe had called Steve's mother, Michelle, and her husband Arlo Korsman, at Diamond Point, Lake George. Most of the people who made up the close circle of friends and family would be present when Bright Star was buried.

Faith felt caught up in a series of events unrelated to anything else in her previous life. Seeing Tom and Morning Dew together was a revelation to her. Her son did not share his private feelings with many people, including his mother. Faith had noticed a look in Tom's eyes when they were at Fort Lewis. It was obvious to her that he cared a great deal for Dew. They were relaxed and comfortable with each other. When the decision was made to come to the house in Montpelier for the night, Faith watched Dew smile at Tom. In that instance Faith assumed that Tom's feelings were reciprocated. At first, she was afraid that they were too young for serious feelings, but then, she was even younger when she met and fell in love with Tom's father, a handsome soldier on the University of Vermont campus.

In the morning, she would drive Tom and Dew back to their dormitories where they could prepare for classes the next day. Joe needed some time to inspect the airplane at Burlington and to meet with his company officials. Faith felt obligated to call Hastings Engineering and give them an update on her activities.

She had given a lot of thought to her immediate future with the company. She was not looking forward to meeting Glenn Hastings again. The question she had been asking herself over the years: "Where do I go from here?" played on her mind until exhaustion overcame the worry, and she slept soundly the rest of the night.

The next morning Faith woke with the pleasant aroma of coffee coming from downstairs. Dressing quickly, she descended the stairs, finding Tom and Dew making breakfast together in the kitchen.

"Good morning," Faith announced, amused to see that Tom was cooking scrambled eggs and bacon in one of her large cast iron frying pans.

"Morning, Mom," Tom answered in good spirits.

"Good morning, Mrs. Hamilton," greeted Morning Dew, buttering some toast. "Can we fix breakfast for you?"

"If you'd like," a surprised Faith answered. She could remember, not too long ago, when Tom couldn't boil water without asking her how to do it! "You've picked up a few domestic skills, Son."

"At forestry summer camp, if you didn't learn how to do something on the stove, you went hungry. You know how I like to eat, so I became a quick learner. We'd be glad to share scrambled eggs, bacon and toast with you, Mom. Dew handled the coffee and toast."

"This summer I did most of the cooking for dad and myself. Grandmother invited us to their cabin a lot, but it was not fair to impose on them too much, so I became comfortable with meal preparation chores," claimed Dew, pouring Faith a cup of coffee.

"Thank you, my dear," Faith took her seat at the table. "Has your Uncle Joe gotten up yet?"

"Oh, yes. He's been up for a while. Generally he takes a long walk first thing in the morning whenever he can. He's done it a lot more since he and Aunt Kay went their separate ways," Dew added, sitting beside Faith.

"What kind of a person was his wife Kay?" Faith asked with some interest.

"She was an opposite of Uncle Joe. You know how he's quiet and thoughtful? Well, she was very outgoing and was nice to me and mother and father over the years. The four of them were together a lot, and when Uncle Scott and Aunt Marie came for visits, they all had a wonderful time. I used to enjoy sitting quietly, listening to them reminisce about the good old days. Aunt Kay always seemed restless as if she was looking for something. I'm not sure what it was, maybe she didn't know either.

"When Marshall left home for West Point, she had a hard time tolerating the long hours demanded of Joe's civilian flying job," Dew continued in that soft melodious voice she shared with her grandmother and mother. "They started drinking and arguing more than ever. They used to laugh a lot and be such fun. That all changed within a year when she got involved with another man. Uncle Joe stayed with us and grandmother and grandfather sometimes at Fort Lewis and at Wells, Maine. He was reckless and didn't take care of himself. We all worried that he would get hurt. He disappeared for weeks at a time. These past few days I've seen a return of the Uncle Joe I've loved. He was always so kind and generous. He worshipped Aunt Kay. Dad said that he was the most skilled pilot he had ever seen."

"It's obvious that he's skilled at his job," commented Faith. "This is a pleasant surprise having breakfast fixed for me by you two young people. Thank you."

The phone interrupted Faith. Tom stepped through the living room door to answer it. "Hello. Yes, Mr. Hastings, my mother is right here."

Faith took the phone from Tom and walked as far into the living room as the cord allowed. "Hello, Glenn," Faith answered with an unsteady voice. "I was going to call a little later this morning."

"I'm sorry to bother you at this hour, Faith, but I wanted to speak to you before Kathleen and I left for Australia. I've thought of you often, and an apology seems inadequate for the disappointment and sorrow I've brought into your life. Can you forgive me?" Faith recognized the ring of sincerity and regret in Glenn's voice.

"I can as long as you and Kathleen are happy. She seems to be a wonderful person. Happiness is such a rare commodity that we must reach for it whenever the opportunity presents itself. I understand your position. I've been getting on with my life. I've also thought a lot about my job, and I don't want personal feelings to interfere with our professional relationship. I've buttoned up the initial phase of my work at Trails End. Would you object if I took some time off to sort out where I'm going from here?" asked Faith, surprised with her spontaneous request.

"Not at all, Faith. You take as long as you think necessary. I understand your need for time. Let me remind you that you will always have a place with us, and we are proud to call you a partner. If, for whatever reasons, you want to do something different, I want to assure you that it will be a privilege to give you a letter of superb commendation and reference. I pray that somewhere, somehow you can find the peace of mind and direction you've been searching for."

"Thank you, Glenn. I'm sorry things did not work out for us. I'm not bitter about it. Hurt maybe, but not angry at you or Kathleen. Thank you for understanding my need for time.

When I know what I want to do next, I promise that you or Bob Smart will be the first to know. Have a safe trip, Glenn."

"We will and thank you, Faith. Good luck!"

Faith placed the phone on the receiver. Shivers ran through her body. Tears started to collect in her luminous blue eyes. She sat quietly in a rocking chair facing the mountains in the distance, feeling unsure whether she was crying for Glenn and Kathleen or for herself and what might have been. Tom checked on his mother, sensing that something was wrong. He kneeled beside her chair and placed an arm around her shoulder. She grasped his hand and held it firmly.

"I'll be all right, Son."

"I've seen you cry more times than you think, Mom. If I had a magic wand I'd drive away all those things that have hurt you over the years."

Morning Dew witnessed the exchange between them. Dew was drawn to Faith stronger than ever this morning and reached out to embrace her, not knowing the cause of her grief.

"Remember what you said to me, Mrs. Hamilton?" Dew asked softly in her ear. "Knowing that someone else cares does help. I haven't known you very long, but I care for how you feel. I've really known you ever since I've known Tom. He talks a lot about his mom. I thought he was just bragging, but I found that his claims were justified. I understand why Tom loves and respects you the way he does. I do, too." Faith ran her fingers through Dew's coal black hair, touched by her words.

"Thanks for caring, Dew. I don't know what came over me. I didn't mean to make a spectacle of myself."

"How about more coffee," Joe suggested from the kitchen. "I just came in from a good walk, and I could eat a bear." They all chuckled over his exaggeration and returned to the kitchen to complete breakfast. Tom continued to do the cooking on the stove. Joe had not been kidding about his appetite. He ate six eggs, ten slices of bacon and five pieces of toast with orange marmalade. Dew was constantly filling his coffee cup, pleased to see her Uncle Joe the way she liked to remember him.

Later in the morning, they headed towards Burlington where they helped Tom and Dew get settled into their dormitory rooms, making certain that each had the supplies they needed for different classes. They were going to continue their respective jobs in the school cafeteria which paid for all of their meals at school and gave each some pocket money for personal use. Joe insisted that Dew take an envelope of money that he slipped into her pocket. Faith had given Tom a separate checking account for his use as needed.

Dew asked Faith and Tom if they would come to her mother's funeral. Faith hesitated at first, not wanting to intrude on what would be an emotional gathering of family and friends, but when she saw the look on Dew's face, she changed her mind and promised they would be there. Faith watched Tom and Dew from her rear view mirror as she drove the car out of the dormitory parking lot. The fact that her son was fast growing into an adult had not occurred to her until that moment. Dew came up to Tom's shoulder. Faith saw a contented look on both of their faces.

"Well, Joe," announced Faith, stopping the car at the Coast Guard Base on the waterfront of Lake Champlain. "I wish you luck with your company. Thanks for being so thoughtful on the trip from Fort Lewis yesterday. It was nice to see an old friend."

"It was my pleasure. When I finish with the plane and my company, I'm going to fly down to Lake George to see Arlo and Michelle. Thanks for putting me up for the night. I couldn't help but notice that you were distressed about something this morning. I don't mean to pry, but is there anything I can do to help?"

"No, I've got to climb that mountain by myself. Thanks for offering to help though," she answered.

Joe reached out and grasped her right hand with his. "I've enjoyed my time with you, Faith, and hope that you and I can be friends. My life has been so mixed up lately that I've run out of direction for tomorrow. I'm trying to get back on track and resolve some things on my own. I can relate to climbing that mountain by yourself. I've got a couple that look intimidating to me, yet, I'm going to give it my best shot. I've heard it said, and would like to believe it's true, that you can see beyond the horizon from the mountaintop. I've also heard it said that not everyone who starts the climb completes it."

"You will, Joe. We can never have too many friends. I'd like to think that we're already friends, and I've enjoyed your company also."

Joe lifted her hand and kissed it gently. "Lady, you've made my day. Thanks for the lift. I'll be in touch about Bright Star's funeral. I'm glad you and Tom are going. You're good for Dew. She needs your friendship. So long, Faith, until next time."

"Until next time, Joe," smiled Faith, waving to him as he walked toward the lake.

The funeral for Ensign Dawn "Bright Star" Jackson was scheduled for a warm sunny day when the leaves were full of color and still clinging to the branches of the hardwood trees as if they wanted to prolong the beauty and innocence of fall for as long as possible. Wells, Maine was burying one of its own. It was a sad day for those townspeople who had known Star. Her love of life and rich capacity to reach out and touch other people's lives was her most endearing trait and most lasting legacy. The teachers that watched her grow from a young child to womanhood were never disappointed in the person she became.

The night before the funeral, there was a special service at the church for the immediate family and close friends. This gave them a chance to spend some quiet reflections with their beloved Star. It was a time to say good-bye and a time to recall all of the memories that bound them together into a remarkable family that had sacrificed so much for the right to be free.

Arlo and Michelle Korsman drove in from Lake George with Joe Lance as a passenger. Scott and Marie also arrived at the Leroux home that afternoon. Faith, Tom and Morning Dew arrived mid-afternoon at Wells. Faith and her son were welcomed to the fold with sincerity and grace, which erased some of Faith's initial misgivings. Steve, Mark and Bright Cloud were relieved when they were informed that friends and neighbors would be responsible for catering all of their needs for food and drinks. They had contracted for several rooming homes that would be available for the next few days to house and care for those who came from far away. Several tables in the Leroux home were filled with foods and refreshment of every description.

Those who had assembled at the Leroux home were escorted to the church by a small contingent of sailors that had accompanied the casket to Wells. The Catholic Priest received them with a prayer asking that they open their hearts and let the hand of God reach out with love, comfort and strength to accept the tragic loss they had come to mourn. Let Him help carry the burden.

Silent tears and trembling lips manifested the pain that most felt in their hearts. Steve looked as if he was traumatized and on the verge of passing out. The pain was more than he could deal with. Dew refused to look at the casket on the alter. She clung to her father's arm and was comforted by Faith who sat on the other side of her.

The kindly Priest announced that they should feel free to spend as much time as each one needed and left them with their private thoughts and feelings. Silence and emotions filled the room as a young Army infantry captain with a spotless uniform covered with ribbons walked respectfully down the aisle of the church. He knelt at the altar, crossed himself and walked directly in front of Mark and Bright Cloud. He held out a letter for them with his left hand while he saluted courteously.

"Mr. and Mrs. Leroux. I'm Captain Leslie Hancock. I have been requested to deliver this letter to you. The person who wrote it is physically unable to deliver it in person. I believe you will find the letter self-explanatory. May I add my own sympathy for your loss."

"Thank you, Captain," answered Mark with tear-stained eyes. The Captain saluted them again and quietly left the church. Mark turned the letter over to Bright Cloud. She carefully opened and read it aloud in her unique melodious tone of voice:

AN OPEN LETTER TO THE PARENTS OF DANIEL-JOSEPH AND DAWN LEROUX, FROM RICHARD HANSEN, A FORMER STUDENT AT WELLS HIGH SCHOOL.

September 25, 1969

Before any more years pass into eternity, I want to take this time to express my deepest sympathy for your tragic loss and to apologize to you, your son and daughter for a wrong I've been burdened and troubled with for most of my adult life. I am not sure if you remember me, but I was a classmate of Bright Star's when she was a Junior in high school. I have a confession to make about an act that took place in our Junior year that has filled me with shame and revulsion over the years.

I was the boastful loud-mouthed person that insulted Dawn and the rest of her family members of similar race. I had asked her to go to a prom with me. She graciously refused with her traditional kindness. I should have walked away then, but I was an ignorant braggart at that time and my ego allowed me to rudely tell her that I didn't want to go with her anyway. In the company of classmates and friends I told her that her skin always looked dirty to me and that I might have caught something if I had touched her. It was a vile thing to say to another human being and I regret the choice of words. Your son, Daniel-Joseph, four years younger and thirty pounds lighter, challenged me as he attempted to defend his sister's honor. He whipped me completely and fairly there on the school playground. At first, I was furious that he had beaten me so easily. In time I held your son in high esteem for the courage and devotion he displayed in defending his sister.

114

A year later, we moved away from Wells. I joined the Army after high school graduation and have served for almost thirty years. I recently returned from Vietnam and was visiting old acquaintances in Wells when I heard about Dawn's funeral.

I hope that you can forgive me. My heart aches that I did not have the courage or the opportunity to tell Daniel-Joseph and Dawn, in person, that I was terribly wrong and apologize for my intolerant and insensitive remarks. What a vicious person I must have been to want to reach out to two of the nicest people on this earth and intentionally insult them. I haven't been able to forgive myself! I just wanted you to know that I share your grief. Maybe God is punishing me after all these years. I recently said good-bye to my only son, Captain James Hansen. He came home to us in a casket the same as your Son and Daughter.

I ask for your forgiveness.

Respectfully yours,
Richard Hansen
Colonel, United States Army

Chapter Twelve

The church was quiet and Bright Cloud's distinctive voice could be heard by everyone. Mark and Bright Cloud were surprised and dismayed by the unexpected communication. They knew what had taken place with Hansen. It was so long ago that they had forgotten the incident. The fact that Hansen had not forgotten made his apology and sorrow creditable.

"I can forgive him," said Bright Cloud. "I'm sure Star would do the same thing." Mark nodded his head in agreement, thinking that such a confession was the work of an honest man and a tribute to the goodness of their beloved daughter and son.

Everyone returned to the Leroux home in a reflective mood. The hour was late and the emotional climate did not lend itself to small talk. Steve and Morning Dew remained with Mark and Bright Cloud for the evening. The others retired to their reserved lodgings located in Ogunquit on the rocky coastline. Faith and Tom were assigned rooms with a view overlooking the ocean. A full moon rose out of the east lighting up the waves on the water. Faith watched the water for a long time before she retired. She was born and raised miles away from the coast, so any chance she had to view the ocean was an exciting event for her. She scanned the star-studded eastern sky searching for the "little dipper" and the North Star. They seemed to have a special glow tonight. A feeling of sadness came over Faith as she thought of Bright Star and the kind of person she must have been. God must have a need for those special kinds of people or He wouldn't call them home so early in their life. It was the same rhetorical question she had pondered for years, questioning why it had to be Thomas who was taken?

116

The next morning everyone began arriving at the Leroux's home to lend support and a show of unity that had always existed within their exceptional circle of friends and family. Scott and Marie arrived at the same time as Faith and Tom. Scott was in uniform with row upon row of ribbons on his chest. He was a handsome man with a distinctive presence about him whether he was in uniform or not. His lovely wife, Marie, was dressed in a dark blue dress with a black veil covering her head and shoulders. Faith thought they were a charming couple.

Arlo and Michelle surprised Faith. She had a mental image of the couple that was far from reality. Arlo was dressed in his Marine dress blues. He looked as if he had been poured into the uniform. His muscular shoulders and chest presented a figure one did not easily forget. Michelle had an energetic vitality that belied her white hair. She exuded warmth and confidence with a no-nonsense attitude. The attraction the couple shared for each other was evident. They remained close to one another as much as possible.

Joe Lance was dressed in his Marine greens and was the only one to wear a Sam Brown belt. His lithe trim physique was a lot more evident in his tailor-made uniform. Faith thought he looked different today. The close military style haircut and a clean shave helped make a difference. He was a proud man and wore the uniform with dignity and grace. When he first got out of the car he looked around and saw Faith. He walked over to meet her and Tom who was dressed in a dark brown suit which accented his slim youthful build. It was his high school graduation suit.

"Good morning, Faith and Tom." He hardly recognized Faith. She wore a black dress with a short black blouse. A small beret style hat sat on one side of her head at a rakish angle with a long black veil that fell over her shoulders. Her natural blonde hair with streaks of gray was pulled on top of her head making her look a little taller. She wore no make-up except for a small amount of red lipstick to accent her lips. "You're lovely, Faith, I can't believe you're the same person."

"This is a solemn occasion, and I could not come any other way," she explained modestly. "You look nice in your uniform. The ribbons you wear are a tribute to your service. I recognize the Distinguished Service Cross and a Silver Star."

"You have keen eyes, lady. Come, we should go inside. May I escort you to the door?" Joe asked, offering her his right arm.

"There are five men in uniform, with two general officers and three full colonels. That's a lot of talent for such a small group of people," claimed Tom.

"It represents a lot of patriotism and sacrifice, and I'm proud to be a part of the group," said Faith, taking Joe's arm.

Steve met Joe, Faith, and Tom at the kitchen door. Steve wore his Air Force blues. He looked drained and distant. His eyes had a glazed hollow shine to them. Joe gave Steve a bear hug. "Hang in there, Steve. You can do it. How's Dew holding up?"

"Dew had a rough night," recalled Steve, turning to Faith and Tom. "Faith, I want to thank you for being so good to Dew. Thanks for bringing her to Wells. I worry about her. She doesn't let her emotions show with me, and I can't tell how she's doing. Maybe I'm too blind with my own grief."

Steve looked so alone and lost that it was only natural for Faith to reach out and embrace him, offering comforting words: "She'll do all right. She's a strong girl. You have to take care of yourself before you can help anyone else. Dew and I have hit it off very well, and I'll try to help where I can. She's a wonderful girl that any parent would be proud of."

"Thanks, Faith," said Steve. "Here come Mark and Bright Cloud."

The uniform that Mark wore on his last day in the Marine Corps, twenty-four years ago, still fit him. He wore more ribbons than any of the other service members. When Bright Cloud joined him in the kitchen, he asked her to help with his Medal of Honor sash. She kissed him on the bare forehead and placed the medal around his neck, making sure it was straight. "It's my privilege, Colonel Leroux," she whispered in his ear.

Marie took a cue from Mark and Bright Cloud and reached up to fasten Scott's Medal of Honor around his neck. "You brave old soldiers," claimed Marie, looking around the room at the five uniformed men. "How lucky we are as a nation to have men like you and women like Bright Star defending our liberties. My heart aches when I see Steve and Dew without my dearest friend, Star. I'm a better person today because of her." Marie started to cry. Scott held her close to him, straightening the black lace around her face.

"It's a sad day for everybody, but the Bright Star we all remember so well would want us to continue with the same spirit and passion for life she displayed every day she was with us," Scott said with a firm upper lip. "We're all better persons from knowing her. I remember how she greeted me on that hospital ship in Tokyo Bay. I was a physical and emotional wreck. Within a short period of time, she had me back to normal and anxious to return to duty. With precious memories and inspiring legacies of generosity that fill our hearts, we're blinded by tears because the pain is deep and long lasting. We know that she'll be pleased when smiles, once again, return to our faces." Scott's dark piercing eyes glistened in the morning sun, and he buried his head in his wife's long brown hair.

"Come everyone," announced Bright Cloud. "It's time to leave for the church."

The small Catholic Church was filled to capacity with a large group of neighbors and friends already congregated at the front door. Faith and Tom followed the others through a side door to the front rows of the church. Bright Star's casket was draped with an American flag. In front of the casket was a small table with several pictures of her. Faith studied them and was drawn to the largest picture in the center of the table. It showed Bright Star standing proudly in her blue Navy Nurse uniform with her long black hair flowing loose about her shoulders, looking towards the sea with a pensive smile. Her beauty was legendary and Faith was awed by the happiness radiating from her eyes.

The priest completed the celebration of the Mass and introduced Arlo to the audience. He left his seat and walked to the pulpit, adjusting the microphone for his added heighth. He looked from side to side at the congregation and rested his eyes on Bright Star's casket for several seconds before starting to speak.

"Today we bid farewell to Captain Dawn Marie Jackson, a brave and courageous nurse who died bringing aid and comfort to the wounded in her care. Most of you will remember her as Dawn Leroux. Those of us who were privileged to be a part of the family circle called her Bright Star. Her brother was killed in combat in World War Two and has gone on ahead of his sister to prepare a final resting place for her at his side.

"Star's death is the end of an era that started in an isolated wilderness outpost in the Canadian north. Star's mother, Minnie, died in childbirth; her paternal father, Flying Eagle, was killed during the First World war. He never saw his beautiful daughter, but he promised that he would always be as close to her as death allowed." Arlo paused in his eulogy and looked above the heads of those in attendance at the church, remembering the way a small child of the forest had touched his heart. He loved her as if she were his own.

"Those of us who knew and loved Star were rewarded by the rare gift she had of making those around her feel special. She was one of the most beautiful people to grace our gathering of friends and family. The source of her beauty came from within. Her compassion and dedication for those less fortunate are legendary in the forested community she served so faithfully.

"I'll always remember the first time I saw her. She was about four years old. Her parents, Mark and Bright Cloud, brought her to Washington, DC, where we observed the dedication of the Tomb of the Unknown Soldier, November 11, 1921. Later in the evening we visited the Tomb a second time and witnessed a sign from Heaven, a gift given to Bright Star, and proof that the remains within the holy crypt of the Tomb could be those of her father, Flying Eagle.

"Flying Eagle has kept his promise over the years and given a significant number of signs that he has truly been close to Star and her family. Now that she has joined him in that land beyond our horizon, we can be certain that there is rejoicing and celebration of their reunion.

"We who have to say good-bye will always remember her indomitable will and inherent goodness. Grace and dignity accompanied everything she did. She was a joyful daughter, a loving and caring wife, and an inspiring role model for her daughter who shares her mother's beauty and temperament. Bright Star follows in the footsteps of Flying Eagle and Daniel-Joseph, adding to their legacy of sacrifice."

"As for me, I'll remember her when I search the night sky for the north star that guides our destiny. She is the quiet hush of a new day's birth, the gentle murmur of waves lapping against the rocky shore, and the whirr of soft winds combing the branches of tall trees. I'll think of her when I see the first flower of spring and the honk of geese overhead on their return flight to the northern wilderness, signifying a renewal of life. She was conceived in love and died in violence. May her journey through eternity be blessed with peace, and may her guardian angel continue to watch over her."

Arlo returned to his seat with quiet solemnity. Michelle reached out to take his hand for comfort. The priest solemnly announced that the committal ceremony would take place at the cemetery next to Daniel-Joseph's grave. The family group was taken by limousine provided by the townspeople. Faith, Tom and Joe rode together to the cemetery.

The Navy ceremonial team accompanied the casket to the graveside where chairs were provided for those who might need them. The priest waited until the crowd had gathered around the grave and started to read his prayers in a slow deliberate manner. When he was finished, the Navy squad of seven men fired three volleys in tribute to the fallen nurse. Off to the side of the gravesite, a lone sailor raised his bugle into the air and played "Taps." The haunting refrain echoed clearly across the garden of stones, a last mournful farewell to a fallen comrade.

The silence of sorrow settled over the scene as the last notes faded away into the distance. Nobody spoke or moved for several moments. The Navy ceremonial team folded the American flag that had covered the casket. When it was completed and tightly folded into the size of a small pillow, the Navy chief walked to Steve, saluted, and presented the flag: "This is presented to you by the President of the United States on behalf of a grateful nation."

Steve received the flag with a firm set to his jaw, returning the sailor's salute. He was fighting tears as he held the flag, close to his heart. Dew reached out to touch the flag leaning her head against her father's shoulder, her heart filled with longing for the comforting arms of her mother one more time.

The crowd slowly began to thin. The Army Captain who presented a letter to Mark and Bright Cloud the night before helped guide a wheelchair to the side of the grave. The person in the chair wore an Army uniform with a Colonel's silver eagle insignias on his shoulders and a green beret on his head. Around his neck he wore the Medal Of Honor. The colonel had lost both of his legs, and the left sleeve of his military jacket hung loose against his body. Faith watched with amazement as the soldier was wheeled close to the casket. She could not take her eyes from the man's face. He had strong angular features with pockmarked skin, but it was his eyes that caught her attention. They were dull gray in color and sunken into his head. They had a lifeless haunting stare that frightened Faith. His eyes were glued to the casket as if he was trying to see through it. The Colonel leaned over his chair and placed two red roses on Star's casket, speaking in low tones: "I pray that you can forgive me."

Tears ran down his cheeks. With the torment of genuine remorse he placed his hand on the casket and said in clear tones: "Sleep well. Goodnight, sweet princess." The soldier held his right hand on the casket for several seconds as if he was caressing it, remaining motionless with his eyes closed.

Eventually, he directed his aide-de-camp to help him roll the wheelchair to where Mark and Bright Cloud were sitting on the chairs at the side of the grave.

"I'm Richard Hansen. You have my sincere sympathy. I realize that my apology is long overdue. I hope that you can forgive me," Colonel Hansen confessed in a wavering voice.

Bright Cloud reacted instantly to the beseeching eyes of the soldier. She stood up from the chair and shook his hand, then leaned over the wheelchair and embraced him. "We are not vindictive people, Colonel Hansen. I'm sure our Bright Star accepts your apology with the same spirit it is given. May God be with you, Sir."

Mark stood beside the wheelchair, saluted Hansen and pointed to his own Medal Of Honor. "You and I are members of a select fraternity. Your valor has wiped clean any need of an apology to me, Colonel. My wife has said it well. God bless you."

Colonel Hansen was visibly moved by his reception from Mark and Bright Cloud. He was unable to speak, but his eyes met theirs and spoke more forcefully than words could ever tell. Faith and the others lingered around the casket watching the lonely figure being wheeled out of the cemetery. They would always remember the soldier's gaunt look of despair.

Chapter Thirteen

Faith and Tom left Wells for Vermont late in the afternoon with Morning Dew and Steve as passengers. Everyone was physically and emotionally drained. There was a consensus of opinion that one of the best ways of honoring Bright Star was to stop mourning and get on with each of their lives. Steve was anxious to return to Fort Lewis and refused an offer for him to stay with Mark and Bright Cloud at Wells for a while longer. He and Star had moved to Wells for several of their annual summer vacations from Fort Lewis school and infirmary routines. It was a welcome break from the difficult winters of the northern wilderness. Yet, reluctantly Steve declined their offer because he knew that he could work his way through this tragedy easier at Fort Lewis. He felt closer to Star there and had more memories of the years they had spent serving the forest people.

Steve had succumbed completely to the magical appeal of the northern forest. The solitude and stillness satisfied a yearning for a simple life that had developed after his performance in the Korean War. He had little desire to be anywhere else. The forest people accepted him as one of their own and were proud of his selfless commitment to bringing the gift of knowledge to the northland.

"It's going to be late by the time we get to Burlington," said Faith, driving over the Connecticut River between New Hampshire and Vermont. "Does anyone object to staying at Montpelier?"

"I was hoping we could do that," responded Dew enthusiastically. "I wasn't anxious to return to the dorm tonight."

Steve, riding up front with Faith, turned around and held out a hand to Dew. "Are you going to be all right, Honey? I worry about you. You're all I've got now."

"I'll be all right, Daddy. I'm just cried out for now and feel exhausted. I'm not ready to face my friends at school just yet. Tomorrow will be better for me."

"Joe will be coming up from Lake George tomorrow with the plane. I was planning to head back to Fort Lewis unless you want me to stay longer. Would you like to come back with me for a while?" Steve asked, uncertain about what was the best thing to do for her.

"You two can make that decision easier in the morning after a good night's rest," added Faith. "You're welcome to stay as long as you want."

"Thanks, Faith. You've been a great help to us. I agree with you, a sound sleep is in order. I'm exhausted, too," admitted Steve.

"Of course you are. It won't be much longer now that we've crossed over into Vermont."

The balance of the trip to the house in Montpelier was made in silence. Steve had dropped off to sleep with his head against the back of the seat and the window. Dew and Tom rode quietly. He could feel the power of Morning Dew's presence beside him. The funeral was obviously difficult for Dew, yet Tom felt that she stood up under the stress remarkably well. It was during the committal service at the cemetery that he truthfully admitted to himself that he loved her. Watching her weep over the loss of her mother, he felt a desire to reach out and hold her and share the sorrow that engulfed her heart and shattered her world.

Dew had tried to rest, closing her eyes for several miles. She had seen what was in Tom's heart. Without a word, Dew reached across the seat of the car taking his hand in hers, holding it firmly. He returned the pressure, hoping that it was a true manifestation of feelings for him instead of thanks for the support he tried to provide during this traumatic period of her life.

"Well, we're here," announced Faith wearily as she turned off the ignition key.

Steve woke suddenly, surprised that he had dozed off. "I'm sorry, Faith, I should have shared the driving with you."

"I didn't mind. I'm familiar with the roads," Faith answered, opening the door of the glove compartment for a flashlight. "Come, let's get settled in. Is anyone hungry?"

"I could eat something, Mom," admitted Tom, opening the car door for Dew.

Faith quickly opened the door to the house, removing her hat and veil as soon as she stepped inside to turn on the lights. Tom showed Steve around the house while Faith and Dew filled the electric coffee maker and started to prepare some sandwiches. Tom pointed out the guest room that Dew would have.

"You can either sleep in my room on the second twin bed, or you can use the large couch in the living room. Both are quite comfortable. Mr. Lance slept in the room with me."

"Thanks, Tom. I can sleep anywhere. Your room sounds good," answered Steve, returning to the kitchen. "You have a nice home, Faith. I hope we're not a bother."

"Steven Jackson," scolded Faith. "How dare you make a statement like that after the gracious hospitality Tom and I received from everyone at Fort Lewis! Now sit down and help yourself to whatever appeals to you. Let me know if something is missing. We put in a reasonable supply of groceries before leaving for Wells."

"This is fine. That coffee smells great. I'm too keyed up and tired to be hungry, but a cup of coffee and something light will taste good and settle me down."

"Please help yourself. I have some hot water on if you want some cocoa, Dew." Faith watched her take a seat beside her father.

"Yes, I'd like that," Dew answered. "I can make it myself, Mrs. Hamilton. You must be as tired as the rest of us."

"All right, dear. You know where things are."

"Daddy, you mentioned that the teacher you had contracted for the eighth grade at Fort Lewis had to back out because of illness. What are you going to do?" asked Dew, selecting a peanut butter and jelly sandwich from the large plate on the table.

"I'm not sure, Honey. I haven't thought very much about it. Maybe I can get one of the nurses from the infirmary to pinch hit as a substitute. I'll have to cross that bridge when I get back to Fort Lewis."

"Would you mind if I went back with you to teach as a substitute?" Dew suggested thoughtfully. "I haven't been in school long enough to earn the credits necessary to teach, but. . ."

"No buts, young lady," replied Steve emphatically. "You are going to continue in school without interruption just as your mother and I had always planned. You aren't having second thoughts about school are you?"

"No. It was just a thought that maybe I could help. Skipping a semester would not be that much of a big deal."

Tom frowned at the conversation taking place and remained silent on the subject. His mother saw his reaction to Dew's offer. Faith agreed with Steve. Once she had started in school, it was for the best not to break it up unless it was absolutely necessary. The rest of the evening was filled with small talk until everyone retired for the evening. It had been a long stressful day and thoughts of a soft warm bed were welcome by all.

Later that evening, Faith reviewed the events of the day as she watched the changing shadows cast by the full moon on the distant mountains. The funeral kindled some of the old feelings she thought had been put to rest long ago. The finality of death was the most difficult concept to accept. No more chances to exchange feelings or thoughts. If an unkind word was passed before it could be explained or apologized for, feelings of guilt lingered. It made her feel old and insignificant as if she was losing the ability to control events in her life.

Faith, once again, woke up the next morning to the pleasant aromas originating from the kitchen where Tom and Dew were preparing breakfast. By the time she made herself presentable, Tom and Steve were already eating breakfast. Dew was fixing toast on the very slow electric toaster on the side counter.

"I guess I'm the lazy one this morning," announced Faith self-consciously. "You two youngsters have got breakfast preparation down to a science."

"Come here, Mrs. Hamilton," requested Dew, holding a chair for her. "I'll get some toast for you. It'll only take a few minutes to prepare an egg if you want one."

"If you don't mind, Dew, that would be nice," Faith answered, pouring a cup of coffee.

"Coming right up."

"I slept like a log," acknowledged Steve. "It's as quiet here as it is in Fort Lewis. Breakfast is delicious. I didn't realize that I was hungry until Tom and Dew insisted on feeding me."

"Steve, I have some questions about your Fort Lewis School," stated Faith with a determined look on her face. "I couldn't stop thinking about it after I went to bed. You mentioned to Dew that you were losing one of the teachers. Is there a possibility that you'll need to hire another teacher?"

"Yes, but I haven't determined whether it's to be permanent or on a temporary basis," Steve answered. "Why do you ask?"

"I've given it a lot of thought. I have enough educational courses to my credit that I obtained a teaching certificate in Vermont. As a matter of fact, I taught for two years after graduating from college during the war. Maybe I could do the job for the winter or for a short period of time if the teacher does decide to return."

"What about your job with Hastings, Mom?" inquired Tom, dumbfounded at her sudden interest in taking a teaching job in the wilderness during wintertime.

"I've had a feeling, these past few weeks, that it might be good for me to select the jobs I want to work on instead of being full-time on the Hastings' payroll. I could pick up the Trails End job in the spring."

"We'd be pleased to have you take over the class, Faith. Are you prepared for the fierce winters that are commonplace in northern Canada?"

"I'm sure I could handle them," she admitted with confidence. "The isolation and solitude will give me an opportunity to get better acquainted with myself and plot a new strategy for my life. Right now, I feel as if I'm just drifting along without any clear goals in mind. I did enjoy teaching even though it was years ago. I'm certain the school board will give me a recommendation if necessary."

"You've been thinking about this, haven't you, Faith?"

"When are you returning to Fort Lewis?" Faith asked.

"Tomorrow, weather permitting," answered Steve. "I thought I'd take today to be with Dew and help get her settled in school. Joe will be flying in from Lake George."

"Would you mind if I returned to Fort Lewis with you?

"No, not at all. Are you sure this is something you wish to do? Remember, it's a rather primitive settlement with limited facilities. Sometimes we're unable to fly in or out for days at a time. What if you tried it and didn't like it?" questioned Steve seriously.

"I'll never know unless I try. I promise to never leave you out on a limb."

"I believe you, Faith. You certainly are decisive, I'll give you that." Steve was pleased with the sudden turn of events.

"We can take Tom and Dew back to school as soon as we finish eating breakfast. Tom can keep the car at school after we leave for Fort Lewis. That way he can check on the house once in a while."

"It sounds like a plan to me. It'll save me a lot of work. Once the school year has started, it's difficult to hire teachers. Consider it a deal."

Tom and Dew listened to the exchange with interest. For days now he had a feeling that his mother was ready to take on a new challenge. It was typical of her even though he was surprised at the suddenness of her decision-making process. Dew was amused and thought that Faith would be good for the school.

Steve placed a phone call to Arlo and his mother at Lake George to discuss plans for their trip to Canada the next day. Joe suggested that they leave Burlington early in the morning. He told Steve that Mark had called that morning to announce that Colonel Hansen, the wounded soldier at Bright Star's funeral, died four hours after leaving the funeral. The unusual circumstances of his appearance and death was a subject of reflection and wonder. Dew interpreted his tragic presence at the cemetery as a compliment to the legacy of decency her mother shared with her family and close friends.

"I'm not surprised that he died," said Faith. "I saw something frightening in his eyes that I'll never forget. What a pitiful figure."

Steve kept his thoughts to himself. He glanced at Dew for some response. She met his eyes with a soft smile which told him that she was all right. "Well, I'm ready to leave for Burlington."

Faith's mind was filled with things she needed to do to get ready for the trip to Fort Lewis, so she suggested that Steve take the automobile with Tom and Dew to Burlington. She would be able to say good-bye to them in the morning when they dropped the car off for Tom. Steve agreed with the idea and spent most of the day with Morning Dew, visiting locations around the campus and ending up eating at the cafeteria where she and Tom worked.

"This is a beautiful college campus, Honey," Steve said over a sandwich and bowl of soup. "Tell me, Dew, is there anything between you and Tom? The two of you seem to enjoy each other's company. I'm glad that you're friends."

"Tom is very quiet and serious most of the time," she explained to her father. "You don't have to worry about me, Daddy. We're just good friends, and I think that both of us like keeping it that way. I'm glad you like him. I have a class I should attend this afternoon. I'll see you in the morning before you take off for Canada. I know that you worry about me, Daddy. I worry about you, too. The emptiness we feel will heal in time. I miss her so much, and was so proud of her when she left the last time for Korea. I hope that I can be like Mother."

"You're very much like her my dearest girl. Hold your head high and always be proud. Your mother had great faith in the future, and I see that same source of strength and spirit in you. I love you, dear girl. You've always made your mom and dad very proud. I'm going shopping for some personal items and a supply of current books that I promised for our Fort Lewis Library. See you in the morning, Honey."

"Thanks for being such a nice dad," Dew cried, falling in his arms.

That evening, Faith completed packing her suitcases for the extended stay at Fort Lewis, uncertain that she was bringing enough warm clothing for the northern latitudes. Steve had assured her that the Hudson Bay Store carried a line of outer clothing for extreme weather conditions if she ever needed them.

Satisfied that she had enough, Faith went downstairs to her favorite room in the house, the study. The view of the mountains from her desk chair never ceased to calm her. She was selecting a few books from the shelves for her personal use at Fort Lewis when she noticed car lights coming in the driveway. She unconsciously checked her watch; it was eight o'clock and she assumed that it was Steve. A few seconds later there was a knock at the door.

"Come in, Steve. The door is unlocked. I'm in my study off the living room."

"I didn't realize it was so late," Steve explained, taking a seat across from Faith. "I got bogged down at the college book store. If I was to buy all the books I wanted and really need at the school, we'd have to use a larger plane."

"Have you eaten anything?"

"Yes," replied Steve. "I wanted to get back so that you wouldn't worry about the car. I don't drive very often. There are no automobiles at Fort Lewis. It was great driving your

Ford. My, what a pleasant study, Faith." He checked out the extensive collection of books filling shelves that took up one whole wall of the study, from floor to ceiling. A large portion was filled with books pertaining to soils, water and the environment.

"I admit this is my favorite room," said Faith, packing some books in a briefcase. "There's a growing interest developing in the country about our environment. We have only one earth, and we need to husband our natural resources."

"Would you characterize yourself as a believer or follower of some of the more prominent environmental organizations?" asked Steve casually.

"Hardly," cried Faith emphatically. "You've hit upon a subject that I have strong feelings about. Most of the groups such as Sierra Club, Greenpeace and others like them, are not as interested in promoting wise stewardship of natural resources as they are in obtaining power to control their use by promoting their own agenda of preservation and limited usage of our land by man. It's a power struggle for them. They have powerful financial and bureaucratic government resources that assist them to advance their point of view.

"The sin of the environmental propagandist is that they seek to validate their views by giving them a rational basis. They claim to support research, but they consistently ignore science and research findings that refute their propaganda. They essentially want to control every aspect of our lives and the land we use and see us return to the days of the cavemen. Each group contains a lot of 'little Napoleons' lusting for power to control. I've always thought of myself and others like me as professional environmentalists interested in using science and wise stewardship in caring for the land in a responsible way. The 'greens' are interested in denying man the rights God gave us to work the land. Many of the activists are poor rich people who've never done a day's work in their lives." Faith paused and laughed at herself. "You should not have asked me that question, Steve. I apologize for carrying on about it."

"I can see that you've given the issues careful thought," chuckled Steve. "Over the years I've had a chance to observe how the Native Americans have been able to survive in such a harsh land as the northern boreal forest. The fact that they have survived is a tribute to their courage and ability to adapt to the environment. A lot of the fanatical academic-type environmentalists believe that man should reject modern society and its accompanying technology for our own welfare. I have a hard time with that concept. Even the native Cree still living off the lands have no desire to turn the clock back to the time when they followed the caribou herds which supplied them with food, clothing and shelter. There was a lot of hard work and drudgery involved. Starvation, illness and despair were constant companions."

"I've been wondering, Steve," commented Faith as she started rummaging through her desk drawers. Steve noticed a large number of old letters in one of them. "I have an old syllabus here somewhere that covered one of the classes I taught years ago in a small town on the Connecticut River."

"If you're talking about subject and grade requirements, Faith, we have all of that at the school. In Canada, the guidelines provided by the Provinces are detailed and specific about the level each grade is expected to obtain. They leave a lot of room for the teacher to handle the class as they deem essential, but at the end of the term year every class in the Province must be on the same parity with each other. The teacher that taught the class last year left a lot of material behind along with an interesting daily diary of her observations and thoughts about teaching in a frontier-like community."

"I'm glad to hear that," sighed Faith. "Since I've made the commitment to teach for a year, I've been thinking a lot about my ability to perform in the classroom."

"You'll do just fine," claimed Steve. "If you didn't have that feeling, I'd be concerned about how thoroughly you've thought this thing through. A year from now you'll have a lot of pleasant memories of teaching and living on the edge of civilization. You'll love the people, and I have a feeling that you'll be enriched by the values the people live by. Their traditional existence as they've always known it is on the verge of extinction. In order for them to survive, they must adapt to the ways of the western white man. Yet, knowledge and technology, which they embrace passionately, is helping some of them to maintain and preserve some of their ancient customs and traditions. A grand wedding of the old and the new."

"Do they resent the intrusion of progress on their traditional hunting and fishing lands?" asked Faith. "I'm beginning to understand your enthusiasm for teaching and envy the level of satisfaction you've drawn from it."

"Yes and no. The Canadian expansion into the North Country is taking place one step at a time. The native people are an important part of the movement. They see it as their last chance to be players in something bigger than their traditional tribal councils, and they're rising to the challenge. If they remain as spectators and oppose the movement, then they'll be scattered to the winds, and they know that."

"It doesn't sound fair."

"Maybe it's not. Change and progress are a constant influence that has touched the lives of every civilization throughout history. Good or bad, it's reality. Generally, progress is synonymous with improvements in the lives of mankind."

"I guess I'm ready for tomorrow. I've called Hastings, and they've been true to their word. Perhaps I'll be able to handle the engineering and the classroom work at Trails End on a part-time basis when spring comes around. I'll see when that time comes."

"I'm glad you're going to be with us this coming school year, Faith. You'll bring a fresh energy to our forest settlement. I believe I'll turn in. We've got a busy day ahead of us tomorrow."

"Goodnight, Steve." Faith remained seated at the desk. As soon as he left the room, she opened the top drawer of the desk and selected a few envelopes. Turning the writing lamp to shine on the worn yellowing pages of the letters, she leaned back in her chair and was emotionally transported back to 1950. . .

Chapter Fourteen

Two weeks after Faith and Steve arrived at Fort Lewis to open the school year for Eagle Nest, Faith received her first letter from Tom. Constable Jenkins delivered it to her desk just as the class was dismissed for the day. A contented Faith opened the envelope:

Burlington, Vt.
September 15, 1969

Dear Mom,

A few words tonight to let you know that my schedule for the year is a full one. I'm taking eighteen credits this semester and the next one, which is about all I can handle. I'm into more forestry courses now than liberal arts subjects. One of my subjects is Elementary Agronomy. I'm aware of your expertise in the field and am more appreciative of the highly technical subject you specialized in. I better get a good grade in that course or you'll scold me!! (Ha-ha).

I wanted to let you know that I drove out to the house yesterday to check on the water pipes. I shut the water off and drained the lines including the toilets so that they would not freeze on us. I may not be able to get back before cold weather sets in.

I received your short note about starting to teach the seventh and eighth grade students. I have a feeling that you are going to do well and wish you luck in your new adventure. I'm glad we went to Fort Lewis for a visit. Now I can picture your surroundings and have a better idea of what you are doing.

I've never talked much about it, Mom, but I want you to know how proud I am of your accomplishments. I'm anxious to graduate so that I can enter the work place and remove some of the financial burden you carry. I'd like to be able to care for you the way you have done for me. Thanks for everything. I love you, Mom.

A few words about Kimberly. I suggest that you keep this between the two of us. I'm afraid the close relationship we have shared up to now has deteriorated. She has become infatuated with one of the very popular football and basketball players on campus. I don't mind telling you that I'm disappointed. We still talk and are still friends, but it has become "awkward" for both of us. The boy's name is Ray Ellis. He comes from a wealthy influential family and seems to get by with adequate grades even though he parties a lot. I'm sorry to say that Kimberly seems to be attracted to the exciting kind of relationship they have going and doing things that most of us at school are unable to afford. Please don't breathe a word to her father!!!

I've got to run to work, I love you, Mom.

Tom

Faith reread the letter twice. Tom seemed to be doing well. The part about Kimberly was troubling. The small classroom was empty. She looked around the room with a smile. The wall behind her desk was covered with slate blackboards and a separation in the center, half used for the seventh grade and half for the eighth grade. She had twelve children in each class which made the room crowded, but they managed to get by.

One of the first things she insisted on when school started was some type of divider between the two classes so that they would not be distracted with her instructions to their neighbors. It worked better than expected. Several of the students' families donated colorful Hudson Bay blankets to act as partition curtains suspended on a clothesline so that the bottom was slightly above the floor. When it was not needed they could push it to the rear of the room out of the way. Faith recalled a similar system for the rural school she attended in Vermont with four classes in a single room.

Steve poked his head through the front door. "How's our new teacher doing today?" he asked good-naturedly.

"Come in, Steve. I was just thinking about something. This is the end of the second week of my introduction to teaching at Fort Lewis, and I have some questions for you."

"I was going to ask if you had any, but you beat me to the punch. What can I help you with?" Steve took a seat in front of her desk.

"If it's possible, I want an evaluation from you. This is uncharted waters for me and I don't have any reference markers to gauge my progress. Do you have any constructive criticism based on what you've heard from the children and their families? I've set standards for myself, but without feedback, I can never know if they are too demanding or too lenient. Give me your best opinion. I respect your years of experience and don't want bad habits to become standard operating procedures."

"Faith - Mrs. Hamilton," corrected Steve. She was discovering that he had a wonderful sense of humor and never took himself too seriously. He joked a lot with the children, and they loved him for his easy-going mannerisms. "The grapevine is always active here in the wilderness. It has informed me that our new blonde-haired school marm is one who doesn't tolerate bad behavior, bad manners or partial effort in class work. At the same time, the grapevine tells me that she encourages and is quick to reward respectful behavior and good manners. It's easy for a teacher to expect more from a student than they can give, but when a student is functioning at or near capacity they enjoy being rewarded for their efforts. In that department you have gained a large audience that supports you. The kids and their parents also appreciate the way you take the time and patience to help those who are having difficulties. That's a true mark of a good teacher. If every student was an Einstein, it would be a simple job for everyone. It's the less endowed ones that challenge us, and it's those individuals that determine if we are successful or not."

"Are you congratulating me or giving me a lecture?" Faith asked with a gleam in her eye.

Steve laughed heartily. "You have exceeded all of our expectations, Faith. You've set the bar quite high for effort and accomplishment, and I support you for that. The thing I have personally been the most impressed with is your ability to inspire the students to greater efforts academically and socially. In many ways you have the hardest group to handle in a rural environment. The kids are twelve to fifteen years old, yet at home they are looked upon as being older and already young adults. Most of the families prefer that they remain in school. The value of an education was first established by Bright Cloud many years ago when she returned to the community with a degree in nursing. However, there are some families that look upon school as a financial loss because some of the students are fully capable of working on a full-time basis. Years ago many were married at the average age of your students."

"Thanks for the input, Steve," confided Faith.

Steve's playful temperament and stable disposition made it easy for her to work with him. His students in the fourth, fifth and sixth grades responded enthusiastically to him. In his playful way he demanded everything the kids could give and still asked for more. Steve lived in the school compound acting as a monitor and house leader for the male barracks. Another female teacher, a native Cree called Iowana, taught the first, second and third grades and stayed with the girls in their section of the barracks.

Faith was offered the cabin belonging to Mark and Bright Cloud. It was empty during the winter months and provided her with a degree of privacy and an opportunity to cook for herself. The cabin was the only one to have a direct phone hookup to the outside world through the Royal Canadian Mounted Police radio station.

"I just got a letter from Dew this afternoon. She sends her best to you. She doesn't say much about her courses, but she seems to be busy," claimed Steve. "Have you heard from Tom?"

"Yes, Constable Jenkins just dropped it off. Tom seems to have settled into the academic routine without a problem. He's carrying eighteen credits this semester and next."

"That's a good load to deal with. Wish him well for me. I'd better check on the kitchen. You're doing great, Faith. If you let your instincts be your guide, you'll continue doing fine. I'll see you later."

"Thanks for the support, Steve," answered Faith, thinking about the things Tom had written about Kimberly.

She collected several sets of papers to correct in the evening and wrapped herself in a warm parka for the walk up the pathway to the Leroux cabin. As she walked abreast of the infirmary the nurse named Minnie called out to her.

"Faith, could I speak to you for a minute?"

"Of course, Minnie," Faith replied, heading for the open door of the infirmary.

"I wanted to speak to you about a subject patients have brought up. Some of the adults in the village and surrounding vicinity asked me if I would speak to you about the possibility of teaching an adult reading and writing class in English," Minnie requested in her happy-go-lucky way. She was a competent nurse trusted by a large number of the forest people who used the infirmary.

"You tell them that I'd be glad to teach one. I'm available most any evening or weekend. We could use one of the classrooms, or they could come here to the cabin if they wish."

"I believe it will have more meaning if you used one of the classrooms," suggested Minnie. "The atmosphere would be more conducive to serious studying."

"I agree with you. I'd have to speak to Steve first, but I can't imagine that he would object to the project. He may have some materials in the storeroom that we could use. I'm glad you mentioned this to me, Minnie."

140

"I know that some of the adults still remember when Marie used to read to them when she was blind. I was a very young girl then, but I remember how the adults, including my father, were proud to be able to read and understand the printed word in books. It enriched his life year after year."

"Marie is a wonderful person. I've met her twice. Her husband, Scott Taylor, was a close friend of my husband Thomas. It's a small world, isn't it? You tell your patients and friends that I'll be happy to conduct a class after hours for them for as often as they desire. Goodnight, Minnie."

"Thanks, Faith. You have a good night, too."

As soon as the sun sets in the northern latitudes, darkness follows swiftly. Faith noticed that a heavy overcast was rolling across the lake, making the evening hour darker than usual. Sometimes it was difficult to see a hand in front of you. She walked quietly to the cabin where she started a fire in the fireplace. The wood stove was still going, keeping the cabin warm. She fixed a couple of poached eggs on toast for supper and cleaned up after herself. The luxury of a warm shower after a day's work was the most appreciated feature in the cabin. She dressed in warm pajamas and bathrobe for a quiet evening correcting papers and writing a letter to Tom.

One set of papers Faith was anxious to read was an assignment she had given to her eighth grade students. She instructed them to describe in their own words what they wanted to do with their lives, suggesting that they examine their hearts and their favorite dreams to help do the writing for them. "Unleash your dreams and commit them to paper," she had instructed.

One paper in particular touched her heart. It was written by a shy thirteen-year-old girl named Anne Clark. Faith could picture the girl sitting in her backrow seat eagerly listening to every word Faith spoke with her dark eyes bright and intense. The child was courteous and well-liked by her classmates. She was the kind of student that makes a teacher feel that her job is worthwhile. Anne was alert at all times, but her shyness and lack of confidence kept her from participating in many of the classroom discussions which Faith stressed from the beginning. It gave her a chance to understand and to know the students better. It also helped her to gain some insight into the family life of the students. Faith knew that Anne was brought to school by her mother, a Cree, and that her father, a white Scotch immigrant, was a trader in the area northwest of Fort Lewis towards James Bay. He no longer lived with the family which seemed to be extremely poor. The difficulty that Anne had of expressing herself in class was not carried over into her writing. The three-page paper from Anne was a simple and poignant expression from the heart:

Dear Mrs. Hamilton,

You asked the class to write about things we feel in our heart. Sometimes I have the feeling that what I think about things doesn't matter because I'm not important enough to matter. When I was a young girl I used to dream that someday I would be able to go to school and learn things so that I could become a teacher like you or a nurse like Bright Cloud and Bright Star. They have always been my idols.

My mother tells me that I can become anything I want to be if I'm willing to work hard enough for it to come true. I've always tried to do that, but it is hard when my father is at home. He makes my mother cry all the time and is cruel to her. My mother defends my right to stay in school, and he gets angry for that. He drinks whiskey all the time and uses my mother for his own pleasure even in front of me. Sometimes he disappears for weeks, even months without a word from him.

I'm afraid because lately he's been trying to touch my body telling me that I'm growing up fast. I told my mother, and she was determined to have me stay at school for the entire winter. I'm afraid he will come and take me away. I don't know what will happen to me after the year is over. I want to continue school, but it means that I'll have to go to a larger settlement that has a high school. He is strongly opposed to that. One of his business partners keeps looking at me as if he wants to devour me. I hate him. He makes me feel cheap.

I want to be more than a bed partner to a drunken creep, but I don't know how I can prevent that from happening. I don't have any dreams, I have fear instead.

Anne Clark

Faith placed the papers on the table and rushed to her bedroom to get dressed again. Once dressed she ran to the school to speak to Steve, and found him helping some of the mothers clean the kitchen after the evening meal.

"Steve, may I have a word with you?"

"What's wrong, Faith?" asked Steve, alarmed at the determined look on her face. "I'm almost finished."

"Could we take a walk outside?"

"Sure, let me get my jacket." A few seconds later he met her outside the school. "You look distressed about something, Faith. Can I help?"

"Steve, let's walk over towards the dock. I don't want anyone to hear us."

"Okay," Steve replied, falling in step beside her. "It must be important, or you wouldn't be acting like this."

"Steve, I asked the eighth graders to submit a paper telling me how they think about things that are important in their lives and where they want to go from here, promising that it would be a secret between them and me. Now, I discover that I may voluntarily break that vow of trust to protect the well-being and physical safety of one of the children. Do you have any thoughts on the dilemma?"

Steve didn't answer her directly. He looked at the night and turned to look at the school. "You know, Faith, we're the catalyst and springboard for the lives of the kids in our charge. Everything we do provides them with the knowledge and dreams that make a tremendous difference in their future. They continue from this point in their lives in the direction we encourage them to take. We have a moral obligation to create an atmosphere where knowledge and values are learned and understood. Sometimes keeping our word to the children is the most important lesson we teach."

"I understand that and agree with you."

"Maybe I can help you without violating your promise. Over the years I have come to know these children probably better than they know themselves. Sometimes one of them stands out from the group as being special in some way. I can truthfully tell you that I've seen a promise in one of your eighth grade students that touched my heart. Her name is Anne Clark, and I would not be surprised that she might be the subject of your concern."

"I…"

"Don't tell me anything, Faith. Let me finish. I've watched this lovely child bloom more each succeeding year. We have to guard against playing favorites because the others pick up on that very quickly, and we lose our moral authority if they perceive that another person is getting special treatment. Yet, we have a solemn obligation to cultivate that small number of promising students who become our responsibility. It's a delicate balancing act that we must always be conscious of."

"I came to the right person," admitted Faith. "Thanks for sharing your wisdom and experience with me."

"Thank you for feeling that you had to ask such a question. The seventh and eighth graders are a lucky bunch. This year they have a gifted teacher who works not only with her brain but with her heart."

Faith felt herself blushing. "Thanks, Steve. I'm grateful that the children have accepted me in this relatively short period of time so that they trust me with their dreams and thoughts closest to their heart. It's a sacred trust that makes me feel good all over."

"Aha, Faith Hamilton," announced Steve in a serious tone. "Since you came to Fort Lewis you have not only won your student's trust and affection, you have also discovered the essence of being a teacher."

Chapter Fifteen

Faith wrote a letter to Tom after returning to the cabin.

Fort Lewis, Canada
September 21, 1969

Dear Son,

It was nice to receive your letter today. I hope you are not taking on too much of a course load. I'm glad you had the foresight to drain the water pipes at the house. I had completely forgotten about them.

I'm staying at the Leroux's cabin while teaching at the school. I can tell you in all honesty that I'm enjoying the teaching adventure. I teach the seventh and eighth grade classes. They are in that awkward stage of physical growth between childhood and adolescence, but their thirst for an education, which is a direct reflection of their parents, is strong and sincere. It's a wonderful experience, Tom.

I can't help but wonder that the hiking trip we took from the plant had to have been the work of Divine Providence or fate whichever you want to call it. Steve has been very supportive of my efforts. He's a fine teacher, and I admire his dedication to the children in the area.

You'll be pleased to know that I've been asked to start an adult reading-and-writing class after regular school hours. I spoke to Steve about it tonight. He was enthusiastic and offered the use of any material in the storerooms from the first grade level that would be applicable to adults. Steve suggested that I stick to the basics, starting with letter and number recognition. I'm excited about the project.

Don't be discouraged by Morning Dew's discovery and attraction to a way of life she's never known. I'm sure it's just a phase she's going through. Continue to be her friend. I know that you have strong feelings for her, but you'll have to be patient, Son. She's a lovely girl, and it's only natural that young men around her will want to court her. Do not despair and do not limit yourself to Kimberly, especially if it appears that she seriously prefers to be with someone besides you. The world is full of all kinds of people, and we must listen to our hearts when we make a choice. Well, I've preached enough, Son. I just don't want you to miss the chance of meeting other nice young ladies that you may enjoy being with. I'll keep our secret.

The fireplace embers are beginning to die out, and I am tired. The nights are dark and long up here. I'm looking forward to the winter months. If I successfully handle the severe weather, then I'll know that this was a wise move for me to make.

I'm proud of you, my dear Son, and love you.

Mom

The next morning Faith was sipping a second cup of coffee when she heard the whipping pulsation of a helicopter landing on the police dock. She had a feeling it might be Joe. His company had sent mechanics to make repairs so that the helicopter could be flown to New York State for a rebuild of the frame and engines. A few minutes later, a knock sounded at the door.

"Come in. The door's open," she hollered.

"Hello, is anyone at home?" asked an excited Joe. "I thought I'd bum a cup of coffee if you don't mind."

"Come and sit down. There's plenty of coffee left. How about a piece of toast or something?"

"Just coffee, please. I ate breakfast at Trails End. I'm doing the daily shuttle for a few days."

"Then your machine is fixed?"

"No, it's going to require some extensive rebuilding, so I'm using another craft just like it. How are you doing with the kids? You look comfortable with your decision."

"I am, Joe. I can't believe that I've already been here for two weeks. The children and parents have been just great. I'm going to do an adult reading and writing class."

"Sounds as if you made a wise choice. I'm glad for you. I can't stay too long. I know you have a class to get to. I just wanted to say 'hi' and let you know that, up to now, I've been true to my promise to leave the booze alone. I admit that a couple of times the temptation was difficult, but I'm slowly climbing that mountain we talked about."

"I'm proud of you, Joe. Thanks for sharing your accomplishment with me. I've been wondering how you were doing. Does your company work up here in the winter time too?"

"Sure, we fly year-round. The weather has to be monitored a little more faithfully in the winter, but the cold doesn't really interfere with the helicopters much. There's a slight loss of lifting ability in the severe cold, but the larger machines handle it well. I also want to tell you that I've purchased a piece of land. I've never owned a piece of real estate in my life. I'm thrilled about it. We'll pass papers by spring."

"I'm so glad for you. The joy of independence and self-sufficiency that ownership generates is a wonderful experience. You deserve it." She saw a more relaxed and focused Joe.

"Now that I've taken the plunge, I understand what you mean. Well, I've got to run. Thanks for the coffee. Do you mind if I stop by to see you once in a while?"

"I'd take that as a compliment, Joe. Please do. Have a safe trip wherever you're going," replied Faith.

"Is there anything I can bring you from the civilized part of the world that you'd like or need?"

"No, I'm all set. Good-bye and good luck. Continue to climb that mountain. I'm working on mine, too."

"Thank you for being a friend. I've changed since you walked out of the wilderness into my life. I. . ." Joe started to speak but the presence of Faith's warm lips could not be denied. He placed his arms around her and kissed her. She returned it.

"So long, Joe. You take care of yourself."

"I promise. You know the first time I saw you sitting at the table with Bright Cloud and Colonel Leroux, I thought you were the loveliest lady I've ever seen. I know now that I was right."

"You have a gift of making people feel good. Thanks for brightening my day."

"The pleasure was mine. Those kids are lucky to have such a pretty school marm. Good-bye, Faith."

"Good-bye, Joe."

Faith watched him walk down the path toward his helicopter. There was a spring to his step and contentment in his eyes. She looked at herself in the mirror above the sink. "Faith, is something happening to you again?"

The air was colder with a bite that penetrated warm clothing. Faith could see mist from her breath as she walked to the Eagle Nest. Steve met her at the door.

"Good morning, Mrs. Hamilton."

"Good morning, Mr. Jackson. Joe Lance seems to be making progress."

"I've had that feeling, Mrs. Hamilton," Steve declared with a raised eyebrow. "It's time to ring the bell."

Faith stepped through the door hanging her coat in the small cloakroom at the rear of the class. "Good morning, everybody."

"Good morning, Mrs. Hamilton," the class responded in unison.

"Before we get into our regular studies, I want to take a few minutes to thank all of you for the wonderful set of papers you turned in to me yesterday. I was touched by the breadth of your topics and the honesty they conveyed. Writing from the heart usually brings out our true thoughts and feelings about things. I want to remind all of you that these writings and others we'll do throughout the year, will be kept in strict confidence between you and me. I give you my word." Faith looked from the seventh to the eighth grade students. They understood what she was saying. She made eye contact with Anne when she pledged her word. Anne smiled and her eyes shined brightly.

"I have just one final word on these papers. I'm going to keep them until the end of the year. Many people like to keep a diary or a daily journal of important events in their lives. If any of you would like to do that, just take an extra notebook from the supply on my desk. If you want me to review it, I'll be glad to. The important thing is to use the journal as a means to express your thoughts about anything you think is important to you. Now, the eighth grade can begin the arithmetic problems on page nineteen of your book while I review math problems with the seventh grade."

The day went quickly. Faith noticed that the students, especially the boys, were different around her after she made the announcement about the papers. A bond had been formed between her and the students by the essays they shared. Most found it easier to communicate in writing than to express themselves in person. She was pleased at the level of intimacy she had been able to reach with them in such a short time. Over half of the two classes accepted her offer of a notebook at the noon break. Anne was one of the first in line.

Winter came to Fort Lewis with all its fury. Faith had experienced a lifetime of severe winters in northern New England, but the weather at Fort Lewis was beyond comparison. Low temperatures of forty degrees below zero and swirling snow in such velocity that unprotected skin would instantly freeze was typical of the winter weather. The wind howled and screamed with such intensity that sometimes it was impossible to sleep. Imaginations could run wild listening to the inhuman intonations outside. They often sounded as if someone was near death. The weather had been especially life-threatening just before the last days leading to Christmas break. School was scheduled to resume the day after the New Year. Many of the wilderness dwellers traveled to Eagle Nest to bring their children home for the holidays. The Quebec Education Bureau had contracted with the helicopter company to transport those children beyond reasonable foot travel back to their homes.

Joe was selected to fulfill the contract at the school. The day after school closed was a clear, cold day with light winds, ideal for flying. Joe had already shuttled several loads of about five children apiece. The only students left were Anne Clark and two seventh graders who lived the furthest away, and they were scheduled to be on the next shuttle.

The village was relatively empty of people. Most of the men were at the forest harvesting operations north of the outpost. Suddenly Anne's father made a surprise visit to the village to get his daughter. He had been drinking, and his two younger companions also wreaked of cheap whiskey. Anne spotted the men as they came out of the Hudson Bay Store and started running for the school building. The only adult at the schoolhouse was Faith.

"Mrs. Hamilton, Mrs. Hamilton, my father's coming to get me. . ." Anne screamed in a high-pitched voice, running through the dining area of the dormitory.

"What are you saying, Anne?" asked Faith, following Anne out the rear door of the building.

Anne climbed on top of piles of firewood in the storage shed behind the school, frightened and hysterical. Fear filled her eyes as she pointed to the men coming around the rear of the school building. Faith immediately understood what was happening and defiantly stood her ground confronting the three men.

"I want Mr. Lance to take me home to my mother," pleaded Anne. "I don't want to go with my father."

Faith seized an axe from a nearby chopping block and stood between Anne and the men: "Anne has the right to go with whomever she wishes."

One of the men made a quick move, distracting Faith while one of his companions sneaked behind and hit her a savage blow across the ear. She fell to the ground, dropping the axe. One of the younger men climbed on the wood pile, grabbed Anne by an arm and yanked her to the ground.

"I want to go home with mother," Anne screamed defiantly.

"I'm your father, and you're coming with me." He was a short and stocky white man with a heavy gray beard. He spoke perfect English, but his words were badly slurred. He was drunk.

"No, I don't want to go," protested Anne, trying to wrench free of the iron grip the men had on her arms.

The snow was too deep for walking. The men had stashed two snowmobiles in a small grove behind the school. They dragged Anne to the waiting machines. Faith was still hurting when she heard Anne's pitiful cries of protest. She tried to stand so that she could see what was taking place, feeling dizzy and disoriented. She knew it was futile to go against the three men, so she ran as fast as she could towards the police station, yelling at the top of her lungs to get someone's attention. Constable Jenkins was in the radio room when he heard Faith's voice. He ran to catch Faith as she collapsed on the snow from exhaustion and fear.

"My God, what is it, Mrs. Hamilton?" he demanded, trying to comfort her by placing his jacket under her head. When he heard her say that Anne had been abducted against her will, Jenkins drew his revolver and fired three shots in the air to summon help.

Minnie heard the shots at the hospital. Three shots always meant that something was wrong. She glanced out the window and saw Faith lying on the snow and started running towards her. Steve had been taking a shower when he heard the shots and bolted from his cabin.

"Minnie, would you please look after Mrs. Hamilton? I'm afraid we've got some ugly business taking place behind the school," requested Constable Jenkins firmly.

"Yes, I'll look after her, Constable."

Jenkins ran behind the school to see what was going on. All he found was one of Anne's mittens. A large area of ground had been disturbed around the snowmobile tracks indicating that the men had trouble with Anne before leaving the area. The tracks were heading northwest around Lookout Mountain. He hurried back in time to see Steve and Minnie helping Faith towards the infirmary. He raced to the radio room and sent out an alert notifying all receivers what had happened. His first response came from Joe Lance.

"Fort Lewis this is Red Dog. I'm on my way back to Fort Lewis. I am low on fuel and am diverting back to Trails End for replenishment. I'll be at Fort Lewis in twenty minutes."

Steve rushed into the radio room before Jenkins had signed off. "Constable, tell him that I'll be airborne in ten minutes. I've replaced the pontoons with skis. There isn't much time before it gets too dark to pick up the trail. I'm sure I can locate it as soon as I get in the air. I'll scout the direction the machines are headed and vector Joe to their positions."

"Fort Lewis to Red Dog, please pick me up at Fort Lewis as soon as you refuel. Steve will be airborne and can direct us to their location. If we find them, I can be dropped on their line of advance to stop them. Do you read me? Out."

"This is Red Dog, I read you Constable."

Faith, against Minnie's protests, left the infirmary and was standing outside the police barracks listening to what was taking place. Steve almost bumped into her on the way to his plane.

"Faith, you shouldn't be here."

"Yes, Steve. I'm going with Joe and the Constable. Anne may need me, and you can't talk me out of it."

Steve shrugged his shoulders and continued on his way. Within minutes his Norseman was warming up while he removed an improvised tent which protected the engine and cockpit from blowing snow and ice. Faith confronted Constable Jenkins while he was busy inspecting and loading his revolver. He also grabbed a U. S. Army surplus M-1 carbine and a couple of ammunition clips. He pulled on his heavy service parka and started out the door.

"Mrs. Hamilton, I can't force you to stay, but I wish you would. It could get dangerous out there."

"Isn't that all the more reason that I should go along to help Anne if she needs me? Please, Constable, I insist on going."

"Come, we'll go by the dock where Joe will pick us up. Are you all right, Ma'am? You took a heavy blow beside the head. Your ear looks swollen and tender."

"It hurts some, but I'm sure it's nothing compared to the trauma Anne's father is subjecting his daughter to as we speak. Time is of the essence, Constable. I've been informed and promised to never reveal it to a soul that Anne is fearful of sexual assault by her father and the men with him. If they touch that girl, I'll kill them with my bare hands."

"I hear Joe's helicopter in the distance. Your revelation is safe with me. I'll see that justice is done."

"I don't doubt that, Constable. The girl was hysterical and feared for her safety. Please keep what I've told you to yourself. I think God is on my side with this one."

"I'm sure He is, Mrs. Hamilton," consoled the young policeman, pulling her parka tighter around her neck. "You don't want to get cold."

Joe brought his helicopter straight into the dock, dropping rapidly to pick up Jenkins and Faith. She climbed into the rear seat. Constable Jenkins took the passenger seat beside Joe. Pausing a moment for them to fasten their seat belts, Joe rammed the helicopter to full power, lifting and traveling forward at the same time, barely missing the bell tower on top of the school.

"This is Red Dog calling Bluebird."

"Bluebird to Red Dog. I've got their tracks in sight. There are two snowmobiles running in a line. The two younger men are in the lead machine. Anne and her father are following them. They're running in excess of fifty miles an hour. Take an azimuth of 280 degrees from the school building. Is Faith on board?"

"Red Dog to Bluebird, affirmative. Am on course. Do you have any idea of their destination? Out."

"Bluebird to Red Dog. I believe they're heading for a cabin about fifty miles from Fort Lewis on the track being followed. I have them in view and don't believe they've spotted me yet. I'm keeping slightly to their rear and as far away as necessary to be able to follow them. Those machines make a lot of noise. Out."

"Steve is correct, Joe," confirmed Jenkins. "They should be approaching the cabin soon. You know it might be worth a try if we gave the track a wide birth, flanking the snowmobiles, and proceed to the cabin as quickly as possible. Hopefully we'll get there first and wait for them."

"Sounds good to me," acknowledged Joe. "I'd feel better if you weren't here, Faith. This could get rough. Red Dog to Bluebird. We're going to flank the route to the cabin in an attempt to reach it before they do. If we're on the ground we can stop them easier. Maintain your position and let us know if they deviate from present track. Out."

"Bluebird to Red Dog. Roger, good luck."

Joe maintained the lowest altitude possible commensurate with safety and turned the engine to maximum throttle. Much of the noise from the rotors and engine would be absorbed by the snow on the ground and the tree branches. Jenkins directed Joe to come in from the rear of the cabin on the same axis as the snowmobiles were traveling. He noticed a small clearing close to the cabin and quickly dropped the helicopter in the snow, cutting the power before they touched the ground. Jenkins buttoned his parka, checked the carbine and leaped from the seat, hitting the ground at the same time the helicopter touched down. He ran for the corner of the cabin with his rifle ready.

Joe unfastened his safety belt and turned to Faith. "Do you know how to use one of these?" he asked, handing her a stubnose .38 revolver.

"Yes, I'm familiar with firearms. I was a good shot," she responded, accepting the weapon with her gloved hands.

"You stay inside the machine where it should be relatively safe. I have my service automatic and am going out to back up Jenkins. These guys are going to pay for what they did to you."

He was gone before Faith could say anything. The cabin was in clear view. The forest was deathly quiet. If she listened carefully she could faintly make out the sound of engines droning in the distance. Joe and Jenkins were on either corner of the cabin. She was fearful for Anne's safety and afraid for Joe and the brave young policeman. A few minutes later two bobbing headlights could be seen in the distance through the forest. They were coming directly at them. The lead machine came on the right side of the cabin where Jenkins was watching for them.

When the lead snowmobile came abreast of the cabin, Jenkins leaped in plain view with his M-1 carbine already on his shoulder. He placed eight shots in the engine compartment of the snowmobile with the two men aboard. The engine sputtered and stopped. The momentum of the machine carried it past the cabin coming to a halt close to the helicopter. The second snowmobile with Anne on board tried to run over Jenkins. At that moment the courageous young Anne rolled off the machine, landing unhurt in the snow. Joe saw his opportunity once Anne had departed the sled. He raised his automatic and fired four rounds in the engine compartment. The engine broke into flames immediately stopping the machine.

Anne's father leaped from the burning machine, drawing his sidearm. Jenkins and Joe reached him before he could level the weapon. He dropped it and quickly raised his hands in the air. Joe stood up to see what had happened to the other men when he saw fire leap from a handgun near the helicopter.

Faith watched in silence as the two men got off the snowmobile seeking cover in nearby small tree growth. They had not noticed her in the helicopter. She grasped the revolver with two hands and continued to watch the men. It took only a few seconds for the act to play itself out. To her, it was an eternity. One of the men raised a hand with a pistol. Faith fearfully caught her breath. Without hesitation she pushed the revolver out the open door, aimed and fired at the same time as the man on the ground pulled the trigger of his automatic. He fell on the snow with a curse. Faith leaped from the seat, holding the revolver on both men, prepared to use it if they did not raise their hands. The one that was hit rolled on the ground and held his empty hands outward toward Faith. The other was glad to hold his in the air in plain sight. Joe was hit on the right side of his chest underneath his arm. The shot spun him around before he landed in the snow.

"Mrs. Hamilton," cried Constable Jenkins. "Are you all right?"

"Yes, Constable. I've got both men covered. Where's Anne?"

"She's fine. Joe has been hit I'm not sure of his status." Jenkins rushed to place handcuffs and wire stays on the three men.

"I was hoping that it would be a wild shot." Faith placed the revolver in her pocket and ran to Joe's inert body. The white snow beneath him was covered with blood.

"Joe, you're hurt," she cried, feeling someone kneeling beside her. It was Anne. She placed her arms around Faith and hung on tight, weeping in deep throbbing gasps for breath.

Joe started to stir and searched for his automatic in the snow. He had dropped it when he fell. "Your automatic is here beside you, Joe," said Jenkins, handing it to him. "Are you hurt bad?"

"It burns, but I'll be okay. It felt as if it ricocheted off my ribs. Are Faith and Anne safe?"

"Yes, we're safe, Joe. I should have fired sooner," Faith apologized. "I was afraid for all of you." Faith turned away from Joe and took the scared and horrified Anne in her arms to comfort her. "Everything will be all right, Anne. Nobody is going to harm you." Anne shivered from the cold and blind fear.

"If you had not fired when you did, it's possible that the assailant might have been able to shoot several more times, injuring or killing any of us. You acted with courage and used sound judgment," claimed Jenkins. "Thank God Joe had an extra weapon in the helicopter, and that you were able to use it effectively."

Joe had managed to pull himself to his knees with Anne and Faith helping him. "Give me a hand back to the helicopter. It's getting cold out here, and darkness has already settled in."

Faith looked at the large spot of blood in the snow and winced without saying a word, insisting on wrapping her scarf around his waist to cover the wound. They helped him climb into the pilot's seat where he immediately turned on the radio.

"Red Dog to Bluebird, we have culprits in custody. Anne is safe."

"Bluebird to Red Dog. I have adequate fuel and will follow you in to Fort Lewis. Well done. Out."

Constable Jenkins herded the three prisoners into the cargo compartment of the helicopter, securing hands and feet to hooks attached to the walls with a liberal amount of rope the same way he would any kind of freight.

"Everybody clear?" asked Joe before starting the engine.

"Are you sure you can do this, Joe?" asked Jenkins. "We could hold up for the night in the cabin and call in Police or Air Force assistance."

"I don't feel too bad right now, Constable."

"I yield to your judgment. Crank it up." Jenkins thought Joe was still in a state of shock but respected his decision. If they were to stay at the cabin, it would have been a long, uncomfortable night.

Faith climbed in front with Joe. "Anne, you come up here with me. We can share the seat and the safety belt. Come, let me hold you." A tearful Anne climbed over the seat and wrapped her arms around Faith. "I was so afraid!"

Joe started the engine and began liftoff straight up so as to not touch any of the surrounding trees, turning on the aircraft lights.

"Bluebird to Red Dog. I have you in sight. Thank God Anne is safe. See you back at the village. Out."

"Are you all right, Joe?" asked Faith, concerned for him.

"I hurt. The slug felt as if I was hit by a hammer. My head is clearer now. I would not have placed you in danger if I had any doubts."

"I know that."

"You were magnificent down there, Faith. I'm glad you came along."

"So am I," Anne agreed, still clinging to Faith.

Joe positioned the helicopter towards the school building and gently lowered the craft onto the dock, just as Steve's ski-equipped plane touched down on the frozen surface of Lac Diamante. Joe turned off the engine and radio without a word and passed out, slumping over the controls.

Chapter Sixteen

Faith saw Joe relax his grip on the controls of the helicopter and quickly released the safety belt holding her and Anne in the same seat. "Anne, Mr. Lance has fainted," Faith exclaimed in a loud voice.

Constable Jenkins ignored his prisoners for the time being. He, too, had seen Joe collapse. Jenkins opened the pilot's door, released the seat belt and lifted Joe out of the helicopter and placed him on the wooden platform.

"Can one of you run to the infirmary to tell them we need a stretcher here?"

"I can do that, Mr. Jenkins," Anne volunteered, running up the path toward the infirmary.

Faith climbed out of the helicopter and kneeled down beside Joe.

She removed her gloves and felt his face and neck, relieved to determine that he was warm to the touch. His pulse was rapid. She shined the flashlight up and down his body looking for additional injuries. The gunshot wound was still bleeding. The side of his hip and pant leg was saturated with blood. "My God, he's been bleeding ever since we left the forest."

"We'll get him to the infirmary as quickly as possible, Mrs. Hamilton. They have a supply of blood plasma, and I'm sure that we can find a match of his blood among the villagers if we have to do a transfusion. I'll help bring Joe to the examination room. Then I'll come back to secure the prisoners in our holding cell."

Steve came running to the wharf, unaware that Joe had been hit. "What's wrong?" he demanded. In the darkness he was not certain who it was lying on the dock.

"It's Joe, Steve. He was shot and has been bleeding heavily."

Steve kneeled beside his friend and checked for a pulse. "It seems strong," he reported grimly.

"I have a stretcher, Constable," declared Anne, jumping on the wharf with it in her arms. "Nurse Minnie is setting up a blood plasma apparatus."

Steve and Constable Jenkins took the stretcher and rolled Joe on it. "Faith, maybe you and Anne can walk beside us, steadying Joe so he won't fall off while we rush him to the infirmary." Faith and Anne positioned themselves opposite each other as the four walked rapidly up the pathway. The faithful Minnie was waiting for them, and opened the door. All hands helped lift Joe from the stretcher to an examination table.

The first thing Minnie did was sterilize an area on Joe's left wrist with alcohol before she inserted a needle in his vein to start the life-giving plasma. Then she started cutting away his clothing for a thorough examination. Steve removed Joe's belt while Faith and Minnie started to remove the clothing around the wound. The massive blood loss around the left rib cage had already started to clot. Minnie poured hydrogen peroxide over the affected area. Bubbles of bloody material started to form all over the wound as if it was boiling. Constable Jenkins excused himself so that he could properly secure the prisoners.

"Constable, when you have a chance, would you please place a call? We need a doctor for Mr. Lance. I believe the Air Force has one at Trails End."

"Will do, Minnie. I'll also place a backup to Lac St. Jean."

"I'll help you with the prisoners, Constable. Our friend Joe here, is in good hands." Steve turned to go with the policeman and almost bumped into Anne who was waiting outside the room, still in shock. Her eyes were filled with horror. He took her in his arms and hugged her.

"This has been a terrible ordeal for you, Anne. I'm so sorry that it had to happen. If nothing else comes out of this sordid mess, you have proof that we value your safety and well being above everything else. Our brave Constable Jenkins and dear friend, Joe Lance, have shown great courage in trying to protect you."

"I know that, Mr. Jackson," Anne's eyes filled with tears. "They were wonderful. The minute I saw his helicopter in the forest, I knew that I'd be safe."

"I'm taking her to my cabin for the night, Steve," Faith told him.

"That's a good idea," Steve agreed, leaving the infirmary.

Minnie continued cleaning and examining the wound. The bullet had not penetrated the rib cage. It scraped along one rib, breaking it in the process, deflecting the bullet. She tried some smelling salts under Joe's nose. He slowly moved his head away from the strong stimulant and opened his eyes, recognizing Faith and Anne.

"I must have passed out," he said in a weak voice. "I don't remember landing."

"You landed us all safely," Faith told him. "Just rest, your wound has bled a lot."

"It would help replenish lost blood if you could take something for liquid, water, ginger ale or orange juice," Minnie whispered in his ear.

"Water."

Minnie went to get him a glass of water with a straw when Constable Jenkins returned with the prisoner that Faith had shot. He was a small framed man with dark complexion, long greasy hair and a straggly beard. His eyes darted wildly from side to side, checking everybody in the examination room.

"We have another one, Minnie. Two gunshot wounds in one evening has to be a record for you. It's his left arm," instructed Jenkins.

"Bring him to the table next to Joe. Help him take off his shirt. I'll be right with him."

"Do as the nurse suggested," demanded Jenkins firmly. The prisoner resisted the pressure the policeman had on his good arm. "Don't make any trouble with the ladies in the room, or you'll regret it. That's a promise."

161

Faith and Anne followed every movement of the wounded man as he removed his jacket. Fear filled Anne's eyes, and she grasped Faith's arm. "It's all right, Anne," comforted Faith. "This piece of human garbage isn't going to hurt you anymore. He likes to hit women." The man sneered in disgust at Faith. "I owe you one, but this is for Anne and Joe." She squared herself in front of him and delivered a swift kick with all the strength she could summon to his groin. He let out a howl of pain and dropped to his knees.

"Mrs. Hamilton, control yourself," exclaimed Jenkins, picking him off the floor.

"I apologize, Constable, but it was an impulse I couldn't resist. Anne and I are going to my cabin. What can be done about notifying Anne's mother? She'll be worried."

"Corporal Rand is on his way to Fort Lewis to assist me, Mrs. Hamilton. I'll divert the shuttle from Trails End to take Anne home if she wants. It's coming in the morning with an Air Force doctor. It also has some provisions for the school kitchen."

"Thank you, Constable," Faith said. "We'll leave Joe in Minnie's competent care. Before we go, I'd like to say how much I admire the dedication and courage you displayed tonight."

"I thank you too, Constable," exclaimed Anne, standing on her toes to kiss the young officer on the cheek.

"It was my pleasure and my duty, but thanks for mentioning it. Anne, you're lucky to have a teacher like Mrs. Hamilton. Try to put this unpleasant business behind you. Goodnight and rest well."

Joe was conscious enough to recognize the man on the table beside him. "Constable, come closer to me."

"What is it, Joe?"

"I have a confession to make to you. I'm not proud of it, but it's something that should be done. The three prisoners in your custody are the same ones that I've purchased whiskey from several times over the past year or so. If you need me to sign an affidavit or statement to that effect I'll do so. To think that I helped to enable scum like these men to exist and contributed to their profits. It makes me sick and ashamed."

"Thanks, Joe. I've had my suspicions for a while about them. I'll work up a statement for you to sign. It'll help put these guys away for a long time."

Faith insisted that Anne take a warm bath or shower first thing while she got something to eat. They were starved. She mixed up a batch of pancakes, and placed several sausage links in the frying pan before putting on a tea kettle of water to heat for cocoa. Suddenly, Anne called for her in an alarming high pitched voice from the bathroom.

"What is it, Anne?" Faith asked. She saw a look of shame and fear in her eyes. "Are you hurt?" Anne was reluctant to answer when Faith recognized the source of her concern. She had started her menstrual cycle.

"Oh, Honey, there's nothing to worry about. I've got what you need." She pulled Anne's wet hair away from her face and in a calm, natural tone tried to reassure her that it was a completely normal phenomenon, and every woman's body went through the same thing. It became evident to Faith that her mother had not prepared her daughter for this moment in her life. Faith went to her closet and brought a fresh change of under clothes for Anne when a knock came at the door.

"Come in," hollered Faith.

"It's me, Steve. I just wanted to check that everything was okay with you two."

"Anne's taking a bath right now," informed Faith. "She's tired, hungry, and still in shock. I think she'll be fine in a while. I'm fixing something to eat. Would you like to join us?"

Steve hesitated a second and agreed. "Something does smell good. I'd be pleased to dine with you two ladies."

"Make yourself comfortable, Steve. I promised to brush out Anne's hair after she was finished with her bath."

"I'll make a pot of coffee, if you don't mind," offered Steve.

"Please do. I'd like a cup, also."

After Anne dried herself, Faith supplied her with a colorful pair of flannel pajamas with red polka dots and a maroon bathrobe. "Your hair is still wet. Do you want me to do it up in braids?"

"If you want. My mother used to do it like that when I was small."

"You have beautiful hair, Anne, so thick and full. When I finish with the braids, I have some red ribbon that will look nice." Anne looked in the mirror and smiled at herself.

Steve had just completed putting the coffee together on the small gas range that Bright Cloud frequently used to cook on during the summer months when Anne and Faith came out from the bathroom.

"Well, Mr. Jackson, how do you like Anne's braids? I noticed that Morning Dew wears her hair like this."

"My, is this the same Anne Clark?" teased Steve. "You certainly are a lovely young lady. I studied sculpture once, and I can tell you that you have beautiful facial bone structure. You should smile more often. It makes your whole face light up. Are you two as hungry as I am?"

"You bet," Anne answered, sitting at the table beside Faith.

The three ate pancakes and sausage until they were ready to burst. Steve saw a more contented Faith. She looked after Anne with a mother's natural instinct. The real miracle of the sordid ordeal that had just taken place was that the girl was transformed into a more confident child. She drew strength and confidence from the fact that she was worth something. Four adults who knew her took risks to save her from an ugly fate. That reality was emphasized by the bloody wound she had seen on Joe Lance. A rejuvenated Anne Clark had come out of the bathroom. Her affection for and loyalty to Faith was obvious.

"Does your head still hurt, Faith?" asked Steve.

Anne reached up to touch her face with a grave look. "It's still warm and swollen, and a black and blue spot has developed on your cheek. Are you sure you're all right?"

"In the excitement I forgot all about it. I'll take a couple of aspirin before I go to bed. Have you heard anything about word getting to Anne's mother? She must be worried sick when Anne didn't show up as expected."

"Jenkins said he sent word to the Mistassinni Patrol area near where Anne lives. They've probably notified her. A doctor is being flown in from Trails End in the morning. Perhaps they can take Anne home. Jenkins told me what took place out there tonight. I can see that you have taken steps to care for Anne, and I applaud that. What I want to know is how are you taking care of yourself? You very likely saved Joe's life, perhaps others, at the confrontation. You intentionally and courageously shot a man."

"If you're asking me, would I do it again? The answer is yes. I was terribly afraid. At the time, my adrenaline was running wild. I have no regrets or remorse about my actions. I'm just thankful that Joe had another firearm to pass on to me. Without it we would possibly be faced with a disaster of major proportions right now."

"You've answered my questions. I was worried that you might be brooding about things. You're a strong lady, Mrs. Hamilton. I know it isn't polite to eat and run, but I want to check on Joe again and cover the engine of my plane before it gets too cold. Good night, Anne. I'm happy that things turned out for the best. We'll see about getting you home as soon as possible. Good night, Faith."

"Good night, Mr. Jackson."

Faith made up the couch beside the fireplace into a bed for Anne.

"Remember now," instructed Faith. "Keep yourself well-covered. The fire will burn down, and it will be colder in the cabin. You stay put until I get up to put wood in the stove. I hope you sleep well. You're safe here, I promise. Good night, Honey."

"I'm scared to think how things might have turned out, and I'll never forget that all of you risked your lives on my behalf."

Faith pulled the comforter around her neck and kissed her on the cheek. "You've already made me proud of you, Anne."

Outside of the warm and comfortable cabin, the intensity of the winds increased. Howling and shrieking sounds shook the log structure as if Mother Nature were venting her fury.

Loose snow was pummeled against the windows like grains of sand. The village was sheltered from driving northwest winds by the huge rock formation known as Lookout Mountain, but when the winds were moving in a circular configuration, they were often accelerated by the mountain of granite. Anne and Faith were so exhausted that they slept through the storm. By morning the weather front had passed, and a fiery sunrise illuminated the frozen surface of Lac Diamante.

They were in the middle of eating breakfast when they heard the shuttle helicopter buzz the village. It was bringing the Air Force doctor. Faith saw Jenkins running up the pathway towards them.

"I think he's coming for you, Anne. Get your stuff ready," predicted Faith, stuffing a few things into Anne's bag. "Hello, Constable Jenkins."

"The helicopter will take her now."

"Did the doctor come?"

"He's over there now, Mrs. Hamilton. How's our girl doing this morning?" asked Jenkins, taking the bag from her. He noticed the braids and smiled in approval.

"It was nice staying with you, Mrs. Hamilton." Anne gave Faith a last minute hug. "I'll be back in a week. Thank you for everything."

"You look especially lovely this morning, young lady," added Jenkins, opening the door. "By the way, Steve has a surprise. Morning Dew came in on the shuttle helicopter."

Chapter Seventeen

Faith watched the helicopter carrying Anne back to her mother rise above the village and disappear in the wilderness on a northern track. A part of her was still with the innocent young Anne. The admonition Steve had given Faith about playing favorites had been in her thoughts all night. It would have been easy to ask Anne to stay with her at Fort Lewis. She had the feeling that Anne would have stayed, too, but it was right and proper that she return to her mother, who probably needed the comfort of the child's presence more than Anne needed her.

Their reunion may be a bittersweet gathering. The atmosphere of terror that hung over the family for so long would soon be removed by the courts. The father's absence meant that the family would lose whatever financial support he sporadically provided. Steve had told Anne that most of the families of the North Woods labored on very meager finances. It was a way of life that had not changed for centuries.

Smoke was billowing from the chimneys all over the village. It was bitterly cold outside. The windows of the infirmary were completely frosted over. Faith thought of Joe and wondered how he was doing. Anne's departure gave her a chance to calmly review what had taken place the day before. She went to the coat rack on the wall and removed the revolver Joe had given to her. It was a Colt.38 stubnose revolver in like-new condition. She swung the cylinder sideways, removed the empty casing in the chamber, and positioned the cylinder so that the hammer was over the empty chamber. She planned to return it to him and replaced it in her jacket pocket.

The Christmas break from teaching allowed Faith to think about a trip out to Lac St. Jean where she could do some shopping for things she could not purchase at the Hudson Bay Store in Fort Lewis. Dressing warmly, Faith walked to the police station to talk to Constable Jenkins. He invited her inside.

"It's cold out there," he declared, rubbing his hands together. "I've just put on a kettle of water for tea. Would you join me in a cup, Mrs. Hamilton?"

"I'd like that, Constable. How badly was the man hurt that I shot?" inquired Faith, accepting a steaming hot mug of strong tea.

"Nurse Minnie was not too sure, but there's a chance the bullet broke his arm bone. The Air Force doctor is up there checking him and Joe out. He'll stop by when he's finished. I secured the prisoner to the hospital bed and left him there for the night. Anne is probably home by now."

"That's one of the things that I wanted to talk to you about. How will the family get by if the father goes to jail?"

"They live beyond my patrol so I'm not familiar with the family. A friend of mine in that patrol has told me that the small trading post the father ran is capable of providing a living for the mother and Anne. Her mother is a Cree, and they have a tendency to look after their own better than many of the poor whites in the North Country. The mother has a brother who could help her run the post if she wanted to. There will be more assistance available from the Bureau of Indian Affairs, no matter what else happens. The family will at least be able to eat and survive."

"I'm glad I stopped by. I'd feel guilty sending Anne back to her home if there was a chance they did not have the essentials to eat and dress adequately."

"Most of them live on the edge, Mrs. Hamilton. Anne's situation isn't any worse or better than most others. Now that we have the father in custody, the threat of physical or emotional abuse from that source is removed from the family. That in itself should be a relief to them. He's a bad hombre all right, especially when he's been drinking. I'll be able to put him away for a long time. Joe's testimony will see to that."

"Joe's testimony?"

"Yes, he claims that Anne's father has been the source of a lot of the whiskey he's consumed in the past year or so. I always suspected it but couldn't prove it. Joe has come a long ways in a short period of time."

"Was he that bad?"

"Oh, Mrs. Hamilton, it would tear your heart out. He's one of the nicest persons you could ask for when he's sober. Once he gets too much liquor in him he becomes a raging lion. I've had to restrain him several times. I've often thought he had a death wish when he's drinking. It was reassuring to work with him yesterday. It was the same old Joe Lance we all love and respect. I see that our doctor has completed his rounds," Jenkins mentioned as a lone figure passed his window. He got up from the table to open the door. "Come in, Captain James. We have hot tea on the stove. Would you like a cup?"

"I'd love one, Constable," answered the young Air Force Captain.

"This is one of our teachers, new this year. Mrs. Hamilton, meet Captain James."

"I'm glad to meet you, Captain."

"The pleasure is mine, Mrs. Hamilton. You're the one that shot the prisoner."

"Yes, I am."

"You're a strong woman, Mrs. Hamilton. You probably saved Joe Lance's life."

"How bad is his wound?"

"It's superficial. He did break a rib, but it'll heal as long as he doesn't overdo. He'll have shortness of breath and some pain for a while. He's lucky though, another eighth of an inch and he would have been killed by the bullet. Thanks for the tea, Constable."

"Can we ship the prisoner south today?"

"Sure, he'll be in some pain. I had to set a bone in his arm. Right now he'll be fine with a heavy compression bandage. You people in the village are very well served by Minnie and the other nurses. They have a passion and competence for their work that would be the envy of any hospital in Montreal or Quebec."

"They do live up to their titles of 'Angels of the North.' It's a remarkable institution," Faith remarked, finishing her tea and rising from the chair. "Thank you for the tea, Constable Jenkins. It's been nice meeting you, Captain. Have a good day."

"And the same to you, Mrs. Hamilton."

Faith stopped by the infirmary to check on how Joe was doing.

"Our patient is doing much better, Mrs. Hamilton," greeted Minnie. "I just came on duty, but the nurse said he had a restful night. Go ahead in. He's drinking coffee."

"Thanks, Minnie." Faith turned into a small room with two beds. Joe was the only patient. "Good morning, Joe."

"My day has already improved with your presence," answered Joe, sitting up in the bed. "I saw you walk by a while ago and was watching you come up the path to the infirmary."

"I can't get away with anything, can I?" Faith smiled. "I'm glad you're feeling better. I spoke to the doctor."

"I'll be back to normal in no time. I've been thinking about the trip back to Fort Lewis. I should not have taken the chance. It was a bad judgment call."

"What's done is done, Joe. We're here safe because of you and Constable Jenkins. We have that to be thankful for."

"The doctor said you probably saved my life. It took a lot of spunk, and I thank you."

"It was a natural reflex. The creep was intent on trying to kill someone. I was afraid that he had," she answered modestly in a low voice. "When will you be able to walk?"

"The Doc said it was up to me. I don't feel that bad this morning. He said that moderate exercise would be better for me than lying around being idle. I'm going to get up and move around later today. I've broken ribs before. They hurt if you move too quickly, but they mend in a week or so."

"Is there anything I can get for you?"

"Yes there is, Faith. Could you go to the chopper and remove my overnight bag in the cargo compartment? Constable Jenkins told me that he has my service automatic. The bag has got a clean change of clothes and my shaving gear. I don't want them to take that stuff if they decide to move the helicopter."

"Sure, I'd be glad to. Incidentally, what do you want me to do with this?" asked Faith, holding the revolver.

"I've carried that around with me since Korea. Do you have a personal protection weapon?"

"No, I've never felt a need for one."

"I give it to you as a gift if you're more comfortable with it. It's an ideal sized purse weapon."

"I'll accept your offer. I've been around firearms all my life and have shot them a lot. I'll admit that it will give me a greater sense of security. Thanks."

"You're welcome. A firearm is a strange gift to give to a pretty lady. I hope that the next offering will be more appropriate."

"Now I know you're feeling better, Joe Lance. I'll see you later," she said with her heart pounding. She leaned over and kissed him softly on the lips.

Faith didn't feel the cold air outside. The warmth she was experiencing filled her heart. She walked briskly to the helicopter to get Joe's overnight bag. He watched her from his bed. There was a vibrancy about the way she walked and moved. He made a vow to himself: "Joe Lance, that lady is worth any mountain you've got to climb. Don't mess up your chances."

Faith soon returned and removed her hood. "Here's your bag as requested."

"Wow, two visits the same morning," kidded Joe. "Thanks for coming into my life."

"I was thinking the same thing. Good-bye again," replied Faith

"Can we say good-bye the same way?" he asked. Faith smiled and kissed him again before leaving the room.

Later that day, the setting sun shined from the top of Lookout Rock, casting long shadows across the deep snow. After hours of correcting papers, Faith made her way towards Steve's cabin, hoping to see Morning Dew, wondering if there was anything wrong. Her knock on the door got an instant answer from Steve.

"Hi, Faith. I see that Anne got off as planned." Steve motioned her into the room near the roaring fireplace. "A fire feels good on days like this."

"Anne was anxious to see her mother. She was in good spirits when she left."

"That's good. Morning Dew arrived on the shuttle. She's at the infirmary to see how Joe is doing. She was pretty upset when I told her what took place."

"I can imagine. I was hoping to say 'hi' to her. Tom had a chance to work at a school research project for one of the professors, so he won't try to make it up here. His mom will miss him, but he's a big boy and must do what he feels is for the best."

"Young adults do have a mind of their own don't they?" mentioned Steve caustically.

"Have I come at a bad time?" inquired Faith.

"I'm sorry, Faith. No, you didn't come at a bad time."

"I was thinking that the next few days might be a good time to get our adult reading classes underway. I want to think about it and work up an outline. First, I want to see what you have in the storeroom for material and plan the class around what's available."

"You have a key to the storeroom. Feel free to use it as needed. If I'm not mistaken, I think there are some film clips available for adult students. Even elementary films help a lot. It's a teaching medium that instructs with visual imagery that the students can easily recall as they want."

"That sounds good, Steve. Well, I was on my way to see Joe. This morning he was noticeably improved from last night."

"Give him my best," replied Steve.

"I will. So long, Steve."

"So long, Faith."

Faith saw Morning Dew sitting beside Joe's bed which was cranked high enough for him to be sitting straight up. "Hello, stranger," greeted Faith.

"Hi, Mrs. Hamilton. I was going to stop by to see you. You had an exciting day yesterday. When Dad told me about it I couldn't believe such a thing at Fort Lewis," exclaimed Dew, hugging Faith firmly. "You look wonderful. Teaching and this brisk weather seems to agree with you."

"I guess it does. How's school going?" asked Faith, feeling that Dew seemed a little uncomfortable with her. There was a hesitancy to her actions and words that usually came forcefully and spontaneously. Dew had trouble making eye contact with her and seemed anxious to leave as soon as Faith arrived.

"School is going great. I'm not doing as well as last year. Oh well, it will come around. I saw Tom before I left. He said he was working at the Agricultural Experiment Station and was remaining on campus for the holidays."

"Yes, he wanted to earn some extra money. I brought a cribbage board and the last few copies of the Reader's Digest for your Uncle Joe here."

"Do you play cribbage, Faith?" Joe asked with a gleam in his eye. "Colonel Leroux told me that your son played a good hand of cribbage. Did he get it from his mom?"

"Maybe," Faith laughed softly. "The last time I played with him he skunked me. I think he was too good a pupil."

"I'm not settled in yet, so I'll run along," said Dew, giving up her chair next to Joe's bed. "I'll see both of you later." She left in a hurry, leaving Faith and Joe wondering if anything was wrong.

"I didn't mean to interrupt," she apologized.

"You didn't, Faith. She was just about ready to leave when you came in. I can't put my finger on it, but Dew seemed different to me. She wasn't her usual bubbly self."

"I had that same feeling, too; but then, I haven't known her very long. Do you play a mean hand of cribbage, Joe Lance?" Faith challenged him with laughing eyes.

"I've been known to hold my own against my old squadron buddies and CO who had the reputation of being the best. Are you challenging me?"

"If you're up to it, I'm ready to see how good you really are."

They played into the late hours of the evening. Faith beat him two games out of three, one with a large point spread.

"I think we better call it a night. I don't want to get you over-tired," Faith said triumphantly. "You really do play a good hand. It's just the luck of the draw."

"You're trying to be magnanimous now," grinned Joe. He had discovered the impish, playful side of Faith. She was a lot of fun to be with. "Thanks for dropping over. I may fake my recovery if you'll visit me every night."

"Maybe that could be arranged. You know, Joe," Faith answered in a serious tone, collecting the pegs and placing them in the compartment on the base of the cribbage board. "I like plain talk between friends. A year ago I fell in love with my boss. He was the first man to make me feel that way since Thomas. It wasn't meant to be, and I had a difficult time getting over it. The lesson I learned from the experience was important to me. I had found that it was possible for me to fall in love again. I'm not and never have been a fickle teenager type. I'm a mature woman almost fifty years old. From the moment I first met you I had the feeling that something meaningful was growing between us."

"I've felt it too, Faith. It's never any good if it's all on one side. When I'm around you I'm at peace with myself and feel whole again. As you know I've had a problem with the bottle this past year or more. I don't want to make any commitments I can't keep. You deserve better than that. I can tell you, in plain talk as you call it, that my first thoughts of you were admiration of your loyalty and respect for your late husband. The integrity and decency that emanates from you is contagious. I admire you for that. I wish I had more to offer than a pledge, but if you'll give me a chance to climb that mountain, I'd be honored to share the top with you."

"We're really strangers, yet, it seems as if I've always known you," declared Faith. "If you want, I'll help you climb that mountain."

"Yes, please do," replied Joe, reaching out to hold her in his arms.

Chapter Eighteen

Faith's first year of teaching at Eagle Nest was coming to an end. It was a year of discovery and fulfillment. She had found a job that was important to her, convinced that man's most noble goal was the pursuit of knowledge and truth. The fulfillment came from the respect and affection of the students she taught. The students were children, mothers and fathers and a couple of grandmothers. The gift and honor of being able to bring enlightenment to people's lives fulfilled a lifetime desire to make a contribution of lasting value. Sharing and introducing a whole new world of information to the forest people made it possible.

Discovery was not limited to the Eagle Nest. During the frigid Canadian winter she and Joe had rediscovered the joy that love was capable of bringing to their lives. It was stronger than a simple infatuation. The joy came from being with each other and being able to say and think what was in their hearts without judgment or criticism. It was based on trust, respect and the recognition that mortal man had limitations. The gift of laughter was perhaps the most rewarding discovery of all. They were free to be themselves and laughed at silly failures.

One event of the winter saddened everybody at the Eagle Nest. Anne Clark's mother died of tuberculosis. Anne was traumatized by the death. A month before her mother's death, Anne's father had been sentenced to seven years in jail for child endangerment and bootlegging whiskey. She became an orphan in a large world she was just beginning to comprehend.

Several days after the funeral Faith asked Anne to come to her cabin after school. They walked up the pathway together in silence. Anne was still in a state of shock and denial. Prospects for a happy future did not look encouraging. She withdrew from her classmates and rarely spoke to anyone. They were worried about her.

"Make yourself comfortable, Anne. I'll put something on for supper. What would you like to eat?"

"I remember that you made pancakes with maple syrup once. I liked that," answered Anne. Since the death of her mother Anne rarely initiated conversation; she simply answered questions. Faith was encouraged that she answered with more than a "yes" or a "no".

"Before we start supper, I want to show you some things I've been collecting for you ever since Christmas break. Come, they're in the next room."

Faith opened the door to the room Bright Cloud used to store her piano. Anne's sad eyes lit up when she saw it. The piano had hit a responsive chord within the child of the forest. "What a beautiful piano."

Faith was thankful to see the despondent air momentarily disappear from her eyes. "It is," Faith agreed. Anne sat on the polished wooden settee and ran her finger over the keyboard. In a split second Faith recognized that something about the piano triggered a response that nothing else had done in days. "You may play with the piano, but first I want to show you what I've got."

Faith placed a suitcase on a chair and opened it. Inside, neatly folded and packed, was a supply of under clothes, socks and personal hygiene items plus several complete outfits of skirts, pants and colorful shirts. "These are basic things a young lady needs to feel good about herself. I purchased them for you the last time Mr. Lance and I went to Lac St. Jean on a shopping trip. Everything should fit you."

"Oh, thank you, Mrs. Hamilton. They smell so nice and clean."

"That's because I put a cake of soap in amongst the clothes," Faith smiled, showing her the lilac-scented soap bar. They laughed with each other. Faith reached out for Anne and held her for several seconds, praying that she could be the one to remove the sadness and dejection from the child's young life.

"May I take a shower and get dressed up in the new clothes?"

"You bet you can," Faith answered, pleased to see her excited about something. "You take your time, and I'll make supper. Afterwards we'll have a desert I picked up in Lac St. Jean. I've missed not having a doughnut with my coffee in the morning, so I bought several dozen and froze them. We'll sample a strawberry-filled doughnut with cocoa after supper. How does that sound?"

Anne placed her arms around Faith's neck. "I love you, Mrs. Hamilton." They wept in each others arms.

"Dear child, you've touched my heart for the past seven months. I've asked you to come here because I want to talk to you about something very important. You can think about it while you take a shower. I've been thinking that if you were willing, you could return to Vermont and stay with Tom and me for the summer. Don't answer now, Honey. You think about it first. Now jump in the shower."

Anne did as she was told. Faith knew what the answer would be. The child's eyes brightened tenfold, bursting to give an answer. Faith was certain in that second that it was the right thing for her to do.

That evening in front of the fireplace, Faith outlined in more detail the proposal she had made. Anne could spend the summer in Vermont. In the fall, Faith planned to return to Fort Lewis for another year of teaching; therefore, a place had to be found for Anne to stay and start her first year of high school. Bright Cloud and Mark suggested to Faith that Anne could come to live with them. She could go to the same school at Wells that Bright Star had attended. It would be possible for Faith to return for short visits a couple of times throughout the winter. In the spring Anne would return to Vermont with Faith.

"I know that it involves a lot of moving around, but what do you think about the arrangement?"

"How do you know that Mr. Leroux and Bright Cloud want me?"

"I've talked several times to them about the situation. They remember you as a younger student. Mr. Leroux taught school for a few months as a substitute teacher, and you were in his class."

"I remember them. Do you think they would let me take piano lessons?"

"I'm sure they would be pleased to do it. You'll bring memories of happier days when their children were young. You'll bring fresh perspectives and spontaneity to their home that both of them will cherish. I'm certain that after a very short time, you'll end up loving both of them the way everyone does. I have no doubt that you'll be loved in return.

"I don't know how long I'll be teaching at Eagle Nest. We'll have to take that one year at a time, but if I decide not to teach, then you can come to live with me. Your home will always be with me. The stay with the Leroux's is only a temporary arrangement."

"When are you and Mr. Lance going to get married?"

"How do you know about that?"

"Everybody at school talks about it."

"I'm not sure. It could be anytime. If we were to marry, would it make a difference to you?"

"No. That's between the two of you. He's a good person. I remember what he and Constable Jenkins did when my father forced me to go with him. He'll always be special to me."

"He's a very special person. I do love him, and it's growing stronger every day. I haven't been this happy in years."

"I like to see you happy. It shows."

"Then it's settled. You're coming to Vermont with us when school ends. I'll speak to Constable Jenkins about the necessary paper work to bring you to the United States. I'm sure it's not a problem."

From that day to the end of the school year in early June, Anne was a new person. She participated more in class discussions, frequently presenting a set of views that required serious thought on her part. She remained a diligent student, and the prospect of going to high school in the United States was an adventure she was happy to contemplate.

One of the subjects that came up during Faith's conversations with Mark and Bright Cloud was a summer job for Tom. Faith told them that he had a few offers in the Montpelier area, but he really wanted to get a job related to some phase of forestry. Mark mentioned that he had volunteered to oversee a land reevaluation study on the Fort Lewis Cree Tribal lands. The Bureau of Indian Affairs had allotted some money for the hiring of temporary help to do the field work, which was basically a forest inventory. Tom was qualified to do that work as an assistant. Mark promised to let Faith and Tom know when he got a firm commitment from the BIA and the Council. He saw no problem with the arrangement. They invited Tom to stay with them at the cabin for the summer. Tom was enthusiastic about the project. The experience would be valuable, and the money would help. Tom looked forward to spending more time with Mark, whom he looked to as a mentor and a friend.

The end of school at Eagle Nest was a joyous occasion for students and staff alike. For Faith's eighth grade students, however, it was the last time many of them would see each other. A small ceremony was arranged to pass out diplomas. It was a proud day for those who had worked so hard to bring the gift of knowledge to the wilderness and for those who received it with humility and grace. Faith met many of the children's parents for the first time at the ceremony. Everyone appreciated her spirit of cooperation and contagious passion for broadening the horizons of the students in her care.

The next day, Faith and Anne were ready to leave Fort Lewis. Joe was taking them to Lac St. Jean in his helicopter where they would make train connections for Burlington. A small group of villagers had assembled at the police wharf to see them off. Joe took their luggage and placed it in the cargo compartment. Constable Jenkins confronted Faith before she boarded the helicopter.

"Mrs. Hamilton, some of the town people have asked me to represent them and to tell you how much they have appreciated your many acts of kindness and the wonderful spirit of sharing that has been a part of your stay with them. You've given of yourself with an open heart. We are gladdened by the fact that you plan to return for another year. Bon voyage to a wonderful lady."

"Constable Jenkins, there was never a day or night that I did not feel safe and secure with you stationed at the village. Thank you for your support, and tell the village folks that, come fall, we'll pick up where we left off. Good-bye." Faith was touched by the show of appreciation. She gave Constable Jenkins a hug and waved to the people watching.

"So long, Anne. Take good care of Mrs. Hamilton."

"I will, Constable," she replied, kissing him on the cheek.

Joe helped Faith into the front passenger seat and Anne in one of the rear seats. "Buckle up good, Anne. This is the beginning of a remarkable journey for you. Enjoy the ride, young lady."

The helicopter lifted slowly from the mooring pad. Joe took it up and around Lookout Rock so that they could see the village and Lac Diamante at the same time. Anne watched through the side window. It was the first day of a dramatic change in her life. She looked out across the landscape. Small teardrops gathered in the corners of her eyes. Faith turned to grasp her hand. Anne squeezed it firmly. She dearly loved this school teacher and was excited about the future, but that did not lessen the sadness that filled her heart. The North was her birthplace and even though she had some bad memories of her childhood, she loved her native land. She wiped away the tears, trying to hide them from Faith.

"That's all right, Honey. I understand how you must feel. We'll come back as often as you want."

Two hours later, Joe set the helicopter down on a pad used by the Trails End shuttle. The Air Service that Joe worked for had a repair and parts station next to the pad. A Jeep Wagoneer had been placed at his disposal.

"We'll leave the helicopter here. I'll drive us into the village where we can grab a bite to eat near the train station," Joe said, checking his watch. "We've got two hours before your train pulls out."

Anne had never been outside of Fort Lewis except in helicopter rides back and forth to her home in the northern forest. Her first marvel was the size of Lac St. Jean. She was amazed at such a large body of water. Her next wonder was the Wagoneer. She had never ridden in an automobile!

"Do you have an automobile?" she asked Faith.

"Yes, I do. Not as nice as this vehicle, but it runs good. We'll show you how to drive, too."

"Me driving an automobile?" Anne smiled.

"I envy you. There are so many wondrous things that you're going to see for the first time. We take it all for granted. The technological ingenuity that has gone into building parts of our civilized world are so much more magical when viewed in person than seeing them in pictures. You'll remember this day for a long time, Honey."

"Look at all the houses," Anne pointed out as Joe drove down a busy street in a small town bordering the western shore of Lac St. Jean.

They went to a restaurant near the railroad station where they used the rest rooms and ordered lunch.

"I don't know about anyone else, but I'm hungry for a juicy beef steak and a glass of milk," claimed Faith.

Anne was reading the menu list and was amazed at the assortment of foods available. "Is beef like venison or moose?" she asked innocently.

"Some people like it better," explained Joe. "Personally, I like a good thinly sliced venison steak as well as I do beef. Why don't you try a beef steak, Anne. I'm going to have one."

"All right, I'm going to have some milk, too. Sometimes when you brought fresh milk to the school, I liked it."

They ordered their meals and took their time eating. When they were finished with the main meal, Faith and Joe insisted that Anne try a hot fudge sundae with vanilla ice cream for dessert. She ate one and eagerly asked for seconds. Joe checked his watch as Anne took the last spoonful of her sundae. "If you eat any more, you'll burst," he teased.

"You're right. It was good," she confirmed triumphantly.

"We should get your bags and head over to the station." Within a few minutes the steam-engine train came around a turn heading for the platform. It was huffing and puffing with black smoke billowing from the tall smokestack. It blew jets of steam beneath the wheels as it shuddered to a stop.

"Whow, it looks and feels as if it was alive." Anne exclaimed with wide eyes, hanging on to Joe's arm as the train drew closer.

"I'm going to miss you, Faith. I'm glad you're going home though. You must be exhausted after the long winter and steady diet of classes. I'll keep in touch. I love you," Joe whispered in her ear.

"I love you, too," answered Faith.

Joe released Faith and turned to Anne, placing both hands on her shoulders. He looked into her bright eyes. "Young lady, I'm going to depend on you to take good care of Faith. Sometime in the future I hope that I can take care of both of you." He hugged her and gave her a kiss on the forehead. "I hope you find happiness in this new life, Anne. I love you, too, and I want to always be there if you need me. Don't forget, you're not alone anymore. Until next time."

"Until next time, Mr. Lance. Thanks for everything," Anne replied with trembling lips.

They boarded the train, taking a seat where they could wave to Joe standing on the platform. Watching him slowly disappear as the train pulled away from the station, Faith thought what a difference ten months had made. Joe had come into her life when she was at an emotional crossroads, looking for something that gave meaning to her existence. First he became a friend and slowly won his way into her heart. She was determined to bring happiness to both of their lives. Joe's acceptance of Anne becoming a part of Faith's life was complete and sincere. He had an easy way with children. They responded to his calm manners and serious demeanor. It was easy for Faith to say that she loved him. When he bared his soul and told Faith that he loved her, she knew it was sincere and heartfelt.

"Before we left Fort Lewis I tried to imagine what the towns and cities would be like," Anne told Faith, looking out the window of the speeding train. Her eyes were glued to the houses, factories, automobiles and large boats on the lake. The ultimate fascination for Anne were the bridges that vehicles and trains used to travel over rivers and valleys. She asked Faith if they ever fell down from all the weight they carry. "It's more amazing than I thought. I think I must be dreaming and wonder when I'm going to wake up."

"Besides the bridges, what impresses you the most?" Faith asked, sharing Anne's enthusiasm.

Without hesitation Anne answered Faith. "The most powerful thing for me is the energy and vitality that seems to be everywhere. Everyone and everything is doing something different and always moving."

Faith thought about the answer and was pleased at her perceptive insight. She liked Anne's natural reticence. In that respect she was a lot like Joe. She wasn't much at small talk and spoke freely when she had something to say. She studied the new world around her seeking answers. Anne's mind was like a sponge, absorbing and cataloging sights and sounds of the new world she was just beginning to explore. Her natural inquisitiveness was what made her a good student. Faith liked the studious part of Anne, but it was the generous compassion that made her love the child of the forest. She brought from the forest wilderness better manners and more sensitivity toward others than Faith had ever seen in children of affluent families.

"What do you say if we stay overnight in Montreal? We've got to change trains anyway," suggested Faith.

"I'd like that if you want it."

"I have an ulterior motive," chuckled Faith. "All winter we've been wearing practical clothing appropriate for Fort Lewis. What do you say if we go to a woman's store in Montreal and dress both of us in a complete set of new clothes and maybe

184

a blazer or light jacket? Wow, with a fresh spring color print dress, you're going to be a knockout, young lady."

Anne laughed out loud at Faith's outrageous enthusiasm.

Chapter Nineteen

The train from Montreal pulled into the Burlington station at mid-day. Faith and Anne picked their luggage from the baggage cart and looked around to see if Tom was there. Faith had called Tom the night before, asking him to meet them at the station. Faith was dressed in a light green dress with a dark green blazer. Anne wore a yellow dress with multicolored flowers and white lace around her neck and a light beige blazer. Both wore their hair pulled behind their ears, hanging loose about their shoulders. True to Faith's prediction, Anne was beautiful by any standard applied to her. When she saw herself in a mirror at the Montreal store she was thrilled at the difference a new dress could make.

Tom was in the parking lot watching for his mother when the train pulled in. She had told him about Anne, so he was expecting a smaller, younger girl and passed over the two of them as they stepped from the train. Suddenly he realized that he was looking at his mother in a new dress. His immediate reaction was how pretty she was. The girl with her had to be Anne. He was struck by her beauty and started running towards them.

"Here comes Tom," Faith announced.

"Mom, you look ravishing," exclaimed Tom, holding her. "Your adventure to Fort Lewis must have been right for you."

"It was, but I'm glad to be back home. This young lady is Anne. She's going to become a member of the family. Anne, meet my son, Tom."

"Hello, Tom," she said shyly, not knowing what her reception would be. "Your mother has told me a lot about you. You're taller than I expected."

"Hi, Anne. Welcome to the Hamilton family. Mom told me that you were a pretty girl. Her assessment was correct. I'm sorry to hear about your mother. I join Mom in sympathizing your loss. As you must already know, Mom is a lady who likes plain talk, and I think I inherited it from her. I'm looking forward to being a big brother. If there's anything I can do to help you with anything at all, just ask and I'll be there. Would a hug be appropriate?"

"Oh, yes," Anne answered with misty eyes.

Tom held Anne at arm length and looked down on her with a gleam in his eye and a serious look on his face. "I've got to tell you one thing right at the beginning. Over the years, especially when I became a teenager, I expected to take over and be the boss of the household. I learned a hard lesson and it took some time, but Mom was always firmly in charge." Tom laughed and Anne joined in.

"She's a wonderful person, and I love her," defended Anne.

"So do I," replied Tom, taking her suitcase. In that moment Anne knew that she had come home.

Tom helped them put their luggage in the trunk of the car. Faith was excited and anxious to drive the Falcon again. Tom opened the front passenger door for Anne. He took a back seat. They toured the college campus. Tom pointed out the dormitory where he lived and the cafeteria where he and Morning Dew worked. They drove past the dormitory where Morning Dew lived. "Hold it, Mom. I see Dew over there by the side entrance to her dormitory. She was asking about you the last time I spoke to her." Tom waved his hand to get her attention. Dew recognized the automobile and started running towards the street.

"Hello, Kimberly," Faith greeted her, getting out of the Falcon to meet her. "I was hoping I'd see you today."

"Hi, Mrs. Hamilton. My, you look nice! It must have been a long winter for you," said Dew, watching Anne get out of the car. "Who is this? I feel that I should know you, but I don't."

"This is Anne Clark. Anne, you must remember Mr. Jackson's daughter, Morning Dew, or Kimberly as she's known on campus."

"Hello, Kimberly. You look like your mother, Bright Star, and your grandmother, Bright Cloud," Anne replied, shaking hands with Dew.

"Now I remember seeing you at Fort Lewis. It's a long way from here, isn't it?"

"Coming from the northern forest to all of this," exclaimed Anne, pointing to the beautiful campus around them, "has been like stepping into the future. Mister Lance told me that I was embarking on a great adventure. He was right. I can't believe it's happening to me." The wonder she was experiencing and the depth of her appreciation for Faith's generosity was evident. "Mrs. Hamilton has been wonderful. I hope to go to a school like this someday."

"How old are you, Anne?" asked Kimberly, seeing in the young girl a maturity beyond her years.

"I'm fifteen years old. In a few weeks I'll be sixteen. I'm older than most students in my grade. I could not start school at the time others did because I had to care for my mother who was sick at the time."

"I'm sorry about your mother. Welcome to Vermont. You'll love their place in Montpelier. It's as peaceful as Fort Lewis. Well, I've got to run along. It was nice seeing everybody." Kimberly waved to a bright red Cadillac convertible passing by. The driver pulled to the opposite side of the street. Kimberly climbed in, and they sped off.

"That's her steady boy friend, Ray Ellis. Academically I don't think she's doing as well as last year. They're always on the go somewhere. People change," sighed Tom, watching the convertible drive out of sight.

"She has changed," admitted Faith. "She was polite and courteous but the warmth and sincerity I felt the last time we were together at her mother's funeral was missing today. That's sad. It's probably just a phase she's going through."

"She looks so much like Bright Star," added Anne climbing back into the Falcon.

"I'm anxious to go home," said Faith impatiently. "We'll stop to buy groceries while we're in Burlington. Anne hasn't been in a supermarket yet. We'll go to the supermarket on the road towards home."

The large display and selection of food products from all over the world fascinated Anne. She wondered how it was possible for shoppers to make selections with so many options. The most impressive section for her was the meat, fish and poultry display. She helped Tom pick out a dozen freshly baked jelly donuts.

"They smell so good, it makes me hungry," she smiled. "Your mother has been hungry for a donut with her morning cup of coffee. She had two in Montreal this morning."

As they were standing in the cashier line to check out, Tom spoke to Anne in a low voice: "You watch Mother, Anne. I'll bet she's going to take a few candy bars and place them in the basket. She always has one in her pocket."

Faith grabbed a handful of chocolate bars as Tom predicted.

"You were right, Tom," grinned Anne.

When Faith told him that Anne was coming home to live with them, he was a little uneasy with the situation. She soon erased any doubts he had about her presence in their home. To his surprise he liked her when they first met. There was something fresh and exciting about Anne. Her innocence and modesty enhanced the maturity she projected. Tom liked the fact that she smiled a lot. His mother probably had a lot to do with that. Mom made everybody smile.

"We're home," announced Faith, turning the Falcon into the long driveway. "It's great to be back. I didn't realize how much I missed it until now. You're going to have your own room, Anne. It has a nice view of the mountains and has the sun most of the day."

"I'm so lucky," Anne exclaimed, looking around the fields. Her eyes shone brighter when she saw the house and the barn.

"It's like a picture or a painting. You have maple trees around the house."

"That's right. Their leaf is the symbol of Canada," Tom recalled.

"We'll have to air out the inside of the house and turn the water on." Faith stepped out of the car to open the back door of the house next to the garage.

Tom made one trip into the house with suitcases and opened the front door. "I'll turn the water and furnace on, Mom. It's still a little cold at night."

"Come in, Anne. I hope you're going to be happy here with us." Faith grasped her by the arm and showed her the kitchen, living room, and bath downstairs. "Let's go upstairs. I'm anxious to show you the bedrooms. We have a bathroom on the second floor, too. This is your room," Faith announced with a sweep of her arm. "As you can see, it has three windows looking out over the barn. We can fix whatever you want for curtains around the windows. The closet will hold all the clothes you'll ever need, and the two dressers for your small things should be adequate. The small vanity table and chair were mine when I was your age. The bed is firm, but most people find it comfortable. We used this as a guest room. Morning Dew slept here last summer. This room belongs to you, Anne. You're free to use it as you please. I hope it becomes a safe refuge for you physically and emotionally, a place where you can let your head and your heart fantasize and dream those wonderful visions that one day might come true."

"Mrs. Hamilton," Anne cried, embracing Faith. "Your home is much more elegant than I imagined. I'm the luckiest person in the world to be welcomed into it."

"It's not elegant, Honey. Actually it's quite modest, but I'm glad you like it."

"I love this room. Everything is so neat and orderly and clean. I promise to keep it that way, too. Thank you again for bringing me with you."

Faith had trouble holding her own tears. She wasn't sure how a stranger would accept what she had to offer. The sincerity and enthusiasm of Anne's reaction dispelled any misgivings Faith might have held. "This is going to be a period of discovery not just of the new world around you, but of your own reaction and adaptation to the vastly different way of life than what you had in the Canadian north. It's my hope and prayer that you'll be able to find the real Anne Clark in this climate of love and trust. I hope that the new Anne is someone you like as much as we already do. Before too many days go by, we'll go shopping to pick out some new clothes to add to your wardrobe."

"I wanted to speak to you about that, Mrs. Hamilton. I know that you and Tom are not wealthy people and that you work hard for your money. I'll feel uncomfortable if you spend money on me when you could use it someplace else. I'm proud and thankful just to be here with you. I don't want to be a financial burden, and I expect to do my share of work around the home."

"I know that, Anne. When I don't have the money for things, I'll tell you. I haven't had the chance to spend much all winter, so I have more money available now than ever. I understand what you're trying to say, and I would feel the same if I were you. You must never, I repeat never, think that you're a financial burden. Seeing the way you turned heads in that pretty dress has gladdened my heart. I'll ask only one thing from you, my dear. Don't ever change."

The next morning Tom planned to go in the woodlot to cut firewood. The piece of land they owned had ten acres of open field and eleven acres of forestland, primarily northern hardwoods, beech, birch and maple. The terrain was relatively flat and free of wetlands. Tom had been cutting the firewood for household use for several years. He used the Jeep in the barn and a surplus military trailer to haul the wood from the forest to the storage area behind the barn where the smaller wood was piled for drying and the larger cut-to-length pieces sorted for splitting at a later time. After some heavy negotiating with his mother, he was authorized to purchase a small chain saw to fell the trees, limb them and cut the firewood to stove length.

Tom was eating breakfast when Anne and his mother came downstairs.

"Good morning, early bird," greeted Faith.

"Good morning, Tom. I slept well. I heard a whippoorwill singing outside my window last night. It was so close I got out of bed to see if I could spot it. I've heard them often but have never seen one." Anne was dressed in a Hudson Bay flannel shirt and a pair of pants.

"Are you hungry?" asked Tom. "I'm prepared to be the cook if you'll let me know what you want to eat."

"I'm going to have some coffee and a big delicious donut," declared Faith, pouring herself a cup of coffee.

"I'd like some of that wheat cereal you bought yesterday," Anne suggested.

"Maybe after your cereal you'll want a donut and a glass of milk. My taste for donuts is big enough that you two better take some before they're all gone," teased Faith.

"I'd like that."

"I had a few things I wanted to say to you this morning, Anne," Tom announced in a serious tone. "I hope that by now you realize that your presence in our home is welcome. Therefore, having said that, you should feel free to eat and help yourself to whatever is in the house without asking permission. It is our intention and hope that you will share in our family team effort. No one stands alone unless they really want it that way. In regards to privacy, you'll soon learn that Mom guards her personal space with conviction. Everyone has that time in their life when they just want to be alone and want others to honor that desire. That is not an affront to us. Everyone needs time and a place to reflect on any of a number of things in life. What I'm trying to say in a very round about way is that if I come around being a nosy pest when you prefer to be left alone, just tell me to 'bug off' and I'll get the message and leave."

Anne laughed out loud at his attempt to make a serious thing sound humorous. It was his way to say welcome again, and she appreciated his thoughtfulness. It was typical of Tom, and Faith was proud that her son felt a need to say it.

Later that morning Anne followed Tom to the barn where he showed her the Jeep. "When my father got out of the Army in 1946, he and my mother bought this place. He purchased the Jeep at an Army surplus sale. We've been using it ever since to plow the driveway and get firewood out of the forest. It's not registered, so we don't take it on the road."

"What do you mean by register?"

"It's a fee and permit every person must obtain for their cars and trucks to be able to use the public roads. Some of the money is used to build and maintain the roads and bridges. We pay it to the towns and state which is the same as your Canadian province."

"I understand."

Tom opened the hood of the Jeep and described that he was hooking up the battery so that he could start the engine. Then he got behind the wheel, pulled the choke and stepped on the starter. The engine started immediately. Motioning for her to climb in the seat beside him, Tom backed the Jeep out of the barn and drove slowly around the field near the house showing Anne what he was doing with the clutch, accelerator and the transmission shift lever. The shift pattern was on a metal tag on the glove compartment door in front of Anne. She memorized the "H" pattern shifting sequence. He pulled the two levers on the floor to show her how the Jeep reacted in four wheel drive and low range around the field again.

"It sounds more powerful like that," described Anne.

"It is much more so," Tom agreed. "Would you like to drive the Jeep? I'll leave it in low range so that it won't go fast and you can get used to the feel of steering it."

"Wow," she smiled. "What if I have an accident?"

"Just remember the three floor pedals are the clutch, brake and accelerator. When you want to stop, simply push in on the clutch and then push the brake, leaving the clutch disengaged until you move the shift lever to neutral position."

She climbed behind the wheel. Tom turned off the engine and had her go through the declutching, starting and shifting routine with the engine shut down. Ready for a first run, he calmly coached her in starting the engine and engaging first gear. She slowly released the clutch, and the Jeep lurched forward.

"That's okay, Anne. It always jumps like that in low range. You did good. Leave the shift lever alone for now and concentrate on following the tracks I left around the field. Don't run the engine too fast. Treat it as if you had an egg under your foot and didn't want to squash it."

Anne smiled at that bit of information. There was a determined look on her face. She was focused and intense about what she was doing, giving no indication that she was nervous or intimidated. She appreciated Tom's patience and calmness. After several laps he had her shift the lever out of low range and take the jeep around the track, shifting gears and increasing in speed. She stopped and started several times and brought the Jeep in front of the trailer tongue as Tom directed her to do.

"Now put the shift lever in reverse and back towards the trailer," instructed Tom calmly. She did as he directed stopping the Jeep a foot from the trailer. "Now shut off the engine and I'll hook up the trailer." She got out of the driver seat to help him lift the end of the trailer into the pintle hook on the Jeep. "You did very well. You're a quick learner. Now all it takes is practice."

"Your mother's car does not have a shift lever like the Jeep."

"No, it has an automatic transmission and does not have a clutch. We can show you that later. Her car is easier to drive than the Jeep, but then you have to be familiar with the rules of the road."

"It sounds complicated."

"It really isn't, you'll see."

They spent the rest of the morning working in the woodlot. Tom cut enough trees down to fill the trailer twice. After he cut the tree down, he showed her how to mark the tree with a measuring stick and a lumber crayon so that he could cut the tree into stove lengths. She loaded most of the wood onto the trailer as soon as he cut it. It became evident to Tom that she was accustomed to hard labor, for she worked tirelessly through the morning and did not appear to be weary.

The weekend went quickly. Tom and Anne worked two days, getting as much wood as possible piled in the storage area behind the barn. Those pieces of firewood too large for the stove were placed in different piles which would have to be split at a later date. Over the weekend Anne felt as if she had known Tom all her life. They worked well together and were exuberant over the amount of wood they had produced.

Anne adapted quickly to her new surroundings. It was as if she had been reborn in a different world. She loved helping Faith around the house cooking, cleaning, raking leaves and picking up dead branches that had fallen off the trees over the winter months. She had found Faith's library on the first day, and it became her favorite sanctuary. She loved the privacy of her bedroom, but there was a calm attraction for her in the library that she could not describe. One evening, when Tom was in his room studying and Faith was busy in the kitchen, Anne grabbed one of several books of poetry that Faith had accumulated. She sat in the large chair at the desk and became absorbed over some of the verses. She was reading the poem *Annabel Lee* by Edgar Allen Poe and was hypnotized by the lines. A tear welled in her left eye and rolled down her bronze cheek as she read the last stanza of the poem. She slowly read it over again and was touched by the sadness of a lost love.

Faith looked through the door quietly, not wanting to disturb her. Anne wiped away the tear and lifted her eyes from the book to the mountains in the distance. They were draped in darkness. A shiver ran through her body as she thought of her mother and wondered if her father could ever think of her as Poe did of the dead bride in the poem. She saw Faith's reflection in the window pane.

"I didn't mean to intrude on you, Honey, but the look on your face was so sad, you made me feel that way too."

"Some of these poems are so beautiful. They describe in simple words feelings that I find it difficult to talk about."

"This library is my favorite room in the house. I can relax completely in here. I'm glad you find it the same way. Just about every emotion and experience that mankind is capable of having has been captured by the great poets and writers through the ages. That's what makes books, especially poetry, so meaningful and timeless."

Early Monday morning Faith and Anne took Tom back to college. He had a work shift at the cafeteria that afternoon and evening. He bid them good-bye and walked across the campus. Faith had privately talked to him about his thoughts on Anne's sudden appearance in the family. When he first heard the news, it made him uncomfortable that his position within the family was going to be shared by a total stranger who might be unable to assimilate into the family relationship that existed between him and his mother.

Anne dispersed his fears in a very short time. She joined as a team player with a willingness and expectation to do her share. The way she looked up to him as a big brother made him feel taller than his six foot frame. Being present to watch Anne absorb all that was taking place around her was a growing experience for both Tom and his mother. They had taken so many things in their lives for granted! An innocent child of the northern forest showed them how truly fortunate they really were. Food, clothing and shelter, the basic needs of life for mankind, were readily available to them without undue hardships or suffering. Those things they had accepted as commonplace, Anne saw as unbelievable luxuries. In the northland one bad decision or stretch of bad luck could end in tragedy. Survival was the ultimate testament to courage, self-sufficiency and luck. The chasm between the two cultures was deep and wide. They both agreed that Anne was bridging the divide better than they would if their roles were reversed.

Tom met Morning Dew on the campus near the entrance to the cafeteria. He waited for her to catch up to him. "Hi, Kimberly. Just one more week of school! The military ball is coming up, and I've always hoped that I could take you to the ball. May I?" asked Tom. It was more a plea than a request. His feelings for her had not changed even though they barely talked anymore. He had made up his mind that anything more than a casual and light friendship may be out of reach, but he had hoped...

"I'm sorry Tom. Ray asked me to go, and I accepted." She saw the disappointment on his face. "I don't mean to hurt you, Tom. I had made other plans, that's all. You shouldn't take it personally."

"How else should I interpret your answer? If I had asked you before Ray Ellis, would you have accepted?" Tom tested her sincerity.

"I don't know, maybe. . . That's not a fair question Tom," Dew blurted impatiently. "Look, you don't own me."

"I thought I knew you, Kimberly, but the Morning Dew I remember disappeared as if she had never existed. I'm bothered by that fact because I loved her, and I've missed her these past months," Tom confessed, filled with anguish. He walked away, leaving her standing alone to reflect on what he had said.

Kimberly's refusal was not unexpected. He was resolved not to expect anything different from her. Tom was determined to escort someone to the ball, so he asked his cousin, Susan Hamilton, a senior at the University, if she would go with him. Susan was graduating that spring with a degree in journalism. She and Tom had been close friends all their lives. Their fathers were brothers. Susan lived with her parents on a dairy farm on the outskirts of Burlington. She was pleased to have a chance to go with Tom. Her fiancée had graduated the previous year and was serving in the Army in Vietnam. Going to the ball with her cousin sounded like fun to her.

The day of the dance, Tom asked his mother if he could borrow the car for the night and return it the next morning. Faith was relieved when Tom told her about Dew's refusal and Susan's acceptance. Faith had been concerned about Tom. His feelings for Kimberly were keeping him from enjoying himself. Faith was very fond of her niece, Susan. She was a serious girl with a pleasant disposition and positive attitude. She had a few freckles around her nose and a habit of slightly wrinkling her nose when she talked. She was average size and wore her auburn red hair cut short slightly below her ears. She was more cute than beautiful, and everyone liked her out-going personality.

On the night of the dance Tom dressed in his ROTC (Reserve Officer Training Corps) uniform. He had shined his shoes three times until they glowed in the dark. Susan was dressed in a green teal gown with white trim. They were an attractive couple on the dance floor and enjoyed themselves dancing almost every set. Kimberly watched the two as they danced and laughed throughout the evening. Tom acknowledged Kimberly, but made no attempt to introduce Susan to her and Ray. As the evening drew to a close, Susan asked Tom if the lovely Native American girl was the one he was carrying the torch for.

"How did you know?" asked Tom, thinking that he had successfully kept his thoughts to himself.

"I've noticed that every time we came around the ballroom near the girl known as Kimberly, you tensed and tried to move away," acknowledged Susan, looking up into his eyes. "Don't apologize for having feelings, Tom. She's a pretty girl, and any young man would find her attractive. You have much to offer the right girl. Don't waste it on someone who's unworthy."

"I never associated Kimberly as being unworthy."

"I'm not saying that she is, Tom, and I don't mean to hurt you or stand in judgment. What I am saying however, is that her boy friend is a lout if there ever was one. He may be charming and rich, but he is nothing but a playboy. A good-time-Charlie. I know because he has gone out with some of my friends. Kimberly doesn't seem to be his type, but the choice is hers."

Tom thought about Susan's remarks and had to agree with her assessment of Ray Ellis. It did not make him angry, for Susan was not one to make rash statements or to put another person down. She had a habit of speaking her mind like his mother. When he drove Susan home that evening his Uncle Bob was relaxing in front of the television set. He asked Tom if he and his mother wanted a puppy. They had two left from a litter of five. One of them was the "runt" of the batch, a lively alert puppy with cute markings. Tom told him he would have to speak to his mom first and would get back to him.

Very early the next morning, Tom called his Uncle Bob to let him know that he would take the puppy and would be there in a few minutes. An hour later, Tom pulled into the driveway at Montpelier. He noticed that his mother and Anne were sitting at the kitchen table eating breakfast. He walked into the kitchen with a box under his arm and a smile on his face.

"Have you eaten breakfast?" asked Faith. "Anne and I are having French toast."

"Good morning, Tom," greeted Anne, glad to see him again.

"I'm all set Mom. Hi, Anne. I've got a surprise. I probably won't be around when you celebrate your birthday later this summer, Anne, so here's an early present for you. Happy Birthday."

"For me?" Anne cried excitedly, looking at the box he had placed on a chair between her and Faith.

"Be very careful when you open it," he warned.

Anne was nervous, not knowing what to expect as she lifted the flap on the cardboard box. Suddenly the puppy poked her head out the top of the box and started to lick her hands. She screamed out loud as she picked up the puppy and held her in the air.

"She's so cute and soft and friendly," she exclaimed, holding the puppy to her neck. "Thank you, Tom. It's so thoughtful of you. I love her already." The puppy was white and silver on the head and most of her body except for a black streak down the back and tip of her tail. Her ears were erect except for the upper third which flopped down over the rest of the ear. Tom had tied a big red ribbon around her neck. The short tail wagged continuously as the pup ran around the room checking everybody out.

"I got her from Uncle Bob. He said that she was a mongrel with a lot of wire-haired fox terrier blood, and that we should have her fixed in a few weeks. He also emphasized that a spayed female makes the best kind of household pet," added Tom.

Anne held the puppy in her lap. Faith and Tom had always had a dog and missed not having one. Faith picked the pup from Ann's lap and held her while scratching her neck. The puppy was a soft bundle of energy. The minute Faith placed her on the floor, she went directly to Anne with tail wagging for attention.

"Now there are a few things that will have to be settled," Tom said, looking at his mother. "I know that Mom has some thoughts about dogs in the house, so she should spell out the house rules, and you've got to come up with a name, Anne. Uncle Bob pointed to the brown spot on her side shaped like a penny, so that's what they called her, but you can give her any name you want."

"I like Penny. That spot on her side does look like one, doesn't it?"

"Then Penny it is. I also have a collar, a leash, a combination food and water dish and a bag of Purina Puppy Chow," said Tom, emptying the bag.

"Thank you, Tom," said Anne appreciative of the gesture. She reached up to kiss him on the cheek.

"You're welcome."

"It's a very thoughtful birthday gift, Tom, and we'll all enjoy the puppy. Since you know me better than Anne does, I'll mention a few ground rules for Penny. We'll make a bed for her out of a couple of blankets that she can use in the house. She's welcome in the house, but she stays on the floor. You may have her in your room at night if you wish, Anne. There's plenty of room outside for her to exercise and play. The porch can provide shelter from snow and rain as she needs it."

"I knew you'd say that, Mom," grinned Tom.

"Those rules sound reasonable, and I'll see that Penny obeys them. I had a dog once when I was small. I'm going to train Penny to be obedient so that everyone can enjoy her.

Thank you again, Tom. I love her already, and I think Penny is beginning to like me."

And so an alert little fox terrier with floppy ears came into their home, and within a short period of time did what puppies have been doing for centuries, found her way into their hearts. Anne and Penny became constant companions.

A few days after Tom gave Anne the puppy, the subject of names came up. Anne asked Faith if she could call her "Mother."

"I've been thinking of that, Honey. I would never attempt to replace your mother. She was a good woman, and she loved you very much. I don't want to overshadow her memory, but if you would like to call me Mother, I think it would be nice."

"You've been more than a mother, you've been a friend and a teacher, too. Mrs. Hamilton is beginning to sound too formal," Anne confided. "I want to show you how much you mean to me and the title 'Mother' seems appropriate."

"God Bless you, Anne," responded Faith, hugging her and kissing her on the top of her head. "You've given this family so much by just being yourself. Now that you've settled into our home, I could not imagine not having you with us. I'll miss you when we have to part this fall. Mr. Jackson is looking for a commitment from me for the coming year. I think I'll take it. What are your thoughts on the subject? Will you be comfortable staying with Bright Cloud and Mr. Leroux for the winter months? I'll try to come back during Christmas time."

"I'll miss you, too, but I'll be all right. They're not strangers to me, so it'll be easier than when I left home to be at the Fort Lewis school dormitory. Can I bring Penny with me to Wells?"

"Of course you can. I have a feeling Penny is going to win them over like she has Tom and me," Faith reassured her. "There is one other thing I want to discuss with you, Anne. You're a young lady and I know that you have not had much experience handling money the way we use it down here in the United States. I'm going to give you a weekly allowance of ten dollars to start."

"You don't have to, Mother. You work so hard for your money. If you really want to do this, I promise to do my share of work around the house."

"You've been wonderful, Honey. You have a fine sense of responsibility and compassion for others. I've admired those qualities from the first day I saw you sitting in the eighth grade classroom. That's why I think you should have the opportunity to manage a small amount of money that's yours to use as you choose. You can spend it all at once or save it; the choice is yours, and I'll never judge how you use it."

"I've been thinking ahead, Mother," answered Anne, conscious of the fact that she used the word for the first time. "I have four years of high school ahead of me. If I save at least half of the allowance each week, maybe that will help for college."

"That kind of choice is valuable, Anne. However, I want you to know that whether you have saved your allowance or not, college will be available. I promise you that."

"I'm so glad that you came to Fort Lewis to teach. Otherwise I would never have known you. Sometimes I wake up in the middle of the night remembering how it was in our cabin north of Fort Lewis, and I'm afraid again. Penny sleeping on the floor beside me seems to sense those moments, and she'll poke her nose in my hand. It's almost as if she wanted to show me that I'm not alone anymore. I have much to be thankful for. I keep repeating those words, because it's true."

Faith and Anne took Tom to Wells, Maine, so that he could travel to Fort Lewis with Bright Cloud and Mark Leroux. He was looking forward to the job of inventorying the tribal lands under Mark's supervision. Faith noted a slight deterioration in the way Mark moved around. She told Tom to look after him as much as possible and realized her request was unnecessary. Tom's affection and respect for the elderly gentleman was complete.

Before Faith and Anne left Wells, they asked Bright Cloud to play the piano for them. Bright Cloud did a medley of selections mostly from Chopin. Anne was mesmerized by the music as she watched Bright Cloud's supple fingers race along the keyboard. Her final selection was "Canadian Sunset," and it triggered a determination that Anne shared with Faith on the way back to Vermont.

"Someday I'm going to play a piano the way Bright Cloud does. I'm saving my allowance money for a piano."

Chapter Twenty

The first week after Tom left Vermont, Faith and Anne went through the house, giving it a thorough cleaning. New curtains were put up in the kitchen and Anne's room. On one of their shopping trips they went to the movies to see the classic film "Gone With the Wind". It was a stirring experience for both of them. They cried at the ending. On their way home that evening Anne mentioned how horrible war could be to a family. She asked Faith if her husband Thomas was affected by the war experience.

Faith replied: "The war did make him a little more quiet and reflective. He kept things that happened during the war to himself. I wanted to share some of that horror with him, but he adamantly refused to revisit those experiences with me."

"My father was a veteran of the Korean War. Canada fought there with the Americans."

"I knew that. Was he wounded in the war?"

"No, I don't think so," Anne recalled. "Mother said he started drinking heavily afterwards, and it just got worse with time. She did say that before the war, he was a responsible, caring man."

"I'm sure that's true, Honey. It could have been any number of terrible things our men had to endure. Alcohol helped some to forget."

"I was always afraid of him, and so was my mother. At times he was a monster. If I had stayed at home, I believe my mother would have killed him if he touched me. He tried once, and there was a terrible fight."

Faith never pressed Anne for information about her life at home. The fact that she could talk freely about it without becoming upset was a measure of the progress that she had made in assimilating to her new surroundings. The minute they turned into the driveway, Penny jumped off the porch to meet them, her tail wagging like a windmill.

"Isn't it nice to be greeted like that when we come home?" questioned Faith.

"She's such a good dog. She learns quick. I've got her to sit, lay down, and roll over by voice command and hand signals. It's fun to see her all excited and happy when she does what I ask her to do."

"I've enjoyed watching the two of you appreciate each other. Come, let's go in the house," said Faith, anxiously unlocking the door. She placed her purse on the kitchen table and continued to the living room where she turned on all the lights and returned to the kitchen with a smug look on her face.

"Anne, would you put these pads of paper we bought on the desk in the study?" Faith asked, handing her several notebooks. Anne went into the study by way of the living room where she screamed in delight.

"Mother, there's a piano in the living room. It's beautiful!" An upright piano was placed against the living room wall with a bench filled with music books and sheet music of every description. Her mouth was opened wide.

"How did you manage this?" Anne questioned, sitting on the bench, feeling the keyboards with her strong hands.

"I'll explain," Faith confessed, as excited as Anne to see that the surprise was complete. "When we came back from bringing Tom to Maine I spoke to my brother-in-law Bob about a piano. They had this one and wanted to get it out of the cellar where it had been stored for years. They cleaned it up and had it tuned. Bob called yesterday; that's why I suggested we take in a movie. Bob and his hired hand delivered the piano while we were gone. Now you have a piano and some music stuff to start. I have another birthday present for you. I've made arrangements with a music teacher at the Montpelier High School to give you lessons as often as you want at the house."

"Oh, Mother. Every day you spring surprises on me," Anne embraced Faith. "I understand why Mr. Lance loves you the way he does. You're so easy to love. Thank you, thank you for taking me into your home and heart."

They received a letter from Tom right after Anne's birthday:

Fort Lewis, PQ

Dear Mom and Anne,

I'm enjoying myself in the wilderness up here. The weather has been warm, but the nights can be cool. The black flies are just starting to be a problem. I've never seen them so hungry or so plentiful. It would be impossible to work in the forest without head nets for protection.

I think of the two of you often. You certainly left a large reservoir of good-will in the village, Mom. Everyone asks about you and are pleased that you're coming back for another year. It's nice to know that other people appreciate the fine qualities my mom brings to any task she undertakes.

We had a nice visit from Scott Taylor and his wife Marie this week. They wanted to make sure that Mr. Leroux and Bright Cloud were doing well, they're very close friends. General Taylor is a fine soldier. I'd follow him anytime anywhere. Just before they left, he took me aside and made me promise to inform them how they did over the summer. He gave me his permanent address. They're on their way to Germany now.

I'm sorry to say that Mr. Leroux is not doing as well as last year. When we go fishing in the lake it's difficult for him to get in and out of the punt. Last summer he did it several times with ease.

The inventory of the tribal tract is going well. It's exciting to work in a forest so far removed from civilization. The attraction of the wilderness is a subtle thing that slowly grows on a person. I've fallen completely under its spell and am gladder than ever that I made the decision to study forestry. Mr. Leroux

206

is quite demanding on the quality of our work. His original Forest Management Plan completed in 1922 remains as a tribute to his qualifications and vision for the area.

I hope you had a nice birthday, Anne. Now that I've had a chance to live in the wilderness environment, my respect and admiration for your people has increased. By the end of summer you'll probably have Penny trained well. She's only a mongrel, but frequently they are the best type of pet. I hope you are enjoying her.

I see Joe Lance once in a while. He and Mr. Leroux are very close friends. He took me in his helicopter around the tribal tract so that I could get a bird's eye view of the land. It was exciting. Mother, I know that the two of you have strong feelings for each other. We never talked about it before I left for Canada, but if you and Joe can find happiness together, you certainly have my blessings. Your loyalty to father has been proven over and over again, but life goes on. I've seen you struggle for years alone, so if Joe Lance is the one to win your heart, don't hesitate to reach out and take the happiness you deserve.

Good-bye Mom, good-bye Anne, I'll see you soon.

All my love,
Tom

The summer months were passing quickly. One day in late August Joe asked Faith if he could pick her up and take a trip to the Maine coast for the day. Anne had a piano lesson that day and promised to look after the house while they were away. She teased Faith that sometimes adults don't need kids tagging along. Joe drove in the yard with his Jeep Wagoneer early the next morning in an expansive mood. He met Faith at the kitchen door, grabbed her in his arms and twirled her around.

"I've missed you, Joe."

"I know it's been a long time," apologized Joe, setting her down on the ground. He kissed her and still held her close. "Are you ready to travel?"

"Yes, I'm ready."

They said good-bye to Anne and headed for the Maine coast. As they drove over the Kittery-Portsmouth bridge into Maine, Joe became more and more excited. He turned off Route One at Cape Neddick and started climbing the road leading to Mount Agamenticus. On top of the mountain, Joe slowly drove past the State of Maine fire tower to the west and stopped in front of a partially completed log cabin located on a prominent overview of the ocean. He pointed out Boone Island and the Isle of Shoals.

"This is the ten acre piece of land I purchased. I was hoping that the cabin would be completed when I showed it to you, but it has taken longer than expected."

Faith was spellbound with the view. The cabin walls and roof were completed, and the porch half way around it was almost finished. At the front of the cabin above the porch, an observation platform was built with stairs leading from the porch deck.

"What a beautiful location, Joe. When you told me about buying a piece of land, I would never have imagined it to be this grand." She put her arm around him, and they climbed the stairs to the observation platform together.

Joe was nervous and excited. Faith loved seeing that side of him. In many ways he was like a small boy anxious to reveal a secret he had successfully kept until now. Faith felt tenseness in his body. When they reached the platform he pointed to the horizon and turned to look into her eyes.

"I waited until this platform was completed, Faith. From here we can see beyond the horizon. I wanted to tell you that I've climbed the mountain and claimed it. Now I want to share it with you. Will you marry me?" Joe held a ring in his hand. "This belonged to my mother, and I'm sure she would have wanted you to have it."

Faith's vision began to blur as a warm glow filled her heart. She replied: "I knew that this day would come, but I didn't expect it to be like this. I'll be proud to be your wife!" Tears of happiness filled her blue eyes. She rested her head against his chest, feeling warm and secure in his arms. How wonderful it was to love and be loved in return. It was a moment they would always remember. She looked up into his smiling eyes. "My dear Joe, for a long time I've wanted something more than what my life has been. Now you come along and fill my days with happiness. My heart cries out that you deserve the best, and I will try to be worthy."

"Not a day has gone by that I haven't had you in my thoughts. I can still picture you that first morning at Mark and Bright Cloud's cabin. I was so ashamed of the man I had become. Even then I felt the strength and integrity that's so much a part of you, Faith. I fell in love with you then, even though I knew I was not worthy. I drew strength from you, my dear lady. If you had not come into my life when you did, Lord only knows what would have happened. You've given me the will to change my destructive behavior. You did it without a word of chastisement or warning. You did it by being yourself, and I love you so much for being the wonderful lady you are."

They spent the rest of the day at the cabin. Joe had brought a picnic basket packed with food and thermos bottles of coffee. They toasted their engagement with two warm cups of coffee just as the sun was setting behind the cabin. The long shadows cast by the sun ran almost parallel with the pounding waves on the ocean, illuminating the crest of the waves and darkening the trough appearing to accelerate the flow of water to shore. A crescent moon began to rise out of the east before the sun had completely set. It cast a swath of light across the water pointing towards the cabin. They took it as a sign of approval of their commitment to each other.

They set the wedding day for the first week Faith returned in the spring from teaching at Fort Lewis and Anne would be coming home from her first year at Wells High School. Joe agreed that Anne should have the opportunity to do the other three years at Montpelier without interruption and have Faith at home. If Faith wanted to continue teaching, she could always get a job nearby or do engineering as a consultant. Joe admitted to Faith that he was anxious to put roots down and share the life they were anticipating. He was prepared to limit his flying to the company's home base in New York, and he was yearning to plant a garden.

At summer's end, Tom returned to Wells with Mark and Bright Cloud where he stayed for several days. Mark had accepted the fact that his legs were failing him, and that he was going to be confined to a wheelchair. Tom helped a local carpenter build a ramp leading to the kitchen door and the living room entrance. They also had to enlarge several of the door jambs on the first floor to make room for a wheelchair. Bright Cloud had purchased a folding chair that could easily be stored in the trunk of their Rambler Ambassador.

Tom was painting the new ramp additions when a freight truck drove into the yard. He helped the driver lift off a heavy crate from Arlo and Michelle Korsman.

"What could it be?" asked Bright Cloud, coming out of the house.

"It's pretty heavy," added Tom, starting to disassemble the packing material. "Here's a packing slip and a letter to you, Bright Cloud." Tom told her. He began calling her Bright Cloud at her insistence while in Fort Lewis.

"Thank you, Tom," she said, ripping open the letter. "Oh, my! Mark will be surprised. It's an electric powered wheelchair with big wheels for rough ground. How thoughtful of Arlo and Michelle."

Tom completed unpacking the vehicle and carefully read the instructions for its operation. "It's ready to go," he exclaimed, sitting on the seat working the controls. "Mr. Leroux is going to love this. It will enable him to get around with ease and safety." Tom drove it up the ramp to the kitchen and parked on the flat deck. Bright Cloud was amused and smiled at him.

"He can use that to go out through some of his favorite trails in the grove behind the house. This is going to make the disappointment of the loss of his legs so much easier to bear. Come, Tom, take it in the living room where Mark is sitting in his favorite chair."

"What have you got there, Tom?" asked Mark with interest. He had not heard the freight truck in the yard. Tom stopped in front of Mark. The minute he saw the machine, he was anxious to try it out.

Tom showed him how the controls worked and helped get him seated on it. "If you're not careful, Mr. Leroux, you'll get a speeding ticket with it." They both laughed.

Bright Cloud quietly watched from the kitchen door. She had been worried how his immobility was going to affect her Mark. She saw a sparkle in his eyes and a look of determination on his face as he slowly made his way out the kitchen door, down the ramp and disappeared in the pine stand at the rear of the house. A few seconds later, they saw him returning with a triumphant look on his face.

"He's like a kid with a new toy," exclaimed Tom.

"Isn't it wonderful, Tom?" replied Bright Cloud with a mist covering her eyes. Love filled her heart. "I haven't seen him this happy in a long time. He's a very proud man and was becoming more and more depressed with his inability to move around. What a difference such a small machine has made. Thank God."

Two Years Later, June, 1972

Joe and Faith were sitting on the porch listening to Anne play the piano in the living room. They had been married for a year and it was the happiest time of Joe's life. All during his years in the Marine Corps the family was moving from state to state, never being able to put down roots and join a community. He retired with expectations of doing just that when his wife abandoned him for another man. That pushed him over the edge until a miracle happened one day, a blonde professional engineer with a mind of her own, and straight talk entered his life when he was the most vulnerable and desperately in need of a life preserver. She picked him out of the gutter, and with her quiet compassion put meaning back into his life. He fell in love with her completely in the knowledge that God was on his side after all. Their home was an oasis of peace and harmony. Anne played a medley of current popular songs and several country ballads. Joe was a country music fan, as sung by Eddy Arnold, Hank Snow, and Marty Robbins. She ended the session playing a concerto by Rachmaninoff, displaying a passion for the music and a mechanical dexterity capable of making the music touch the heart as well as the ears. Anne's music teacher of two years marveled at her ability to interpret the music and give it "life". She had already played for several school events.

"That was wonderful, Anne. The night is beautiful. Come out and enjoy it."

Anne took a seat in a rocker chair beside Joe. "It's nice and peaceful, isn't it? There's nothing like a warm day in June."

"I never dreamed that old piano from your Uncle Bob could make the kind of music that you can get out of it, Honey. We're so proud of your commitment to music."

"It would never have been possible without you, Mother. Bright Cloud helped me a lot during the winter I stayed with her. She's a good player and has the ability to see the beauty in the melody, too. Music has opened up a whole new world that I never knew existed before I came to live with you…I hear the phone ringing. I'll get it," said Anne, running in the house. "Hello."

"Hello, is Colonel Lance there, please?" a male voice asked.

"Yes, he's here, just a minute, Sir." Anne told Joe it was for him.

"Colonel Lance here. Who's calling?"

"I'm Captain Robert Holmes, a doctor at the Walter Reed Army Hospital in Washington. Your son, Captain Marshall Lance, has been wounded in combat and will be under my care, Sir. Forty-eight hours ago he was in Vietnam on a patrol when his unit came under enemy fire. He was hit by metal fragments from a mortar."

"How badly is he hurt?" Joe demanded in a loud voice, suddenly feeling sick to his stomach. The minute Faith heard his request she came to his side and wrapped her arms around him for support. He held the phone receiver so that Faith could hear what was being said.

"Your son has burns over half of his body. Several bones were broken in his right leg and right arm. I called to assure you that his wounds are not fatal, and that his recovery will be complete. It'll take a while, but he should recover fully and return to duty."

"Thank God for that!"

"You evidently had not been notified of his condition. I'm glad that I called, Sir. If you can make it to the capital, we welcome any input you may have in his recovery."

"Thank you for calling, Captain Holmes." Joe hung up and clung to Faith.

Joe and Faith discussed the situation and planned to fly to Washington the next morning. Just before they left for the airport, Tom drove into the yard with the Falcon. Faith told him what was going on.

"I'm sorry about Marshall," said Tom. "I'm sure he'll be glad to see his dad again and meet mom for the first time. I came over to see if you two would like to come to the Military Ball the night before graduation as my guests and as Honorary Chaperones. That way I can show off my mom and her marine husband to the whole ROTC class. What do you say? It's a week away."

Joe looked at Faith. "I'd love to let the rest of the world see my wife. We could fly to Washington to see how Marshall's doing and come back in time for the Ball and graduation. What do you say, Mrs. Lance?"

"I'd like that, too. Mark and Bright Cloud told us they'd like to attend the graduation and we promised to get them in your Wagoneer. It's important that we spend some time with Marshall. He needs our support now, yet, there's plenty of time to do those things," Faith answered.

"If you and Mom would like to rest the morning after the Ball, maybe Anne and I could take your Wagoneer to Maine for Bright Cloud and Mr. Leroux," Tom suggested, looking across the room at Anne. She nodded her head in acknowledgment.

"Young man, are you implying that a dance will wear us out?" Joe smiled, placing an arm around Faith.

"Things will work out. After graduation we can spend more time with Marshall. I want to get to know him better. If he's anything like his dad, it will be a pleasure. Is this a good time for the item you have in the closet, Joe?"

"Couldn't be better," said Joe, opening the closet door beside the bathroom. He reached for a package on the top shelf. "Tom, you'll soon become an officer in the United States Army and take an oath that is sacred. You'll join the ranks of thousands who have gone before you and sacrificed much in defense of the freedom that we enjoy in this great land." Joe unwrapped the package revealing an Army Officer's sword and scabbard.

"The tempered steel in this sword is a symbol of the commitment you have already made to defend those freedoms. This comes from your mother and me with love and admiration for the young man you have grown to be. Congratulations, Lieutenant."

Tom was not expecting such a gift and could not take his eyes from the beautiful sword. He received it from Joe with a stiff upper lip. "Thank you, Joe and Mom. I hope that I can honor the uniform the way you have."

"The sword is one that was specifically forged for a Master of the Sword at West Point. He's a retired Colonel and a dear friend. Some day I'll have you meet him. His dedication to the military and admiration for those who serve is an emotional experience. When I told him about you, he insisted that I take his personal sword. He claims that the sword is not only a symbol of the nation it defends — it is also a symbol and reflection of the will of the soldier who yields it." It was a solemn moment. Faith and Anne unsuccessfully fought their tears.

That evening Faith and Joe had packed and prepared for their flight out of Montpelier the next morning and retired early. Tom had brought some of his things from college to store in his room before returning to the dormitory. Anne helped him carry some boxes upstairs, trying to be quiet so that Joe and Faith could sleep.

"Would you like a cup of coffee before you return to school?" asked Anne.

"Will you have some, too?"

"Yes," she smiled. "I'm afraid your mother's addiction to the stuff has rubbed off on me. There's a piece of apple pie in the fridge if you'd like it."

"I won't pass up apple pie."

Anne set the table for them and waited next to the electric percolator. She was reflective and quiet.

"Is something wrong, Anne?"

"I've just been thinking about the sword and where you'll be going afterwards. You haven't been home much lately, but you're nearby at college where we know that you're safe. There's something sad about a soldier leaving home for the first time. I know your mom worries about that, too."

"When I leave I'll be depending on you to look after them and keep in touch with me."

"You know I'll do that anyway. I love them, too. It's been like a dream these past two years. I've experienced so much since your mother brought me here. I talk with my friends at school, and so many of them are from homes with divorced parents. Some are afraid of the future. The thing I've enjoyed the most in this home is the atmosphere of harmony and caring that surrounds it. Not every home has that, and the kids suffer from it, mostly in silence. I've enjoyed having a big brother, too, and I'll miss you when you leave," Anne spoke her heart. She poured their coffee and set the percolator on the table.

"Thanks. I'll miss you, too, Anne. Its great having you as a part of the family. I wanted to ask you something. As you know, the graduation is next week, and the military ball is the night before. It'll be my last one at the university. Would you go with me to the ball?"

Anne almost spilled her coffee. "I thought you already had a date for that," Anne mentioned hesitantly.

"No, I haven't asked anyone because I wanted to ask you first."

"I've never been to a formal dance... but... yes, I'd love to go with you," she answered, blushing.

"That's great."

"I'm not much of a dancer you know."

"You haven't seen me on the dance floor," he laughed softly and she joined in. "You'll be the belle of the ball, wait and see."

Anne spent the days before the ball in a state of nervous expectation. Time dragged slowly. The evening of the ball was warm and rain-free, making it ideal for formal gowns and uniforms worn by those in attendance. Tom drove to the house to pick up Anne. He brought a fresh orchid for her and his mother. Walking through the door of the house he saw Anne waiting in the living room. She was a vision of loveliness. Her black hair shined in the light and fell loose around her shoulders. She wore a light pastel yellow dress which complimented her bronze complexion. White lace covered her shoulders and a portion of her neck. A light amount of lipstick accented her lips and mouth.

"You're beautiful, Anne," exclaimed Tom, unable to contain his enthusiasm.

"This is my first formal dress," she said modestly, pleased at his response. "You're handsome in your uniform. It makes you look taller."

"I see you've discovered Anne," said Faith, walking out of the bathroom. She was dressed in a teal blue-green gown. Her blonde hair was done the same as Anne's except that it was cut much shorter.

"You're so pretty, Mom, you could be mistaken for a college girl. I'm glad you're coming. Here are some fresh orchids for you and Anne."

"They're beautiful," said Anne, admiring them. "They're the first orchids I've seen. Thank you, Tom. This is going to be an exciting evening."

Joe came down the stairs in his dress blues and a full compliment of ribbons on his left chest.

"Does a new second lieutenant have to salute a retired colonel?" asked Tom, admiring the service and battle ribbons that Joe wore.

"Always," Joe answered, smiling. "I see two of the loveliest ladies I've ever laid eyes on. Tom and I are two lucky guys."

"Flattery will get you anything, Colonel," laughed Faith.

"Anne and I are going along. I'm on the refreshment committee, and I've got to check on a couple of things before the dance starts. We'll see you there."

"Before you leave I want to get some pictures of Tom and Anne together," requested Faith, picking up her camera. "As a matter of fact I'd also like one of you two in uniform." Pictures were taken of everybody until they ran out of film.

Tom escorted Anne to the Falcon, opening the door and making sure that her gown did not drag on the ground or get caught in the door jamb. They were an attractive couple. Tom stood tall and straight and was proud to have Anne with him. Anne came up to his chin and was her natural self, a little shy and nervous but confident and proud. At the auditorium Tom talked to others on the refreshment committee and was satisfied that everything was all set. He was very attentive to Anne and proudly introduced her to his friends. That made her feel special, and she glowed with happiness at the attention everyone paid to her.

The first half hour of the ball was the period when every couple was evaluated, and votes were cast for selection of the King and Queen of the Ball. The announcer was Colonel Blake, commander of the ROTC unit at Vermont University. He stepped to the microphone on the bandstand platform, holding up his hands for everybody to be quiet.

"Ladies and gentlemen, I have a few announcements to make. First I want to bring your attention to our Honorary Chaperones, Marine Corps Colonel Joseph Lance and his lovely wife, Faith Lance. Would you please come forward so that we can see you?"

Joe escorted Faith across the floor to the bandstand where they waved to the crowd. "I'm the envy of every male in the ballroom," whispered Joe in Faith's ear.

She winked at him. "Maybe I'm the envy of every lady in the ballroom."

"Thank you for inviting us, Colonel Blake," Joe acknowledged him and turned towards the audience. "It's our pleasure to be here to celebrate with you the graduation and commissioning of the senior class. Our country is well served by these proud young soldiers from Vermont. It's an honor and a privilege to salute you." The crowd clapped and whistled.

"Now, ladies and gentlemen," continued Colonel Blake. "Our votes are in and they are unanimous. I proudly announce that Lieutenant Hamilton and his lovely date, Anne, have been selected King and Queen of this Military Ball." Two high backed chairs were positioned on the bandstand for the King and Queen's use throughout the balance of the evening.

Tom was not surprised for Anne garnered praise from every corner. She held his arm as they walked across the ballroom floor. There was a hush to the crowd. Anne's modesty was evident in her slight discomfort at being the object of everyone's admiration and appraisal. Her naturalness and wholesomeness was part of her timeless charm. The beauty of her youth and innocence graced the ballroom.

Faith beamed with pride and fought tears. It was the first time she looked upon Anne as a young lady instead of a little girl. Faith surveyed the crowd to see if she could spot Kimberly. She hadn't talked with her in months. After the crowning ceremony she danced several sets with Joe and continued to look for Dew. A slow waltz started, and Joe suggested that he and Tom change partners.

"You and Anne have caused quite a stir," Faith mentioned to Tom as they waltzed around the floor. "I'm proud of you. Have you seen Kimberly? I've been looking all over for her. Is she here, Tom?"

"Yes, I saw her earlier. She's with Ray Ellis. He's in our graduating class, too. She's awful distant lately. She'll talk, but it's not like it used to be."

"That's too bad," cried Faith, saddened about the turn of events. She thought about Steve and how difficult it must be for him if things are not going well for Kimberly. "I think Joe and I will be leaving after one more set. Don't be too late bringing Anne home."

"I won't, Mom. Thanks for coming. I'll also be over first thing in the morning to get Bright Cloud and Mr. Leroux. You and Joe are a nice couple. He has put a sparkle in your eyes. You smile more often, and that makes me happy for the both of you."

"I love you, Lieutenant Hamilton," said Faith, standing on her toes to kiss him. "Now I think I'll go claim the other man in my life."

Tom and Anne stayed until the ballroom was empty and helped to lock the auditorium. They were tired, but the excitement of the evening still lingered. It had been a special event that awakened new feelings and new expectations of the future. Anne was quiet on the way home.

"Mom and Joe must have danced themselves out tonight," Tom said as he turned into the driveway. All of the house lights were out except the one over the garage door. "This has been a wonderful occasion for me, Anne. I was so proud of you, and I enjoyed being with you."

"It was a special night for me, too, Tom, one I'll remember all my life. Thank you for taking me."

The light from the back door reflected across her face. She was beautiful. Tom leaned down to kiss her. She lifted her lips to him. They held each other close, sharing the wonder of what was happening between them. Anne broke free of the embrace and ran to the house. She watched from the window as Tom turned the car around and left. Tears stained her dress.

Chapter Twenty-One

Tom and Anne left Montpelier early in the morning to pick up Mark and Bright Cloud at Wells, Maine. They were driving Joe's Wagoneer because it could hold Mark's electric powered wheelchair in the rear cargo area along with four passengers.

"Did you sleep well last night?" Tom asked guardedly.

"If you want the truth, I was so excited I had trouble getting to sleep. How about you?"

"I thought about a lot of things, but you were on my mind most of the night. You're a beautiful and desirable young lady, Anne, and you're going to have plenty of young men chasing after you. I'm not a glamorous party type of person and never will be. As a matter of a fact, Kimberly even called me dull and unexciting which is probably correct."

"No, Tom, she's wrong. You have all those qualities real men should have. Sensitivity and gentleness just make men stronger, and it's lacking in a lot of them. You care about people, and that makes you special. It'll make you a good officer. Joe agrees with that, too. As for boys chasing after me, I'm not so sure. I certainly don't encourage it. I try to be friendly to everybody, and I've made some good friends at Montpelier. I detest those creeps that think they can get anything they want from a girl. I think they see me as too independent to bother with, and that suits me just fine. This next year I'm going to play in an orchestra being formed at the school. We'll probably end up playing for most of the school dances. I'm pleased about that."

"That's great, Anne. You've taken to the piano very well."

"I'm younger than you by three and a half years, Tom, and I'm inexperienced in affairs of the heart, but I think people should be honest with their feelings. I love that characteristic about your mother."

"What are you trying to say, Anne?"

"I'm saying that I have feelings and emotions that I've never had before. I don't know what to do about it, and I'm scared. . . I think I've fallen in love with you!"

Tom looked for a spot to pull the Wagoneer off the road and shut the ignition off.

"Dear Anne, you've brought so much happiness to mother and myself. I respect you and have from the start. You're a breath of fresh air that has filled our lives with joy. Trust and respect is a solid foundation to base any relationship on. It wasn't until last night that I realized that I loved you, too." She fell in his waiting arms and cried for happiness.

"I knew that something was taking place last night. I felt it, too. What are we going to do, Tom? I'm just finishing my sophomore year in high school. I'm young and inexperienced, but please don't doubt the sincerity or strength of my feelings. I feel trapped because you're going away, Lord only knows where, maybe in combat. That frightens me more than you know," Anne confessed between sobs.

Tom held her until the sobs stopped and she relaxed. He kissed her jet black hair and thanked God that he had won the affection of such a rare human being. "I think that for now we have a right to rejoice in what we've discovered for each other. You have two more years of high school. After that possibly two or four more years of college if you want to go. I'll be away in the Army at least four years, maybe more.

"If you determine that someone has won your heart, you'll let me know quickly. I promise to do the same thing with you. In the meantime, let's just continue the joy of each other's company. While I'm away we can write and keep in touch."

"I promise to do that," answered Anne, reassured that the future held much to look forward to. "I can tell you that my choice of a career is going to be either a nurse like Bright Cloud, or a teacher like your mother. I'm taking all of the chemistry and math courses I can get in high school; that way I'll be prepared for either one."

"That sounds great, Anne." Tom was relieved that they could be honest with each other about the most tender feelings of the human heart.

"I feel better now. You have the same gift that mother has of creating order out of chaos. Let's take the future one year at a time, but I can assure you that my feelings will only grow deeper and stronger."

"Don't ever change, Anne," Tom pleaded.

Bright Cloud and Mark were waiting for them when they arrived an hour and a half later at their home in Wells.

"Two of our favorite people," Mark exclaimed. "Graduations and weddings are our preferred events. They're always full of happiness and hope for the future."

"I made a deal with Anne. I drove over, and she can drive back. She got her license to drive last winter. Mother says she's doing great. What do you say if we let the ladies sit up front, and we'll be back seat drivers."

"Sounds good to me, Tom." They helped Mark into the rear seat while Anne backed the Wagoneer to the flat section of the kitchen deck where Tom rolled the electric wheelchair over the tailgate into the cargo area of the vehicle. Bright Cloud suggested that they also take the folding wheelchair just in case something went wrong with the motorized one.

Tom sat behind Bright Cloud so that he could see Anne clearer. She was relaxed and confident in her driving. She had the ability to focus deeply on whatever she was doing and block out other things around her. She did the same thing when she played the piano.

"Tom, do you see much of Morning Dew at school?" Bright Cloud asked, concerned about her granddaughter. "We used to hear from her at least once a month, but this year we just got a card at Christmastime. I know that Steve is worried about something, but he keeps it to himself."

"I'm not betraying any confidences, Bright Cloud, when I tell you that she has been going with a student named Ray Ellis

222

for the past year. They're a regular two-some on campus. He's a senior, also. He's popular with his fancy car and apparently has all the money he wants to spend. I still see her occasionally at the cafeteria, but sometimes she doesn't show up when she's supposed to. I don't know why she's changed so abruptly. I liked the old Kimberly a lot better." Anne looked at him in the rear view mirror as if to say: "I knew you had something for her at one time!"

"Steve mentioned that she might stay on campus for the summer to make up some work," Mark added, reserving judgment. He looked at Tom beside him. "How does it feel to be a second lieutenant, young man?"

"It's one of the great thrills of my life, Sir. I notice that you're wearing your Medal of Honor sash. Your circle of friends include some very impressive combat veterans. I hope I measure up."

"I'm sure you will, Tom, but I pray that you won't have to prove it. The last time we saw Joe Lance, he was his old self again. Your mother has been a wonderful influence on him. She mentioned when she called that they went to Washington to see how Marshall is doing. He's one of the lucky ones who's going to pull through without any limitations. Thank God for that."

It was noon when Anne drove into their Montpelier driveway. Joe saw them coming and was waiting at the garage entrance. He had just completed building a ramp over the back door sill so that Mark's chair could negotiate it with ease. Faith had rearranged the living room, setting up a bed with privacy curtains for them to sleep downstairs close to the bathroom.

"Bright Cloud and Colonel Leroux, welcome to Vermont," Joe greeted them, giving Bright Cloud a warm embrace and shaking Mark's hand through the open window. "I'll give Tom a hand, and we'll have your electric vehicle ready in a jiffy." They lifted the chair over the tailgate and directed it beside the Wagoneer. "With your permission, Colonel, it would be easier if I simply lifted you from the wagon and seated you on your chair. Do you object?"

"The loss of my legs has been a difficult adjustment for me to make, Joe. I know that the alternative is to be an invalid, and I absolute refuse to be categorized in that way," Mark announced with conviction. "I don't object really. My false pride can get the best of me if I'm not careful, but I appreciate the concern and offer of assistance from my friends."

"You can remember better than I when President Roosevelt ran this country for many years from a wheelchair. I understand the pride thing, and you should understand that help is offered in a spirit of respect. Semper Fi, Sir."

"Semper Fi, Joe," Mark replied as he was effortlessly transferred to the mechanical chair. "What a remarkable machine this has been for me. On those days when Bright Cloud thinks I'm a pest around the house, she tells me to go take a ride. She used to tell me to go take a hike!" Joe saw that old gleam in the elderly gentleman's eye and was pleased to note its return.

"And you know what?" Bright Cloud smiled. "He does it, too!"

"It's great to have you two for a visit. We hope you can stay for a few days. Faith was just getting out of the shower when you turned into the yard. She'll be down soon. Come, let's go inside."

"Tom and I will get their luggage. Should we leave the folding chair in the Jeep?" asked Anne.

"Why don't you, Anne," suggested Joe. "We can use that one at the graduation. You must be hungry. We've got lunch ready. Doesn't that Wagoneer go over the road nice?"

"I liked it a lot. It has a solid feel to it and you sit up so that you can see the road and other vehicles around," Anne agreed, holding the door for them to enter the house.

"Bright Cloud and Mark," acknowledged Faith. "Welcome to our home. You'll have to excuse my wet hair, I just got out of the shower."

"You look lovelier than ever, Faith," admitted Mark.

"You and Joe have been a nice match, and it shows," Bright Cloud accepted Faith's embrace. "It's always nice to be with friends and especially young people. Tom and Anne have been a lot of help."

"Take their things into the living room," Faith directed Tom and Anne. "I've fixed up a place opposite the piano where Bright Cloud and Mark can sleep comfortably and in privacy. Joe fastened an assistance bar in the bathroom in case you need it. Please, let our home be your home. If you need anything, you have only to ask."

They ate lunch and visited until mid afternoon when they prepared for the trip to Burlington. Tom dressed in his uniform and came downstairs when Mark mentioned that he had something for him.

"You're a second lieutenant now, Tom, but I'm certain that not too far down the road you'll be promoted to first lieutenant and then to captain. I want you to have these first lieutenant and captain bars. It would please me to know that you'll wear them. They are the same insignia in use today. The Army and Marine Corps are identical. As a matter of fact, an Army colonel gave me the captain bars when I was promoted to company commander in France. They are the same bars I wore on my first trip to Fort Lewis when I met and fell in love with my Bright Cloud. They were lucky for me; I pray that they will be for you."

Tom accepted the four insignias and examined them with admiration. "Thank you, Mr. Leroux. I'll do my best to honor the legacy they represent." He knelt down and wrapped his arms around the fragile Mark and hugged him.

"I have no doubt that you will, Tom."

Tom and Anne left shortly afterwards in the Falcon. The adults would follow in the Wagoneer. Steve had called earlier to let them know that Arlo and Michelle, and Scott and Marie were going to attend the graduation. Everyone was planning to gather at the parking lot entrance. It was a clear day with a few cumulous clouds in the sky, perfect for the out-of-doors ceremony. Arlo, Michelle, Scott and Marie watched the cars as they came through the gate.

Arlo recognized the Wagoneer pulling into a parking space, and they all started walking towards them. It was a happy reunion of old friends. Scott was still in his uniform. He and Marie had come directly from Germany to Arlo and Michelle's home on Lake George. The men were all dressed in suits and ties. The ladies wore colorful spring dresses. Anne and Faith were dressed in the same yellow dresses they had purchased in Montreal two years ago. Anne had also been looking for the Wagoneer from the other side of the parking lot where Tom had dropped her off. She saw the vehicle and joined the group, feeling confident and at ease.

"I wonder where Steve is?" Faith asked, looking out through the lot. "He said he'd meet us here."

"I see him over there," Anne pointed towards the dormitory buildings where Steve was walking towards them.

"I can't tell you how glad I am to see all of you people," Steve cried. When he knelt to hug Mark tears filled his eyes. "Thank you for coming. I just came from Dew's dormitory room. I wanted her to wear something from Star, so I gave her one of Star's ensign insignias, and she completely broke down."

"If we can help in any way, you have but to ask. That's what families are for," Bright Cloud told Steve and held him in a strong embrace.

"Come, we should head over to the soccer field and take our seats," Steve suggested, strengthened by the show of support. "My Lord, I hardly recognized you, Anne. Can an old teacher give you a hug?"

"Of course, Mr. Jackson. I'm so glad to see you again. You've always been a very special person to me. I'll never forget you and your kindness," Anne replied in a soft voice.

"My instincts were right about you, young lady."

Scott and Arlo flipped a quarter to see who was going to wheel Mark to the seating area. Scott won and took his position behind Mark's chair. They walked slowly across the well-mowed lawn. Joe told them that Marshall was in the hospital in Washington.

"You and Faith want to be careful going to Walter Reed. It's in a bad section of Washington," Scott warned, thinking to himself for a few seconds. "Let me see what can be done about getting him transferred to Plattsburg so that you can visit more often together."

"I'd appreciate it, Scott. Thanks for offering," Joe replied.

Arlo looked on in silence, nodding his head in approval. He and Scott were very like-minded individuals, neither used their rank to obtain personal favors, but when friends were in need of a helping hand in cutting through bureaucratic red tape, neither hesitated to use their authority to get things done.

Chairs were lined in neat rows in front of a speaking platform with the graduating class at right angles to the audience so that they could see the graduates. Scott maneuvered Mark's chair to the end of a row of chairs. Joe removed the end chair so that Mark could sit in line with the others without feeling conspicuous. Marie took Scott's Medal of Honor from her purse and, standing on her tiptoes, fastened the sash around his neck. As soon as they sat down, a young army captain from the ROTC teaching unit approached them and introduced himself.

He saluted Scott who returned the salute: "I'm Captain Riley. I hesitate to intrude upon your celebration, but two Medal of Honor recipients in our gathering is something to be proud of. I'd like to acknowledge your presence with your permission, of course."

"You may do that, Captain Riley. I'm Colonel Mark Leroux, USMC (Ret.)."

"I'm Major General Scott Taylor. I believe that I speak for Colonel Leroux, also, when I say that the medal is worn more for the recognition of those who gave their lives in defense of freedom than for our own aggrandizement."

"Thank you, gentlemen. It has been a privilege."

The ceremony started with the acknowledgment of Mark and Scott in the audience. They received a standing ovation. Scott helped Mark stand. The response to the two veterans was strong and long lasting. Afterwards, the individual graduates were awarded their diplomas by the governor of Vermont. Tom received a five hundred dollar award for having the highest grades over the past four years in Military Science. Faith swelled with pride when he walked to the podium to accept the award and his diploma. The ROTC section gave him a boisterous applause.

Morning Dew's name was called after Tom. Those who knew the young energetic lady were shocked. She climbed the platform with hesitant steps and a detached air of indifference. Steve was crushed when he saw his beloved daughter act as if she had too much to drink. Michelle grabbed Bright Cloud's arm and squeezed hard. They both knew what was wrong with Dew. At last, all the questions about her behavior for the past year and a half could now be answered. Morning Dew was under the influence of drugs!

Steve wept openly in shame and embarrassment, burying his head in the palm of his hands. Anne was sitting beside him and placed her arms around his shoulders. The rest of the ceremony and the speech of the well known politician that followed were lost in their shock and disillusionment over Kimberly's appearance. Mark and Bright Cloud were crushed.

Tom had just taken his seat when Dew followed him onto the stand. He watched her, and his heart sank. Tom's best friend for the past four years, Dave Ross, whispered in his ear, "She's been taking drugs. I'm pretty sure she's been getting stuff from Ellis."

"How long have you known?" Tom asked, angry at himself for not picking up on the symptoms earlier. "It all makes sense now."

"At least a year or more. Ellis always has some. He probably got her hooked on whatever it is."

Tom looked around to locate Ray Ellis sitting at the opposite end of the row of seats. He was not sure what he was going to do, but Tom planned on confronting Ellis.

The ceremony came to a close, and tables were set up in the soccer field for drinks and refreshments of grads and guests. Steve immediately searched for Morning Dew and located her talking to Ellis, and approached her.

"What in the world do you think you're doing with yourself, Dew?" Steve demanded, disappointed, hurt and angry. "Who's this young man?"

"Dad, this is Ray Ellis. He's been my best friend at school," Morning Dew answered defiantly. Ray Ellis was a relatively short young man with black wavy hair and medium complexion. He was an attractive man with an arrogant air of superiority that infuriated Steve. He hated Ellis the minute he laid eyes on him.

"I have just one thing to say to you, Ray Ellis. If I find that you're responsible for what's happened to my daughter, I'll personally rip you into little pieces with my bare hands."

"Kimberly," announced Ellis, indignantly. "Has the right to do as she pleases. She's an..."

He didn't finish the sentence. Tom and two of his ROTC friends in uniform grabbed Ellis by the arms, with one pushing from behind. They walked him off the field to the parking lot where his red Cadillac was parked. A University security vehicle was parked blocking Ray's automobile. "Mr. Ellis," the security officer turned to him. "I was called to investigate your auto as being unsafe to operate on public roads,"

"There's nothing wrong with my car," Ellis shouted, still being held by Tom and Dave.

"Oh but there is, Mr. Ellis. You have three broken lights on the car," replied the officer. "I have the authority to search any vehicle if I have 'probable cause' of violations of the laws of this state. My search came up with marijuana and this bag of cocaine."

"You son of a bitch, you rigged all of this," growled Ellis.

"Ray Ellis, you have a right to remain silent. . ." Two Burlington Metropolitan Police arrived at the scene taking Ellis into custody and impounding his automobile for further search.

Dew watched from the field and saw Ray being arrested. She became hysterical, breaking away from Steve's hold on her and ran towards the scene. "You, Tom Hamilton!" Dew screamed. She was filled with rage, pointing an accusing finger directly in his face. "You and your goodie, goodie friends don't know what you're doing. You all make me sick. I hate you! I hate you!"

Tom was stung by the cruel words. He didn't know the enraged Kimberly standing before him. He remembered the full-of-life girl he met at the cafeteria on their first year, and he was saddened even more. Steve was on the verge of collapse.

Bright Cloud came upon the scene sickened at what her granddaughter had become. She stepped in front of Dew and slapped her across the face. The sound could be heard throughout the parking lot.

"You may be under the influence of some drug. I don't know, but it's not an excuse to carry on the way you're doing."

"Who do you think you are...??"

Stunned by the defiance, Bright Cloud slapped her again. "Don't you ever speak to me again in that manner. We came here today filled with pride and high expectations and out of love for my Bright Star's daughter who shares the same heritage and blood as I. You have done something I never thought possible. You've brought shame on our family and disgraced your father. How could you? All we ever did for you was love you, perhaps too much. . . I may never forgive you for this." Bright Cloud turned away and fell in Arlo's supporting arms, exhausted and emotionally drained.

"I hate all of you for what you've done to Ray. Especially you, Tom Hamilton. I'll always hate you."

Chapter Twenty-Two

Two years Later, June, 1974

Faith and Joe had just returned home from Anne's high school graduation at Montpelier High School, picking up the mail at the box beside the driveway. They were hoping for a letter from Tom.

"We've got one," Joe cried, climbing back into their brand new Jeep Wagoneer. Faith waited until they were in the house before opening it. She sat at the kitchen table and read:

Korea, May, 1974

Dear Mom and Joe,

You'll probably be having Anne's graduation sometime soon by the time you receive this letter. I wish I could be there, but duty calls. Things are very tense on the DMZ (Demilitarized Zone) right now. We are on a high alert status.

"I have some good news. I will be promoted to Captain next month. My name is on the list. I'm already wearing Colonel Leroux's first lieutenant bars. In a while I'll be able to pin on his captain bars. Promotion has come a little more rapid than normal for our division in Korea on the DMZ. It seems like such a long time since I've seen any of you. The further away one gets, the longer the separations seem to be.

I've been getting mail regularly from Bright Cloud and Mr. Leroux. They are still recuperating from the shock of Kimberly's drug addiction. Sometimes I blame myself. If I had not been so naïve, maybe I could have spotted the symptoms earlier and helped her. I understand that she's been in and out of rehabilitation centers ever since. What a sad way to live.

I was glad to learn that Ray Ellis got a stiff sentence for peddling drugs on campus. He was a phony all the way. The police found large amounts of drugs in his apartment. For a while I felt guilty about setting him up for the arrest. I acted out of anger and as judge and jury. It could have blown up in my face.

You wrote that Marshall has been released from the hospital in Plattsburg. That's good news. You'll be interested in knowing that several of the older officers in our division have served under General Scott Taylor. They all think highly of him. He's a soldier's soldier, and no one can believe that he's good friends with the family. I'm enclosing a separate envelope for you to pass on to Anne. I've gotta get some sleep! See you when I can.

> All my love,
> Tom

"Here comes Anne," said Faith, watching her drive the faithful Falcon into the driveway. "Wasn't she lovely tonight, Joe?"

"She was the hit of the commencement service," replied Joe. "I like to see the way she focuses so intently on playing the piano like she did tonight. She shuts out everything around her and wraps herself in the music. It warms my heart to see you two interact. She loves you so completely. She's in love with Tom."

"I've known that for quite a while," reflected Faith. "If it's meant to be, I can't see any reason not to let it run its course. In many ways they deserve each other."

"I agree," said Joe. "Before she comes in, I'd like to share something with you that I've been thinking a lot about lately. She's completed her high school and will start college this fall. Anne was lifted, at a very impressionable age, from a primitive environment and has lived in a modern yet modest home with advantages and privileges beyond her wildest dreams. However, she's a Cree, and it would be good for her to touch base with her Cree heritage this summer if possible. Such a revisit to her roots will give her a firmer understanding and appreciation of her heritage and may give her a clearer vision of what the future holds for her. Am I making any sense?"

"Yes, my dear husband, and I've been thinking of that, too. Here she comes. Well, Honey, you're now an alumnus of Montpelier High School. You were fabulous tonight."

"I've enjoyed my high school years." Anne was a serious student at school. She cultivated a large number of friends, students and teachers alike, and worked hard so that she could get financial help for college. Her weekly allowance savings amounted to two thousand dollars.

"Here's a letter from Tom," Faith held it out to her.

"Thank you, Mother, would you two excuse me?" Anne's face lit up when she saw the letter.

"Of course. You go along and be private. Joe and I were just going to have our traditional evening coffee."

"I'll be back and join you," Anne promised, running up the stairs to her room.

Korea, May, 1974

Dear Anne,

A few words with you tonight. I can't tell you how much your letters mean to me. I feel guilty that I can't write as often as I want, but it's impossible while I'm on this DMZ security duty. I hope you understand.

I received a letter from Kimberly last week. She apologized to me for the scene she created at our graduation. I can accept it and forgive her. It still saddens me because she was a wonderful caring person before her addiction. I can honestly tell you that I thought I loved her at one time. It was easy to do, and I don't apologize for having had those feelings, but it's over now. I may be her friend in the future, that's all. I don't hate her, I just think it was a terrible waste that brought misery to everyone who knew her. The family didn't deserve what she did to them. Bright Cloud wrote that Mr. Jackson has adapted to Kimberly's situation. Too bad, he deserved better than that.

I thank God that I was never tempted by drugs. I had a young soldier in my platoon from Iowa that became addicted to cocaine. He was a pathetic case. The Army shipped him out in short order.

I think often of the time we picked up Bright Cloud and Mr. Leroux. My feelings for you have not changed except to grow stronger. At times I feel as if I was unfair to you because you should go out with others when you have a chance. That way you will be more certain of what you want.

I have to run. I send my love by way of the stars and large moon that's out tonight. I do love you so very much, Anne.

Until next time,
Tom

The next morning Faith talked to Anne about going back to Fort Lewis for the summer or part of it.

"The last time I talked with Bright Cloud she mentioned that they were planning to return this summer. Maybe you could go with them. What do you think, Honey? Joe and I will miss you, but it may be beneficial for you to appreciate your Cree roots more. It's up to you."

"I'd like to go back, Mother. I haven't been there since you and Joe brought me to the United States," Anne reflected, pouring a cup of coffee. "I haven't said anything to you, but every once in a while at school, my racial ancestry comes up. Most of the kids think it's unique and interesting and don't think any more about it. I love my friends, but there are a few kids that have made remarks about me being a squaw and imply that I'm racially inferior. I ignore them because I know it's not true. Four years ago I never gave it a thought, but lately I've wondered more about who and what I am. To answer your question, yes, I'd like to go. Bright Cloud would be able to help me in that respect."

"Then we'll see if it's possible," answered a determined Faith. That night when Joe came home she talked with him about it.

"Things may work out so that I can take them north. My boss mentioned that he had a new helicopter for delivery to the Lac St. Jean base of operations. There would be room for everybody and Colonel Leroux's electric wheelchair," said Joe, suddenly thinking about an item he had recently seen in a store in Burlington.

"What are you thinking about, Joe?" Faith asked, smiling at him. She knew that when he became silent like that he had something definite in mind.

"I saw a really neat foam-filled boat about twelve feet long. It would make a great platform for the Colonel to roll his chair onto. It would be relatively stable. He can't use the punt anymore. This one I saw will be much more stable for him and give him a more secure feeling on the water. I have a small two-horsepower electric trolling motor that would be ideal for him. I'll check it out."

They called Bright Cloud and Mark to discuss plans. They were overjoyed that Anne wanted to return to Fort Lewis with them, and looked forward to having her stay at their cabin.

A week later Joe positioned the brand new helicopter over the familiar wooden Mounted Police dock at Fort Lewis and gently settled to a stop. Mark had ridden up front with Joe and was tired from the five-hour trip. Joe said nothing about the plastic-wrapped bundle suspended between the struts of the helicopter. Anne was the first to climb down to the platform. Penny stood in the doorway surveying the new surroundings.

"C'mon, Penny," Anne pointed for her to sit and stay on the wharf. Bright Cloud accepted her helping hand before stepping onto the dock.

Joe untied Mark's electric chair from the cargo area and pushed it around beside the door. He lifted Mark from the helicopter and sat him on the chair as a Mounted Policeman came running from the barracks.

"Hello, Joe. It's been a while since I heard your 'Red Dog' call over the airways. Welcome back to Fort Lewis. It's nice to see you again, Mr. Leroux and Bright Cloud," greeted Sergeant Jenkins. "I can't believe my eyes, but this has to be Miss Anne

Clark. You have grown even lovelier since I last saw you, young lady."

"It's nice to be back. I was hoping that you would still be stationed here. I never forgot what you did for me," Anne said, giving him a hug.

"That was a while ago, Miss. I've been trying to locate your father ever since we had word that you were coming for a visit. I haven't had any luck. He got out of prison a year ago and has disappeared in the north somewhere. My impression is that he headed to Manitoba, but it's only a guess. I'm sorry, Miss."

"You tried, Sergeant. Thank you for that."

Mark led the way up the familiar pathway toward their cabin. There was a wind from the west, and he could smell the distinct aroma of cedar and spruce as the soft breeze combed the forest canopy filling the air with the fragrance unique to the northland — spruce and fir mixed with cedar. He and Bright Cloud returned each year wondering if it was their last journey into the wilderness. They were a part of the legacy, living legends, that the inhabitants talked about over hot tea and roaring fires when the winds howled out of the north. Everywhere they looked they could visualize a part of their lives, and with each succeeding annual trek, the memories become more vivid and the sadness of yesterday filled more and more of their hearts.

The wood box in the cabin was filled to overflowing, and the flickering fire in the fireplace was most welcome. A small bouquet of bayberry was placed on the kitchen table. Anne entered the cabin after ordering Penny to sit outside and stay. The little terrier sat and surveyed the surrounding countryside. A dog barked in the distance. Penny placed her nose in the air to smell the uniqueness of the wilderness land.

"Where's Steve?" asked Bright Cloud, noticing that his plane was not tied to the dock.

"He's on fire patrol for the Quebec Forestry Department. It's been dry so far. He'll be back by dusk," answered Jenkins.

"I had forgotten how brisk and fresh the air is up here," Anne recalled, slightly apprehensive now that she had arrived.

She didn't know what to expect from the journey. The fact that her father was out of prison and never made an attempt to find out about her hurt a lot more than she let on. For a moment the same empty feeling of being abandoned filled her heart again, but thoughts of Faith and Tom quickly dispelled the sadness.

Joe noticed that she was quieter than usual. He helped carry the suitcases to her room, the same one Faith had used when she was teaching at Fort Lewis. He placed them on the bed and took Anne in his arms, understanding the source of her silence. "You know, Anne, if you have any idea that this might be a mistake for you, I promise to come for you any time you ask me. Faith and I love you dearly, and we only want you to be happy, and that happiness has to be on your terms, not on someone else's."

"I know that, Joe. I believe that I should do this now. My first reaction to being here is not what I expected. I'm almost twenty years old and sixteen of those years were spent being tired, cold, hungry and afraid, especially afraid. I remember that every night I prayed that things could be easier for us. My mother died a bitter, exhausted woman who simply gave up the struggle to stay alive. I understand now how courageous she was to continue for as long as she did. I always knew that she loved me. It's just as well that my father has gone away somewhere else. I'm not sure how I would greet him if he presented himself to me. I can never forgive him for the years that I stayed awake most of the night afraid he was going to return, and desperate because there was nothing to eat and he had to return in order to bring food. We could not have one without the other. The dilemma is what destroyed my mother. It still makes me angry and sick to my stomach."

"That's all in the past, Sweetheart," comforted Joe. This was the first time she had talked about life in the remote cabin. He could recall taking her home from Fort Lewis School a couple of times when he had dropped her off from the helicopter in a clearing next to the cabin. She would look back and wave in a pathetic way, her eyes filled with fear and dread.

"Listen, my dear girl," he said, wondering if this whole trip was a mistake. "You can return with me tomorrow if you want."

"I didn't dream that a human being could be as happy as I've been with Mother, you and Tom. I ask myself now why in the world would I want to leave a real home filled with love and harmony, for a place where I was horrified most of my days?"

"That's a question only you can answer, Anne. Whichever it is, we support your decision and the reason for making it. You're no longer alone, and if this region holds memories that are too painful for you, then what is accomplished by subjecting yourself to the pain all over again?"

"I've been thinking that very thing, Joe, but there are other questions that must be answered too. Bright Cloud, Bright Star, and Nurse Minnie all came from the same region and love the area. There has to be something here that is beautiful besides being ugly. I think I have to stay and try to find that beauty. If I do, maybe it will give me more pride in the heritage I share with Bright Cloud."

The courage and wisdom of the child-woman he held in his arms brought a lump to Joe's throat.

"Are you all right, Anne?" asked Bright Cloud, standing in the doorway.

"Yes, I'm all right. You know, Joe, the beauty I was talking about is represented by this lady," Anne answered, rushing to hug Bright Cloud. She looked over Anne's shoulder at Joe.

"Our Anne is having a little trouble adjusting to her ancestral homeland," Joe replied, looking on helplessly. "Most of her memories of the North Woods are painful. Faith and I would do anything to keep her from being hurt again."

"I understand," replied Bright Cloud. "It's perfectly natural to avoid those things that can hurt us. In regards to our land of the Cree, let me say that there is much that is good and honorable and even noble in the legacy of courage we share, my darling girl. I'll try to point that out to you while you're with us. Come, Faith has fixed us a large box of food to eat so that we wouldn't have to fix anything tonight. Everyone must be hungry."

Bright Cloud had put coffee together first thing upon entering the cabin. They sat and ate ham sandwiches and fruit. On the table was a box Faith had included with the foodstuff with a note for Anne on it: "This is for you, Anne. A sweet bite for a sweet young lady."

"I'll share the jelly donuts with anybody who wants one," announced Anne, thinking how typical it was of Faith.

"Seeing as to how you're going to be that generous, I'll give up a sandwich and have a donut or two," teased Mark.

Joe heard the drone of an aircraft in the distance. "Here comes Steve. You can't miss that distinctive sounding engine of a Norseman."

Steve landed on the lake, noticing the helicopter on the wharf. He pulled the plane to shore and ran to the cabin. "Hi, Joe. Am I glad to see you," Steve exclaimed, greeting everybody. "Wait a minute, who is this young lady? Oh, my, it's Anne. Welcome back. I didn't expect to see you."

Morning Dew appeared in the door, hesitant and unsure of herself. Bright Cloud saw her first and rushed to grab Dew and hold her tightly. "Heart of my heart, blood of my blood, I was afraid I had lost you forever."

"Dew is going to spend the summer with us. She needs it, and so do I," said Steve matter-of-factly.

"I've been to more treatment centers than I want to think about," Dew said and sat at the table and began to tell her story. "Maybe the centers work, and maybe they don't, but in the final analysis, nobody can make you give up the addiction except yourself. Why did I do it? I can't answer that question except to say that at first, I thought it was a real cool way to feel good about everything. I'm not making excuses for myself, for in reality, there are no valid ones. I found it exciting to be with the most popular man on campus. I went from that point to the bottom of the sewer, which is a living hell. I know that all of you had high expectations for me, and I let you down, especially my father, who suffered enough when we lost my mother. I'll never forgive myself for putting him through the torment I did. What's ahead for me? I'm going back to school to make up what I lost, and I'm going to graduate. I'm not going to do it because it's expected of me. I'm doing it because I want it."

"Bravo, Dew. Can Uncle Joe have a hug? More than anyone else in this room, I understand how easy it is to fail to measure up. Failure is a very human characteristic. But courage and discipline are also human traits, and we alone control our destiny. When we fall to the bottom, the lost pride hurts the most. It takes courage and good old fashioned guts to pick yourself back up when you've fallen so low. It can be a frightening journey. Welcome back, daughter of Bright Star and my friend Steve."

"Thank you, Uncle Joe," cried Morning Dew, weeping in his arms.

The next day Joe and Steve assembled the rigid inflatable boat for Mark. They erected steel pipe rails all the way around the craft, which essentially was a float on pontoons. Prefabricated wheelchair channels were placed so that Mark's chair could not run out of the grooves. The locking mechanism was simple to use and sturdy. Finally, they attached an electric trolling motor and an extra battery for a longer, more powerful power source so that Mark could cover any part of the lake he wanted to.

Morning Dew and Anne soon became good friends. They talked for long periods of time and went on walks to the lookout rock and the center cabin, and they canoed around the lake for hours at a time. The Cree Tribal Council welcomed them at their weekly meetings. Half of the time they worked at Eagle Nest cleaning and painting. Their friendship pleased everybody and was especially rewarding for the two young ladies. Dew was much more world-wise, but she lacked the wisdom of maturity that defined the younger Anne. One day they discussed Tom Hamilton while sitting at the Flying Eagle cenotaph north of the village.

"I watched you at the military ball. You love Tom, don't you?" asked Morning Dew.

"Yes, I do and have for a long time," Anne admitted proudly. "We write often. He's in Korea now. You must know that he loved you once but you drove him away. He was hurt for a long time."

"I knew I was doing that to him and couldn't stop myself," Dew admitted, angrily shaking her head.

"Tom Hamilton is a young man worth fighting for. He's a lot like his mother. Did you ever love him?"

"The first time I saw Tom at the cafeteria I knew that he was going to be a good friend and I liked him a lot. Did I love him? I don't know. At that time in my life I thought Ellis represented the good life... how wrong I was. Does Tom love you, Anne?"

Anne hesitated to answer the question. She thought about it and asked herself if she had the right to convey the intimate conversations she and Tom had shared. "I believe that he does." she ultimately answered and let it go at that.

"Grandfather thinks a lot of him. Tom reminds him of his son, DJ. The summer that Mrs. Hamilton sprained her ankle, I was secure in my world. The minute Ray entered it, the more discontented I became with my life and friends. We did things and went places that I would never have done with someone like Tom. For two years I was introduced to a life that left me breathless even though I knew that it was not reality. Now, where do I go from here? Dad and Grandmother especially are hoping that being here in Fort Lewis will help me find direction and a goal worthy of pursuit. So far I'm at a loss for answers except a desire to complete the college credits I need for a diploma."

"Maybe you're just thinking too much about yourself, Dew," Anne observed. "We have an obligation to contribute our share of work and effort for the common good. If we don't do that, then we're simply takers and that is inherently unfair. I thought I would like to be a nurse. After visiting the infirmary and seeing it up close this summer, I don't think it's for me. It's truly a noble undertaking and serves others with a universal need for care, but it's not for me. Faith thought that I'd find

241

teaching more suitable for my temperament. Whatever I decide, she'll support my decision. Don't you want to return to Fort Lewis to teach like your father?"

"I did, once, but that seems a long time ago."

"Maybe you need to work and think about helping others. In doing so, you may discover admirable things about yourself. Right now it seems to me that you don't like yourself very much."

"Maybe you're right, Anne. Maybe you're right. . . We should head back to the village."

"I promised your grandfather to go fishing with him after lunch. I like to fish. When I was a little girl, I fished a lot. Sometimes it was the only food we had."

"I have to confess that at one time I was jealous of you. I thought you were lucky to have won Tom's affection. Now I see that it's the other way around. He's fortunate to have someone like you. I'm so glad that you came up here this summer and that we're friends," Dew told Anne along the trail to the village.

Later in the day, Mark and Anne were off the shore from Mark's cabin fishing when a helicopter landed on the police dock. "That looked like the same machine Joe used to bring us to Fort Lewis," said Anne.

"I'll head for the dock." Mark pulled in his line and steered towards the landing.

Joe climbed out of the helicopter and waved to them. Anne noticed a sober air about Joe and was afraid something had happened.

"Is anything wrong, Joe?" asked Mark.

"We just received word from the Army that Tom has been wounded at the Korean DMZ in a fire fight!"

Chapter Twenty-Three

"We haven't got much time, Anne. Let's get your things. I want to make connections at Lac St. Jean for a commercial flight to Burlington," Joe demanded urgently. "I'm glad to see that you're using the boat, Colonel. Time is precious right now. I'll be in touch to keep you informed of how Tom is doing."

"Please do, Joe," Mark requested grimly. His life had been filled with the pain of sacrifice by those who wear the uniform in defense of the country. He prayed for the young soldier he had come to love like a son.

Anne ran to the cabin and grabbed her suitcases. Joe explained to Bright Cloud and Morning Dew what had happened. "Good-bye, Bright Cloud and Dew," Anne said, embracing them.

"May God be with you and Tom," cried Bright Cloud with tears in her eyes. "Our young men just keep on giving and giving..." They followed Joe and Anne to the platform. Joe lifted off immediately. Anne waved at them through the window. "Poor Tom. I pray he'll be all right. Thank God he's got Anne." Bright Cloud broke down and wept openly.

Two days later Faith, Joe and Anne landed at the San Francisco Airport and took a cab to the hospital at the Presidio, one of the most attractive Army bases in the country. The hospital was a large complex filled with wounded men from the Vietnam War and the sporadic flare-ups at the Korean DMZ.

Joe inquired at the desk where Tom was located. The duty nurse directed them to the tenth floor, room 22. Tom had just completed breakfast and the daily change of dressings on his wounds. Joe peeked through the partially opened door. The nurse told them that Tom was in a bed at the corner of the room between two windows, the only patient in the room. The upper half of his body was wrapped in bandages, leaving an opening around his nose and mouth. The only way he knew for certain that it was Tom, was by checking the chart attached to his bed.

"Is someone there?" Tom asked in a soft voice as if he was half asleep.

"Yes, Tom." cried Faith, running to his side. "We came as quickly as possible."

"I must look a mess!"

"You look just fine to us, Tom." Joe took his right hand in his.

"Is Anne with you?"

"Yes, I'm here, Tom," she replied, holding his hand. It felt cold and damp. She was fighting the tears building in her brown eyes.

"I can't see. The doctor is not sure if my sight will ever return. . ." Tom started to become hysterical. A high-pitched cry of despair released the stark fear that he would never be able to see again. His body trembled as Faith, Anne and Joe looked on helplessly. Joe ran outside for a nurse or a doctor. A few seconds later a doctor entered the room to check on Tom's convulsive outbreak. He ordered the nurse to administer a sedative, and motioned everyone in the room toward the door.

"I'm glad that you've come to visit him. As difficult as it was for you to see Captain Hamilton carry on the way he did, it's an encouraging sign. The sooner he comes to grips with his limitations, the quicker he can start the recovery process."

"What's wrong with Tom, Doctor?" Faith demanded anxiously. "I'm his mother, this is my husband, Joseph Lance, and this young lady is Anne."

"I'm Doctor Bluett, Tom is my patient. He was struck by several machine gun bullets and a mortar round."

"Oh, no," gasped Faith, frightened for her son.

"Take heart, Mrs. Lance. Your son was seriously injured, but I can assure you that his wounds will heal and he can return to a normal life full of activity of his choosing, except, and this is a big exception, he may be blind. His eyes are perfectly healthy, but something has disconnected in the optic nerve that we do not fully understand. We'll just have to wait and see what develops. In the same breath, I caution you against unwarranted optimism."

"How long will it take for his other wounds to heal?"

"Several months to a year. Incidentally, I have just received notification that your son should be transferred to Plattsburg Army Base in New York."

"Did that order come from a General Scott Taylor?" Joe asked, silently thanking his friend.

"Taylor, yes, that was the name. You may visit as long as you want. Tom will be groggy for a while. We can start his transfer in a day or two."

The transfer came the next day, with Tom actually arriving at Plattsburg Army Hospital on the west bank of Lake Champlain before Faith and family could get a flight to Burlington.

Anne visited Tom every day and shared what was going on in her life. She was going to go to the University of Vermont for a degree in Education. She wanted to be a teacher like Faith and Steve Taylor. She had already signed up for classes to begin in September. In two years she could obtain a teaching certificate which would allow her to start teaching in public or private elementary schools.

The schedule Anne made up for classes gave her ample time to take the ferry across the lake to Plattsburg and spend part of every day with Tom. She insisted on accompanying him and participating in the Braille classes Tom attended and as many of the classes for the blind as she could fit into her schedule. She cheerfully and energetically took it upon herself to show her love for Tom by being as supporting as possible and trying to understand what it was like for him to live in a world of darkness.

By Thanksgiving, Tom was able to walk around and come home for short visits. Anne was his constant companion when she was not in school. One weekend she drove with Tom to the cabin that Joe had built on Mount Agamenticus. She drove the same Wagoneer they had used two years ago to bring Bright Cloud and Mark to Montpelier.

"The air is fresh and clean at the coast," said Tom, standing on the observation platform. "I can't see the view but I can feel it, if that makes any sense."

"Sure it does, Tom. Your senses of touch, smell, and sound have been elevated to a high level of awareness as a result of your blindness. You feel textures, hear sounds, and smell scents that most other people have a difficult time with," she answered, holding him by the arm. Tom's acceptance of his condition and adaptation to his limitation was made easier by Anne's faithful patience.

"I couldn't have handled this thing if it had not been for you, Anne. You're young and have a full life ahead of you. I don't want you to be burdened by my bad luck."

"Listen, Tom Hamilton," Anne cried in desperation. "Sure, you've been hurt badly and maybe you'll never be able to see again. That's not easy to accept, but it could be worse. You're not a cripple; you're just blind, and together we can do whatever it takes to minimize its effect. Let me be your eyes if that is what the future holds. I love you, Tom. Mother and Joe claim that love can climb any mountain. You can see the future through my eyes."

"I have a bad feeling that I'm keeping you from getting more out of life."

"Good Lord, Tom, how could any person have more than I? When I came to your home five years ago, I found love and harmony that filled my soul and touched my heart. You, your mother and Joe have made me feel special. Please don't shut me out! I love you with all my heart."

Tom reached for her. She came into his arms and kissed him on both eyes.

"Will you marry me?" asked Tom, squeezing her hard.

"Yes, I'll be proud to be your wife. All I want is to be with you and share our lives together."

They stood on the observation deck that Joe had built. Anne saw the horizon where the blue-green waters of the

Atlantic met the cobalt blue of the sky and described it to Tom. It was a place where sea, earth and sky touched and became one, a true harmonic balance. Tom could not see it, but he felt it as intensely as Anne did.

Sometimes the horizons are within ourselves, each person cultivating a different level. That which is beyond our horizon may not be made clear to us until we have climbed the mountain. To those who make the effort, the rewards are generous, long-lasting, and worthwhile.

The End

Other Historical Romance Novels

BY

Clifton LaBree

A Song for Lisa   A Historical Romance

This is the story of a young American woman captured by the Japanese in the Philippines, 1941. Like most prisoners, she was brutalized and sadistically treated with a cruel disregard for human life. Three years later, Lisa and her companions had reached the low point of starvation and abuse .....

Lake of Three Sorrows   A Historical Romance

A warm spiritually uplifting story of courage, commitment, and sacrifice. This is the story of Dale Cooper, a battle-weary American soldier who served in two world wars.

Flickering Flame (Colonial Series Book One)

A historical novel, about the Cullen family who settled in Portsmouth, New Hampshire, and their participation in events prior to the French and Indian War. Freedom and opportunity were on the march, but it extracted a heavy price. Frontier settlers were ruthlessly killed and butchered by rampaging Indians lead by French officers and Jesuit priests who frequently incited them to greater levels of inhumanity...

Raising the Torch (Colonial Series Book Two)

A continuation of the saga from Flickering Flame, Colonial Series book one, of the Cullen family in Colonial Portsmouth. This is a moving story of love and sacrifice when a small colony had the audacity to fight for independence from their motherland...

Non-Fiction Books

By

Clifton LaBree

New Hampshire's General John Stark, Live Free or Die: Death Is Not the Greatest of Evils

Publisher - Fading Shadows Imprint

A fresh look at one of America's staunchest defenders of liberty and freedom. John Stark was a courageous New Hampshire citizen-soldier who fought in both, the French and Indian War, and the Revolutionary War. His pursuit of leadership excellence on the battlefield distinguished him as one of the most successful combat commanders of the war, and one of the least appreciated.

His selflessness, modest life style, and devotion to the cause of freedom are an inspiration that time has not diminished. He remains today the embodiment of the frugal, independent, and cantankerous New Hampshire Yankee.

Gentle Warrior, General Oliver Prince Smith, USMC

Published by - Kent State University Press. Kent, Ohio, 2001

The Story of one of the United States Marine Corps best General Officer. His flawless performance in Korea is a story that needed to be told.